LIKE *China*

LIKE *China*

Varley O'Connor

WILLIAM MORROW AND COMPANY, INC.
NEW YORK

Recognizing the importance of preserving what has been written, it is the policy of William Morrow and Company, Inc., and its imprints and affiliates to have the books it publishes printed on acid-free paper, and we exert our best efforts to that end.

Library of Congress Cataloging-in-Publication Data

O'Connor, Varley.
    Like China / Varley O'Connor.
        p.   cm.
    ISBN 0-688-09444-9
    I. Title.
PS3565.C655L55   1991
813'.54—dc20   90-43018
                                                                          CIP

Printed in the United States of America

First Edition

1 2 3 4 5 6 7 8 9 10

BOOK DESIGN BY LISA STOKES

*For my family
and for Steven*

The three brothers used to sleep together in the room at the back of the house by the kitchen, Big Dan and Sam on the bunks and Peter in a cot by the windows, where he could see the trees sway in the breeze that came off the ocean. Wind built up on the ocean, Daddy said, whistled over the dunes, flew across the fields and the woods and over the lawns to cool them here in this house on summer days. The morning was clear and cool the day Daddy left, a sparkler Sam said. Light crackled gold in the grass and Peter knew that soon school would let out. God damn, said Big Dan when the pickup was gone and Daddy's stuff from the closet. God damn. Then with a shrug he walked up the dusty road to where the bus would get him and take him to East Hampton High. Sam said junior high sucked, so when Big Dan was gone he jumped the fence and took off through the woods.

Peter used to play with Banjo in the backyard. Throw the ball up against the shed and let it roll through the patchy grass, Banjo barking, scudding on his butt, catching the ball in his big happy mouth, bringing it to Peter. They would play a tug of war until Peter got the ball, threw it back at the shed. One week before Daddy left, Banjo ran away. The second night he was gone Peter lay in his bed, his eyes open, practicing howls, very softly, but like the way he and Banjo always talked to each other. Big Dan and Sam were asleep. Peter could see Sam's black hair, splayed like a spider on the pillow. Big Dan breathed in sharply, then moaned gently in his sleep. A damp breeze wafted in from the window and prickled Peter's nose and his ears.

By the bed his shirt and sneakers were ready. Under the sheet, he had on his jeans. He was waiting for Daddy to stop pacing in the kitchen, for the light to go out. He was going to find Banjo. Already he'd covered the Springs: walked calling by the harbors, the boatyards, the landings that spotted the bay; through the marsh of Acabonack then by the town dump, by Green River and Parsons, where the dead people lay. He went as far up in the Springs as he could, to Hog Creek, where just beyond it, way out past the water, he saw the sad blue-gray shape of New England. Tonight he'd go south and cross over the highway to the ocean side. Walk to the tip of the island if he had to.

Daddy said it was good that Banjo was gone, that they couldn't afford to feed him. But Peter had money from his job. He dug his hand deep in his pocket, felt the wadded-up five-dollar bill the lady had given him that morning for mowing her lawn. He figured he could buy about a hundred cans of Alpo for that much money.

This lady was nice, pretty, with bright blue eyes and silky blond hair he wanted to touch sometimes. Her husband was foreign, maybe an Indian, though he talked like anyone else in New York. When he was there at the house he sat out on the deck fully dressed and smoked cigarettes, a tall glass beside him. It was easy to tell he came from the city. He was handsome, like guys on TV. He had very white teeth. One day when Peter finished mowing the man raised his hand, smoke curling from the tips of his fingers, said, Peter, you did a good job. Once Peter saw the man and the lady hugging on the deck; the man slipped his hands inside the lady's robe, brought his hands up her back beneath the robe and under her hair, wrapped his dark hands around the skin of her neck.

Daddy said forget about the dog, put your mind on things that matter. Peter thought for a moment about what he could put in his mind that would matter, but all he wanted to think of was Banjo. His mind filled with Banjo. In his head he saw a chart, like the ones they used at school, and on the chart was a picture of a black-and-white dog. Underneath the picture the chart said "Dog," because Peter wasn't sure what letters spelled Banjo.

After dinner Daddy said, tell ya what, settle down, get to sleep, and we'll go fishing in the morning, surf casting. Peter liked surf casting. Daddy took him surf casting when Peter was smaller, before Daddy went into—how had Sam said it?—before Daddy went into a decline, after Mama died from the sickness.

At the edge of the sea, boots all the way up and heavy equipment. Silver line in an arc above the water then—ping!—it hits the water. Reeling, reeling, reel it back in, then the line in the sky, then ping in the water. All the day the sun coming down. Light on the rocks, on the shark tattoo on Daddy's big beefy arm. Going home, the shadows getting sharp. Curtains. Mama on the couch, the sun lamp on her sore chest. She says there's my sweet boy, he went fishing with his daddy. Big Dan said Mama got Banjo for Peter when Peter was little. Peter didn't remember.

Under the door the yellow light of the kitchen went out. Peter stayed still in his bed until Daddy was quiet, then put on his sneakers and shirt and crawled through the window, dropped to the ground. The moist ground gave like a cushion beneath his feet. He put out his lips and made a soft howl, listened, but just heard the trees, the leaves brushing, whisper of the night.

He ran to the front of the house and up the short road,

turned the corner off Rappaport to the road that was paved, started walking in slow zigzag lines. The sky was like smoke, it hung in the trees. Peter looked down and saw his legs covered to the knees with fog. It swirled, dispersed, blew away.

Some of the people in the houses had dogs. He passed a house where two little girls in red bikinis played sticks with their dog sometimes, a scrawny little gray thing that looked like a rat. They took it for rides in a wagon. It wasn't pretty like Banjo, it didn't have spots.

The houses grew larger, the lawns got broad. Roofs jutted in angles at the sky. Tall slashes of glass beneath the roofs shined with lights from inside. Dunes appeared at the south of the Springs, and once past the highway they hunched by the houses, protecting the beach. Banjo liked the beach, the sea birds, kites in the sky, the surf. Peter could hear it now, the rush of the sea.

On the beach fog had collected, gathered force into big blustering shapes that blocked out his vision and made the walking tough. But the sand was level, hard-packed. Some light from the moon and the stars cut through. The ocean was black, steel gray where the waves began to crest, hard white coming down. Waves came in rough but steady with a rush and a sigh.

Peter walked until his sneakers were soaked and his eyes felt as though they had sinkers on the lids. He tried a howl now and then, but sadly, called, "Banjo? Cootie dog?" Just the rush and the sigh of the ocean, fog marching thick from the dunes. He felt so sad and so tired that at last he turned back, crossed back over the highway, went back between the houses and down to the bay, starting home. It was quieter here, it was dark. He heard only the lap of the water, the squeak of his shoes; smelled the strong sickish smell of dead fish. On the rough bumpy sand there were long ropy things that drew flies in the light. Then he saw something—

an instant of white, a quick flash, through the fog. Peter strained his eyes. The flash was a lady, the white was her robe; it was the lady whose grass he mowed. She was running down the beach to the bay. Peter dashed for the shelter of a dark clump of grass where the dunes began. A man had come onto the beach, the lady's husband. But Peter couldn't tell if he was chasing her into the water or saving her from it. The fog had passed by, and Peter was afraid he'd be discovered if he ran in any direction, so he kept hiding and watched.

The lady's feet hit the water; it wet the hem of her robe. She looked back at the man who was running down the beach. She walked into the bay till the water was up near her hips. At the edge of the bay the man yelled, and she pushed at the water like it wouldn't move. The man yelled again and she let herself down in the thick, black water and started to swim. The man took off his shoes and plunged into the bay. Her swimming was slow; he reached out to get her and then she went down, then the man went down and the water closed up over them and all Peter could hear was the soft gentle lap of the water on the sand. He looked up at a gull that cried, once, in the sky.

When they surfaced he was dragging her back to the shore. She struggled, thrashed, swinging her arms at his face. He caught her arms and pulled her close to his body, then took her by the shoulders and forced her down under the water, and he held her there, then brought her up, then put her down again. She came up screaming, gasping, her arms in front of her face. The man took her by the arm and dragged her up on the sand. He shouted something into her face. He shook her, then dropped her so she fell to her knees in the sand. He kicked at the sand, he grabbed her hair and brought her face up, forcing her face to look up at him. She swung back her head and fell backward in the sand, but she struggled to her feet, went into a crouch, extended her arms.

When he came at her she swung at his face. He moved back. He kicked at the sand and closed his hands hard into fists, and Peter howled.

Peter howled into the sky. Then he fell back flat in the sand, panting, knowing the man would come get him, kill him. The man staggered back a few steps. His head snapped around to the dunes and he listened. The woman stayed crouching, her arms extended. Peter buried his face in the sand.

He looked up and the man had turned back to the woman. They seemed frozen there, the woman crouching, the water washing up around her ankles, the man standing silent above her. His hands were relaxed. He watched her, looked down at the sand, and then he turned and started walking back up the beach. He went over the dunes to where the lights of the houses were shining.

The woman came out of the sea. Her robe was heavy with water. It dragged in the sand and pulled her shoulders, her arms, her hands to the sand. She sank to her knees, her head drooping, weighted like the robe. She struggled with the belt of the robe and untied it, pulled the robe down off her shoulders to her waist. She fell down in the sand on her side, holding her arms across her chest and she lay there, her hair in the sand. A fog came by and covered her. But then it moved on down the beach and Peter could see her again, the skin of her arms, her shoulders lit softly by the moon. He remembered her name. It was Katha. He said it once, Katha. She was beautiful. He thought she was asleep.

She sat up, the white robe spread around her on the sand. She put her arms in the sleeves and pulled the robe up over her body, secured it with the belt. She stood, swaying for a moment. She looked at the bay then slowly walked up the beach to where the man had gone, to the dunes where the houses shined.

Like China

Peter waited, watching the water lap the dark, empty beach. The water washed over the shoes the man had left on the sand. Peter sprang out of the bushes and ran for home. He climbed in the window and got into bed without taking off his clothes, just his sneakers, wet through from the beach.

. . . four weeks later

Part One—Waiting

Chapter 1

It was a bright morning in July. Katha slid open the long glass doors and went out on the deck. She pulled her robe closer as the air touched her skin, shook back her hair, then went to the edge of the deck and sat with her legs hanging over, the grass on her toes, her arms resting lightly on the rail. It was still—just the gentlest swish of the trees on either side of the house. In front of her the short lawn ran into a miniature field of high cord grass, salt grass that crawled partway up the dunes and then thinned and disappeared. The morning was swimming and nodding with light, both distilled and brilliant, that light of the Hamptons Katha loved and that reminded her of Turner and Vermeer.

From the top of the dunes a long sweep of the bay was visible, and sometimes, from the deck, she heard the pulse of the ocean; on rougher days she could hear it from the house. She hummed softly for a moment, lay her cheek on her arm. The mornings were consistently clear these days, released from the heavy fogs of May and of June when warm air rising from the fields met the cold of the ocean. The ocean gave up its bitter chill, that chill, it was said, which in the spring could stop the heart of a swimmer in his chest.

She lay back on the warm soft wood of the deck and looked up at the sky, watching for the flock of wild mute swans. Three times she had seen them on mornings when she crept out of bed while Tommy was still sleeping, sleeping it off. They flew in a straight white line, and she heard the musical throbbing sound of their wings. Once she thought they were coming but instead she saw geese, an arrowhead of geese in high, rowdy honking flight.

Arching her back, she tilted her head and looked behind her at the house upside down. The light bounced off the broad expanse of glass at the front of the house. Toward the top, on the second floor where their bedroom was, the window was in shade, sheltered by the deep overhang of the shingled roof. The sidings were weathered and gray. Past the trees to the right of the house was the road that led to the highway. The highway itself was in back of the house, beyond a thick hedgerow and a new colonial home that stood in the space where there used to be woods. Then over the highway was the ocean side.

For five years now she and Tommy had been renting in the Springs in the summer. Ever since they were married. Each March they'd leave the winter-clogged city and drive the hundred miles across Long Island to where it forked, then go south. The South Fork in the winter was shrouded in white, a white so cold it looked as barren as a desert. The wind pushed at the windows of the car as they drove through the towns of Southampton then on to the section called the Springs, just north of East Hampton Village. This year they'd found something ideal, a house in the Springs but still close to the ocean.

Katha listened for a moment for sounds from the house, looked again at the vast empty sky. He would sleep for an hour or two more. When he drank himself out in the night, which was most of the time, he slept the sleep of the dead, his arms outflung and his palms open to the ceiling. She imagined him dreaming of smoke and fire. When he woke up he would want her there with him. His hand would move to touch her.

It was strange, she thought, how when real trouble came, when it knocked and then pounded at your door and finally moved in, you felt strangely released. Different things sustained you, definitions dissolved. As the trouble grew larger, old things dropped away one by one. Now she lived day to day like an animal did or a very small child. The natural world of the mornings grew voices, voices more real than the ones she'd once heard. Like magic she could melt into the woods, the farmlands, the ocean and the bays, hear the swamps and the marshes and the scent of sharp pine. She went back very seldom to the city these days, having no need to. Here she hadn't met her neighbors, even liked it that from where she was lying on the deck, if she shifted her eyes from the sky, she could see but one house. Other than Tommy, she rarely saw anyone now. She saw the sly swarthy-faced man in the visor at the general store when she went there to shop, saw the little boy Peter when he came to mow the lawn. She used to be a model, propped in front of a camera, trying to be all the things that others would want. She could hardly remember what that used to feel like. She felt terribly young and also very old, though she was twenty-five. The figure was abstract.

Inside, the phone rang, rang again and subsided. Katha stood, suddenly tensed. She looked up at the window. "Tommy?" She listened, watching the still, smoky, translucent curtain. Somewhere behind her she heard a gull cry. After nearly two minutes the curtain drew away. She went into the house.

"You hear the phone?" he called down from upstairs.

"Who was it?" She waited, then sat on the couch that

faced the glass doors. She drew up her legs and hugged her knees. He was moving around above her; doors opened, something dragged across the floor. She put her chin on her knees, looking down. The polish on her toenails was peeling and chipped. Last week in a flurry of optimism she'd painted them a gaudy shocking pink. Frowning, she tucked up her feet underneath her. Pipes groaned in the walls and the shower went on. She listlessly picked up a magazine from the coffee table, dropped it back. Then it occurred to her that he might be going back to the city, that maybe someone from Stand had called.

"Tommy?" She went to the foot of the stairs. She'd heard the shower stop. He didn't answer. She sighed and went into the kitchen to start coffee. While it was brewing, she leaned against the sink, looking through the glass at the dunes, beyond the deck—the sand shimmered, as in a mirage. Like many of the houses in the Hamptons, the downstairs of the house was designed on an open plan. The kitchen was open to the dining area and the living room, just partially closed on one side by a counter. Behind this main space were the stairs and a short narrow hallway that led to a bath and two small guest rooms. Sometimes when she couldn't sleep at night she snuck down and crawled into one of the beds back there and drew or tried to read.

"Where were you?" he said. His cigarette smoke drifted into the kitchen and then he was there, setting down his overnight bag at the entrance. He slid it aside with his foot.

"What's wrong?" she said.

"I don't want any coffee." He took a bottle of vodka and a rock glass from the cupboard, then made a drink with half Absolut and half orange juice. With his drink he walked out of the kitchen. His hair was wet. He gave a short jerk to his head and drops flew. "Where's my glasses?"

"In your jacket pocket." His leather jacket was tossed

over a chair. She poured herself coffee. "Is it something at the club?"

He stood at the sliding glass doors, looking out and squinting at the light. His eyes were puffy. He hadn't shaved and the shadow on his face made his cheekbones stand out. He looked as long and as lean as a blade, she thought. He looked as though he was standing at a bar.

"It's my mother," he said. "She's in the hospital again."

"On top of everything. Tommy, I'm sorry." He didn't respond. "Would you like me to come with you?"

"No, I don't want you." His words had come fast; his head turned to her slightly, in a warning.

"All right." She looked down at her cup, letting her hair fall forward against her hot face. He knew that her offer wasn't sincere, that she would feel relief when he left. Except once she had never gone with him when he left this summer. He usually left to see about something at Chinese Stand, the club he owned on LaGuardia Place in the city. She heard him come closer, then watched as he put out his cigarette in a shell—an ashtray. He finished his drink, set down the glass, then he turned to her, smiling for a moment.

"Come here," he said.

She left the kitchen and approached him, carefully, timidly at first, but then she rushed and put her arms around him, and she held him as if by holding him hard enough she could alter something, or give him something, or tell him something both too fragile and too strong for words. Then she realized that his arms were still straight at his sides. She pulled back, and a harshness came into his eyes and went over his face. She flinched, and he felt it. She knew he had felt it.

He sat at the edge of the table, took his lighter and cigarettes from his shirt pocket. He lit one. "I don't ask you to do much, do I?" he said. She didn't move. She felt the pulse in her throat.

"But do you think—" he took a piece of her hair, a tip at the ends, and held it. "Will you try while I'm gone to get yourself together? Will you do that for me?" She nodded. He rolled the piece of hair in his fingers as if testing it for color, then he went for his bag and his jacket; she watched as he moved through the room. "I'll be gone maybe a week," he said. "I've gotta stop by Stand when I'm through in Jersey."

"Are you taking the car?"

"Yeah, I'm taking the car. That a hardship for you? You have some appointments?"

"No."

"Look, Kath." He stopped by the door. "The fire set us back. But I've got it handled now, yeah? You want to start believing that?"

"I do."

He slid open the door and went out. She followed and watched from the deck as he walked to the car, his jeans riding low around his slim hips. His wet black hair was lit by the sun. Although he was older than she was, not far from forty, his hair had no gray. She frequently noticed this. After putting his bag in the car, he stood for a moment, one hand on the open door, before he turned back to her and said, "You okay? You'll be all right?"

"I'll be fine," she said, and smiled.

She did hope his mother would get better. His mother, and the club, were the only things he cared for anymore. But she and his mother had never been close, to put it mildly, so she felt she shouldn't say this. It would be the wrong thing to say. So she stood waving, smiling, and watched as the car pulled out of the drive and then vanished through trees.

It was quiet. There was a slight breeze. She looked up at a gull that sliced through the sky, its wings reflecting the wild bright light. Under her hands Tommy's back had felt taut, the muscles coiled tight: his anger was building again. She had been waiting, watching, almost wanting it to come so that it would be over. She rubbed at her neck where it was sore and sat down on the steps of the deck. She could rest now, get back her strength—she had made a mistake. She'd let Tommy know that she was afraid. She looked at the empty drive and the road. She slit her eyes and peered at the sun, felt it warm on her skin. Better, feeling better.

She went into the house and got dressed, in a pair of jeans and a faded blue shirt that came down to her knees. She decided she'd walk to the general store for supplies—there wasn't much food in the house—then get back her bike. It figured that Tommy had taken the car instead of the train; she thought he enjoyed the idea of her being trapped. She'd felt trapped all summer. She put on her shades. Watching the mirror, she brushed her long hair, liking the feel of it, soft, in her hands. With the bike she could go into town; with him gone there were all sorts of things she might do.

In the bedroom upstairs, she quickly made the bed. She threw the clothes he'd left out in the closet. The air was still thick with him, stale. She washed the glass he had used, then emptied the ashtrays, and left the house. Later, she thought, she would go to the beach. Tommy hated the beach. He hated the feel of the sand. He didn't swim. Tommy liked parties and bars and crowds, he liked talking over drinks. What he liked about the Hamptons was the scene, which was just an extension of the city. For her it was different. These days she thought that the green of the Springs, the low hills of East Hampton kept her sane.

She turned out of the Springs and walked west on the highway. Light fell from the trees like pieces of glass. Sometimes she walked east, as far east as Napeague where the ground began to rise, where the land was so narrow she could see the waters of the bay and the ocean at once. The trees there were stunted by wind; some were bent prostrate, their branches, like arms, creeping out along the ground, almost buried in places by traveling sand. She stood by those trees, hearing the wind and the beating of her heart. She would wait then for something to shift, that thing, like a fist, always pressing at her lungs, giving her the sensation of constantly holding her breath, of living underwater. She would feel it give way, feel the blood as it pulsed through her veins. She would know she was alive.

A car passed by, jarring her with the rush of the air as it passed. She was walking too close to the edge of the highway. Up ahead she saw the store, on the left. She moved further up on the shoulder; then stopped, unexpectedly held to a tree she was near—a big oak at the side of the road. Beside it was a flagstone path that led to an old frame house, recently painted barn red; its red edges were bright against the sky. Its sudden significance puzzled her, since she had passed it hundreds of times.

But just beyond it, down a side street, was the house of a painter who used to frequent Stand. She and Tommy had been there to a party some years ago. Two summers back. It was one of those parties of the famous and the hip, of people who had taken that year to Chinese Stand. They went to the party with friends but stayed late and the friends left without them. Tommy was high on attention that night.

When they left they were drunk, staggering wildly on foot up the dark road toward home. The heels of her shoes kept sticking in the earth of the shoulder; Tommy knelt and took them off and carried them for her. Here, where she stood now, they stopped, and leaned against the tree, laughing hysterically at God knows what. The laughter turned to kissing. Headlights shined in their faces. "They'll go away," he said, pressing into her, pressing her hands to the front of his jeans. She stood on his shoes. They heard the voices of their friends, their laughter. "If you're too involved to extricate yourselves, by all means continue. But would you like a ride?" They fell into the car, so happy at that moment. She was blushing; Tommy saw it in the dark.

She got the connection. That was two days before Chinese Stand caught fire, killing the cook and a waitress. From there it had all come down—from the pressure of the debts, his drinking—and yet, she remembered specifically thinking, that night in the car, with his arm around her: I am happy. She remembered with what delight, with what pride, she had thought that if someone had turned and asked how she was then she could have said, I'm happy! Simply, flat out. No qualifications. She had felt the living proof that happiness was real. Here, by that tree, on that night before the fire.

It didn't seem so distant in time as it seemed, oddly, in space. It was as if she had moved far away to a place where she couldn't speak the language and everything was strange, to another country, like China maybe. And it seemed to her now that after the fire, on the day when she'd found him outside of the club and staring bereft at the ruins, it should have been her, as well as the others, he grieved for.

She started walking again. She again grew aware of cars passing by. She saw the people up ahead and just seeing them made her afraid—that was one of the signs of the life she lived now. It wouldn't change, her new life. Tommy was gone, but he would be back. It would get worse. So the doctor had said, the shrink. She had gone to a shrink in the spring when things were looking really bad. You can't control it, said the doctor, or hope it will stop. Do I have to spell out what could happen if you don't leave him now? That was the last she had seen of the doctor. She couldn't leave Tommy, it wasn't his fault.

Chapter 2

The broken bike was shoved under the slats of the deck. Katha knelt down on the grass and pulled it out; the front brake wire was snapped, and the rim was bent. "Damn." She sat back on her heels. Without a bike she'd be trapped here all week. There were two bikes at the house at the start of the summer. After Peter broke this one she'd lent him the other. Poor Peter, he hid the bike under the deck when he broke it, putting branches around it in an attempt, she supposed, at camouflage. It took her a while to convince him he wouldn't lose his job.

Peter was a scrawny little kid with a longish head that looked slightly too large for the rest of his body. His dirty blond hair had a big swatch of white on one side. Most days he stopped by the house to see if there was anything she needed, though Katha hadn't seen him now in three or four days, she realized. When Tommy was here at the house Peter didn't come over so often.

She pushed the bike back where he'd hid it, then went into the house to look up Peter's address in the phone book. She'd called the house once but the phone was disconnected. The Brenners, the people she and Tommy were renting from, had said Peter's family were having hard times, would be grateful for the money they would make taking care of the house. So far, though, she had met no one in the family but Peter. He said he had two older brothers but whenever she saw him, he was alone. Sometimes when Tommy was here at the house she'd see Peter ride by on one of the bikes, his spotted dog Banjo tied with a rope to the handlebars, legs pumping to keep up. She'd wave, he'd wave back. She sort of liked that he was around. He didn't live far. She thought she'd go by.

She ran a few blocks, slowing down when the house was out of sight; the sun was now high in the sky. Deeper into the Springs yards got flatter, greener, more suburban in appearance. Flower boxes and neatly trimmed shrubs framed one-story houses of brick and clapboard. Here and there an old field, awaiting development, lay overgrown with cedars and wild cherry saplings.

When she first came to the Hamptons she wanted a house farther out on the island, in Amagansett or beyond Napeague at land's end, in Montauk. As the island narrowed the landscape got rougher and raw, the greens stripped to browns and grays by the beat of the ocean, its spray bursting up from the rocks toward the houses perched high on the bluffs. But here it was gentle and lush.

Rappaport Lane curved into some woods and dead-ended. She stopped, checking the address again from the paper in her pocket; she hadn't missed it. Through the thin woods she saw a wire fence, then something red in the air that flapped in the breeze. She went through the trees toward the fence, thinking the road continued beyond it—there might be a gate.

But as she got close, she saw that the fence enclosed a squarish dilapidated structure of cement blocks, painted blue but faded and mottled with weather. The yard at the back was littered with trash. Near a worn wooden shed was a swing set, squatting in weeds and covered with rust. A tattered black net hung limp from a line. She spotted a path and followed it into a clearing that opened out to the rest of Rappaport; here was the front of the house, with no number—she hoped Peter didn't live there. Across the street was another house, well maintained and sporting a huge American flag on a pole that rose high as the trees. The gravel road bore sharply past it to the right, probably circling back into the neighborhood.

The house with the flag wasn't it; she didn't want number 444. The blue house was Peter's all right. A broken-down box of bottles and cans spilled off the front stoop. The two windows she could see were blocked out by newspapers, stuck up from inside.

She stayed where she was in the middle of the road. The seclusion was eerie, the stillness. All she heard in the quiet was the flapping of the big crazy flag.

"Hey, lady. You looking for something?"

She took a step back. A tall boy stood at the side of the house, wiping his hands on a rag. He was broad-shouldered and slim, maybe sixteen, and not looking friendly—staring out at her from under hooded brown eyes and a dazzling shock of black hair. He pulled the rag taut in his hands. Another boy, smaller, stood at the other far side of the house, suppressing a grin; when she looked at him he appeared to bow very slightly.

"I was looking for Peter," she said. "He looks after my house. Mows the lawn, that sort of thing." For a moment her voice had been stuck in her throat. She imagined they had come from the back of the house but she hadn't seen them, and they had approached with the stealth of two cats.

"Which house you renting?" asked the tall boy.

"The Brenners'," she said. "You're Peter's brothers, aren't you?" No answer. In front of her, the place where the gate to the fence had been was open and gaping, like someone had sawed it out.

"Peter's not here." The tall boy shifted his weight. He touched the rag he held to his forehead with exaggerated slowness. The smaller boy grinned. "Me and Sam over there look after a lot of the rentals. You wanted something?"

She thought for a moment, then changed her intention. "I have a bike at the house I hoped Peter might look at." That didn't seem to impress them. "It's broken," she added.

"You want Peter to fix it?" The taller boy smirked.

Yes, that was funny, she thought. How old was he, eight? She felt like a fool. She could hear the big flag behind her flapping in the breeze. The boys stood at the sides of the mottled blue house like twin guards. The house seemed to blink in the light.

"Truth is," said the tall boy, "Peter hasn't been around." He shifted his weight again, slowly, and pulled at the rag in his hands—there was something too mature about him, presumptuous. "He's got this old dog. This mangy old dog that keeps running off. When that dog is gone, Peter is gone. Trying to find him, neglecting his chores. I ought to knock some sense into Peter, wouldn't you say?" He waited for an answer that wasn't forthcoming. "Teach him a lesson, yeah, Sam?" Sam laughed, and the sound echoed in the air. "Maybe," said the tall boy, "I should dock his allowance."

The smaller boy bounced a few times, on his toes.

"Peter's done very well for us really," she said. "I can have the bike repaired just as easily at a gas station."

"Me and Sam can fix it."

"No please, don't go to the trouble."

"Ma'am, it's our job," said the boy, with decisiveness.

She hesitated. "I won't be home this afternoon."

"Just leave it outside and me and Sam will take care of it."

"Well—thank you." She backed farther into the road.

"Say—tell Peter I said hello. I hope he finds his dog." She turned and headed for the path in the woods.

"Have a nice day," called Sam.

She dashed through the trees and out into the sun. The road on the other side swayed; she was dizzy. She touched the damp palms of her hands to her face. "God," she said, "damn." Why was she so—frightened, repelled. It was something in their eyes, how they watched her. She had never before encountered resentment here in the locals, like the frightening tangible resentment she'd felt, for instance, on St. Thomas when she went there with Tommy. But then, she had never before seen a house like that house in the Hamptons.

One time, when the sink in her kitchen was clogged, she'd asked Peter if his father might come by and fix it. But Peter said he couldn't, that his father had gone out of town on a business trip to Chicago. That wasn't the house of a man who took trips to Chicago—poor Peter. She didn't want the bike back from him anymore, he could have it. His father was no doubt on welfare, spending what money he had in some seedy bar in Bridgehampton. The mother, a thin, wan, gray-haired woman, scrubbed floors in the mansions on Lily Pond Lane, worried sick about the future of her three young boys, hiding the money she earned from her husband so he wouldn't drink it up; she needed the money to reconnect the phone.

"Katha, stop it," she said. Her eyes swept the neat rows of houses that quietly stretched down the sides of the road. In a garden she saw, like a dream—but it was real—a rainbow hovering over the spray of water from a sprinkler. It was so lovely tears came to her eyes. Everything got to her these days. Bums in the city made her break down and weep. She always knew what they were feeling. She couldn't read the newspaper because she felt personally attached to every disaster. And of course she was. Just because she wouldn't face it didn't mean it wasn't so. Just because no one could walk by her house and see she was in trouble, she was.

Like China

Like—here, these sweet trim houses. Houses all dressed up for Easter. The green of the grass, the bright blue of the sky— a place in a picture. The houses were smug, self-satisfied, when any minute, she knew, they could burst into flame.

From outside she couldn't tell what went on behind their doors. All kinds of things you were not supposed to talk about, think about, see.

She hoped Tommy's mother would die. But she wouldn't. Theresa was chronically ill, but she always recovered. She was a survivor, whatever that was.

"Go to the beach," she said. Go to the beach and forget it. Tonight, she thought, she might ride into town. But all day she couldn't stop thinking of that house, and those boys—of the look in their eyes—so that at the end of the day, coming back from the beach and nearing her house, she almost wished Tommy was there. She wasn't surprised, though, to find that while she was gone, the broken bike hadn't been fixed.

Peter rode slowly home on his bike: it was white and shining with three speeds and red reflectors that winked at the trees. Peter howled a little bit, feeling tired. Near the corner, through trees, he saw the flag going down. Weird Harold. No one liked Harold. He wore green suspenders and a smashed-up peaked cap pulled down over his eyes. He made Peter and Sam and Big Dan clean up the front yard. Sam even planted a shrub by the stoop, but now it was scroungy and dry as a cactus.

Harold spent most of his time in his own yard, raking, hoeing and clipping at the bushes. Each morning he put up the flag, then at sunset he hauled it back down, folded it tight to a diamond and kept it in his house overnight. Big Dan said Weird Harold must have fought in a war and was probably proud of killing some guys. Weird Harold was old, even older than Daddy. Sam said Daddy had a boat with a flag on the side but it sank.

Peter rode fast around the corner to Rappaport Lane; Harold's white house flew by in a streak. He parked the bike out by the shed and went quietly in the kitchen door so Big Dan and Sam and the other boys who were out front watching TV wouldn't hear him. Most of the guys who hung out, Peter didn't like. There was Mike and Roger and skinhead Paul. Mike and Roger were bonacker guys, their father was a clammer. One time Mike and Roger asked Peter to play a new game and then left him tied up to a tree half the night. Paul was okay, except for his skinhead. Paul came from the city and was here for the summer, visiting his uncle who lived two streets over. A guy from upisland named Artie came once in a while, in a car, late at night.

There was a paper bag of food on the counter by stacks of dirty dishes. Peter kicked away rags and papers and the old sick cat, and plunged his hand into the bag, coming up with an apple and a bag of potato chips. He'd eat his dinner out back by his bike, then after a rest, hit the road again to find Banjo when it was dark.

But Big Dan must have heard him when he opened the door.

"Get some milk," said Big Dan. "Your bones are growing." Peter throught about that: growing bones. He got the carton and sat down at the table—Big Dan didn't like him eating outside.

"Where you been?"

"Been looking for Banjo."

"Hey, Sam," said Big Dan. *"Turn down the TV."*

"Talk a little louder," yelled Sam.

But the sound went down lower. Big Dan knocked a pile of comics off a chair and sat down next to Peter, took a comb from his pocket and pulled it real slow through his thick black hair. As soon as he finished, a clump of it fell back on his forehead, above his right eye. "That dog is dead," he told Peter. "Bet some good Samaritan found him all smashed on the highway, took him out to the dump."

Peter ripped open the chips and started to eat.

"Some things are just gone," said Big Dan. He spotted a tear in the wallpaper, peeled back an edge, then pulled a long strip off the wall. He crumpled it up and threw it on the floor. "How long've you been working for the Brenners?" he asked. "Some lady came snooping around today, saying you work there."

"What did she want?"

"I don't like my own brother holding out on me, Peter."

"Daddy gave it to me, Danny. He said the Brenners' could be mine for all summer."

"Yeah? So where's Daddy?" Peter ate another chip; Big Dan reached over and snatched the potato chip bag from Peter's hands. "Where's Daddy?"

"I don't know."

"What I'm telling you, Peter." He gave the chips back. "You can't even fix that lady's old bike, she comes snooping around—how am I supposed to know who she is?"

"I don't know."

"She sees too much, Peter, you know what'll happen? She'll get you put in one of those homes. She'll get me and Sam put in one of those homes." Peter felt bad. Big Dan had told him about this before. "Is that how you want it? You want to put all of us in a home?"

"No, Big Dan."

"*Hey, Sam.* You wanna come in here?"

Sam came in and leaned up against the doorway.

"He says Daddy gave him the Brenners'."

"Yeah?" said Sam. "Wish he gave me the blonde."

"Gimme a break," said Big Dan.

"Hey, nerd," Sam said to Peter. "What d'ya think of my hair, I mean honest opinion, okay?"

Sam's hair was slicked back with what looked like Vaseline. It didn't look good. Sam's hair wasn't thick like Big Dan's, plus Sam had pimples on his forehead so his hair looked better down.

"It looks nice," Peter said.

"Gorgeous." Big Dan picked at the paper on the wall. He took Peter's apple and gave it a toss, then he scraped back his chair and threw the apple, past Sam, at the wall; it landed on the floor with a thud.

"Hey," said Sam, "that's a good apple."

"I'm in a mood," said Big Dan, "I gotta do something." He stretched his arms over his head to crack his knuckles, then he went and got the apple and gave it back to Peter. Peter looked at the apple; it looked all right. He set it back down on the table by his milk.

"Sam," said Big Dan, "you know where's the Brenners'?"

"Out by the highway, not fancy but nice."

"How's it look?" Dan asked Peter. "You seen much for sacking? These people gone through the week or there all the time?"

"She's there all the time," said Peter. "Don't sack it, Danny. I'll lose my job."

"You think I'm not careful?" Big Dan looked more hurt than insulted. "And how do you think you eat, huh, Peter?" Peter didn't know. Big Dan sat back down, took a paper from his pocket and gave it a shake. "You know what this is?"

"A check?" said Peter.

"It's a money order, Peter. For the phone. I gotta think about the phone and Lilco, on top of which now, I've got Harold saying he's gonna report me to the Department of Health. I need this stuff, Peter?" Big Dan put the paper back in his pocket.

Sam came over and took a few chips. He patted his hair, rubbed the grease from his hand on the front of his T-shirt.

"When Daddy comes back he'll tell Harold where to put it. Let me tell ya, that's something I sure won't mind seeing."

"Keep waiting," said Dan. He got up and went to the door, rolling his shoulders a couple of times. "Yeah, I'm in a mood," he said. "I am decidedly, definitely in a mood." He opened the door. "Sam, tell your friends to turn off the TV. We're going on a spying expedition." Big Dan went outside.

"Oh wow," said Sam, "this'll be good. That blonde's got a shape." He wiggled his eyebrows at Peter, he bounced on his toes. "If we're lucky, nerd, she'll be taking off her clothes." Peter went after Big Dan. He jumped off the stoop and hopped through the weeds and junk in the yard to where Big Dan was standing by the shed, lighting a cigarette.

"Don't do it, Danny. That lady, she gave me my bike."

"Thought you stole it. Should have known you couldn't."

Big Dan was smiling; his cigarette glowed in the dark. "We're going on what I call a reconnoiter, capisce?"

Sam jumped out of the house with three other boys.

"Get Frankie and Ben," said Big Dan. "I want a crowd."

Peter watched Sam and the boys go over the fence and take off through the woods, their T-shirts flashing. He looked down at a tire that lay in the weeds, watched how the dark was filling up the space in the middle. He looked at the shadow growing over the chain that Big Dan had put through the handles of the shed's doors; holding the chain was a lock.

"Can I go find my dog?"

"Later." Big Dan crushed his cigarette out.

The bike glinted at the back of the shed.

"Nice bike," said Big Dan. "That's a real nice bike. Listen, that dog'll come back. I didn't mean what I told you before."

"Can I go find him?"

"Not now. I don't want you running off all the time." Big

Dan sat down on one of the swings. "Have a seat," he said. Peter shuffled over and took the other swing. All of the junk in the yard was fading away in the dark, the trash, the buckets, the bricks, the net on the line.

Peter watched the dim square of light in the kitchen, the small back window. Crickets hummed and the fireflies started to dart in the sky. Soon he heard branches snap, the pound of feet off in the woods. "Can I go watch TV?" he asked Dan.

"Negative, Peter. You're going with us."

Sam's whistle came, sharp and high in the night.

Big Dan stood up from the swing. He whistled back to Sam, then stretched up his arms—got two good strong cracks.

Chapter 3

She could hear it, the sea, like a voice saying sh-h-h. The trees, though, were quiet tonight. What she loved most was the sound of the trees in the wind, stirring the night. She lay on the floor in the dark and the darkness spread over her body like smoke—she could smell it, thick, wet and old, but clinging like fingers to her clothes.

If you can't stop thinking about it, the doctor had said, then *think* about it, you know what I mean?

I don't want to, she'd said.

She remembered the air: how it came in the window that night. It was September, with the first hint of autumn, but warm and balmy. She'd gone to bed early that night. When she woke up it was cold. The phone was ringing and Tommy wasn't there. It was four in the morning, still dark, and Ira was calling. He was surprised when she told him that Tommy wasn't in yet, more surprised when she said she didn't know yet what happened. The fire had started at ten and was over by midnight. Two people were dead.

Think about it.

She hung up the phone, turned on the lights and got dressed. She paced back and forth in the loft, glancing every few minutes at her watch; she was torn between wanting to wait for Tommy and needing to see it, the club—or what was left of it.

At five she couldn't wait any longer. She went out, and walked the five blocks up to Chinese Stand. Dawn was just beginning to break. Cabs passed and slowed; she kept walking, then ran.

Tommy was there. He sat on the hood of a car parked in front of the club, staring at the sheet that covered the smashed-out front window. People walked by, unconcerned. She could smell an acrid mixture of char and wetness.

His glasses lay on the sidewalk. She picked them up and then put her hand on his arm.

"Somebody called you?" he said. The lines in his face looked etched into the skin. His eyes were circled and red, but very bright, feverish-looking. His arm and his hand felt cold; he wasn't wearing a jacket. "You want to see it?"

"All right." He wanted her to. He put his feet carefully onto the sidewalk and straightened up, like an old man or someone in shock. Then in an instant he changed and moved briskly, reaching the door before she did so he could open it for her. That gesture at that particular time seemed incredibly strange.

Inside the smell was so overwhelming that for a moment she covered her nose and her mouth with her hand. The wooden floor was flooded with water, in places an inch or two deep. The mirror in back of the bar, the bottles of liquor lined up against the mirror, were coated with soot. Some of the bottles had broken. In the dining room, chairs were pulled back from tables where diners had hurriedly departed. Napkins lay black and soaked with water on the floor. The tableware was preserved by a brackish crust: baskets of bread, cups and saucers, glasses, the crystal bud vases, the flowers. The flowers were strangely unwithered, just black—the petals of the roses, the leaves, the stems.

Like China

Tommy said this was damage from the smoke, that the fire had started in back, in the kitchen, where it had been contained. The kitchen, he said, was completely destroyed; one of its doors had been ripped off the hinges by the firemen and lay, like planking to a ship, at its entrance.

Tommy stood by the kitchen. From the front window a thin shaft of light pierced through the dank air and the blackness; it trembled in the water on the floor.

"I don't want to go in there," she said.

But he seemed not to hear.

"Tommy? We should go home." The drawings and paintings on the walls were blotted by blackness. Water had seeped through some of the frames, making ghostly abstractions against the glass.

"You don't want to see it?" he said.

"No, let's go home." He left with her then, reluctantly. He was weak with exhaustion and let himself lean on her while they waited for a cab. Outside the morning was viciously bright.

"Chet is dead," he said. "Toni is dead."

"I know." She took his hand in the cab. She barely knew Chet and Toni, but to Tommy his employees were like members of his family; he lent them money, he listened to their troubles over drinks after work. He inspired a fierce loyalty in them.

At home he wouldn't sleep. She sat on the couch and he sat in a chair by the window, watching the morning light get stronger. Her hair and her clothes smelled like smoke. She imagined the scent reaching into the fibers of the couch and staying there, trapped in the fabric and the springs. She saw that his shirt was stained by the soot.

"Do you want to talk about it?" she asked him.

"They wouldn't let me see them," he said. "They brought them out in—bags. I knew which one was Toni because she was—smaller. I wanted to see her." He started to cry.

She got up to go to him, but he said, "No, no don't."
She stood watching him, wanting badly to comfort him.
Then he said: *"I killed them."*

"Tommy, don't. You're upset."

*"You want to listen? You want to hear what I'm trying to
tell you?"* He got up and lay his face and his arms against
the window; his fingers moved, clutching or clawing at the
glass.

He turned and leaned next to the window, breathing hard
for a minute but gaining control. He ran his hands over his
face and stopped crying. "I wouldn't make a payoff," he
said. "Ira wanted to and I wouldn't. I had to be a hero,
make a point."

"I don't understand."

He was impatient. "Katha, you own a business in a certain neighborhood there are men who control it, want a
piece of the action." He pressed his head to the wall, looked
up at the ceiling. "For protection, they say." He looked
back at her. "So I say I don't want protection, I don't need
it—I say it's my place. They let it slide, for a while they
ignore my *misguided* independence. What they think is the
store won't last because the boy from uptown doesn't know
what he's dealing with, right? But then I'm successful, so
what do they do? They burn it, baby."

"You know this?"

"I spent half my life with people like this. But I forget
what I come from." He paused. "That's the key, I forget."
He shoved himself off the wall with his foot. He paced by
her, then back. "The police report cites the cause as a deficient stove." He almost laughed.

"Maybe they're right," she said. "I think that's what
you've got to believe until you definitely know."

He grabbed her arm. "Then what when I know?"

"Then—Tommy, don't. You're hurting me."

Like China

"What when I know?" He was gripping her hard, his eyes held her hard. Her hand was going numb.

"Tommy, I don't know." He let her go, and stepped back, putting his hand to his head and saying, "I'm sorry, I'm—"

"It's okay," she said, "never mind." There were marks on her arm from his fingers. The loft now was flooded with sun. She reached out to touch him, to comfort him, but he turned and went into the bedroom, shutting the door. She stood rubbing her arm but knowing she had to be strong. She asked herself what she would do if she found that he had, inadvertently, caused Chet and Toni to die. There wasn't any question: she would stand by him, she wouldn't stop loving him. He wouldn't change in her eyes.

She went to the bedroom. He was lying on his side, facing away from the door, his legs drawn up toward his chest. She lay down beside him on the bed, curling herself to his back, her face in his hair. She draped her arm over his shoulder. His breathing was quiet, like he was asleep, so she silently said I'd still love you, I would still love you, I will still love you. She said it until her lips began moving, until she was saying it, softly, aloud. He finally turned, put his face to her neck, and cried with the abandon of a child. It was then she believed if she just loved him hard enough, he'd be all right.

She never knew for certain the cause of the fire. Rumor said it was arson; there was never any proof. Tommy said that he didn't need proof, that he was convinced, and since he wouldn't listen when she tried to reason with him, she simply stopped talking about it. Tommy preferred to deal privately with his burden of guilt. He became almost covetous of it; but she felt it as the force, the intention behind everything that he did, and in all of the ways that he changed through the next two years.

The day before Chinese Stand reopened he burst into the loft, waving a bottle of Dom Perignon and looking joyous, happier than she'd seen him in over a month. He had bought out his partners in Stand, and sold his shares in Split and Gillorhan's, his other two clubs. This startled her some. Chinese Stand was by far the largest of the clubs, the most expensive to run because of its high-rent location, and the hippest—which, as he'd often reminded her, made continued success unpredictable. Yet, seeing his elation, she said nothing.

"Look," he said, "I can concentrate. At heart I'm a proprietor, you know? Not a businessman. I create an atmosphere, make a place where people go to get away, to imagine. Make the night last. Meet the love of their life. I like to be there, to see it. They're family. I'm there I can see that it's humming, purring, the night machine. And that it's safe."

Ira, one of Tommy's old partners in Stand, had told her that Tommy went in again and again to the fire, making sure everyone was out. He couldn't get Chet and Toni but he kept trying, finally fainting at the door from the smoke. "He cares too much," Ira said. "That's the thing about Tommy. He cares so much that it kills him."

Katha got up from the floor and turned on the light. She felt stiff. The sound of the ocean was gone. She went back to the table where she'd left her dinner—a salad, a big plate of lettuce really, though she'd meant to get something more substantial at the store this morning—and a *Glamour* magazine. She'd bought the *Glamour* because on the cover was a girl she used to know. But the lighting in the picture was off. Maddie's nose looked flat, and the lines of her mouth were extended with a ghoulish purple tint so her mouth looked swollen and bruised. Katha ripped up the cover, in twos and in fours, and put Maddie's poor face with the lettuce in the trash. Then she turned and saw her own face in the sliding glass doors, the face of a woman she no longer knew: shadowy, gaunt.

Her father had said that bad things would happen if she moved to the city. He was so cautious, so tense, he'd made her afraid too. In the year she went to college at Marymount, she clung to the campus uptown, never venturing down to the heart of New York. But as a child she'd gone to the city many times with her parents, and its rich textures, dissonant sounds, and foreign-looking people, who mingled and rushed with the others on the streets—the sense that exciting things happened there, so different from bland, predictable Westchester County where she lived—sent her mind off to uncharted places, to places that scared and compelled her. She'd come home from those trips to the quiet of her powder-blue room, chintz curtains at the windows. She'd sit in front of her mirror, watching her face and dreaming that someday she'd live there, in the city. The thought made her breathless, made patches of pink appear on her cheeks. But she was also relieved to be home, where she could anticipate, wait. Anticipation was sweet and safe.

She went to the doors, put her hands on the glass. No one could know, she thought, how Tommy had once made her feel. Her mother, for instance, when she met him: the lift of the eyebrow that said, it can only be sex. Yes, it was sex, but it was much more than that—it was how he had made her feel whole and accepted, as she never felt before. He had a gift for making people feel good about themselves. She remembered that even her mother had, briefly, been charmed. Sometimes, in bed with Tommy, she pretended her father was watching, could see her with Tommy; and she felt free, like she had escaped and her father was imprisoned, doomed to watch her being free and happy without him for the rest of her life.

The glass under her hands was cool, soothing. She'd felt

so damn good today, almost normal and strong. In the Hamptons, away from the city, alone, she could rest. She could sometimes remember she had lived another life. The nights, though, were bad because nights were the end of things, when exhaustion blotted reason and misunderstandings grew to unearthly proportions.

She slid open the doors and went out on the deck. She could see, beyond the tall grass and the dunes, a slip of the bay. The night air was clear and the moon was bright. But the trees were too still, they brought no comfort, and even alone, with the moon in the salt-fresh air, there was no rest. There was only the blackness of night, and her consciousness of blackness, a tunnel of black that went on and on and never stopped. She turned to go back in the house— she heard something, a rustle in the grass. It seemed to come first from one place and then from another.

Oh great, she thought, now I'm hearing things—maybe the breeze was picking up. But then it was silent. She turned around and looked out across the grass. The rustle came again, then it stopped. Slowly, she reached back against the wall of the house and turned on the deck's floodlights. When her eyes adjusted she saw, in the grass, the eyes of an animal—no. Over the eyes, just above the spiky points of the grass, was the top of a head, then the face of a person. The grass was filled with them—boys, children, their white faces gleaming from the moon in the darkness. She stood for a moment, transfixed, not quite comprehending. The faces were too far away to be clear, except for the eyes, watching her, shining like lights. Someone moved. She heard a slash, then the sound of a switch, a thin branch whipped fast through the air—and she knew, and she didn't know why she'd forgotten Peter's brothers by the time it got dark, why she didn't lock the doors, close the drapes. She felt her heart pound in her throat. The branch sounded again, with a whistling sound. "Get out!" No one moved. She was shaking. She knew they could smell her fear, that it drew them here, made them come closer. *"Goddamnit, get out of here or I'll call the police."* They moved back. The grass started swishing all over the field. She ran to the rail of the deck and watched as they swarmed up the dunes. One held a branch as if it were a torch or a sword.

Two of them were Peter's brothers, she was sure. And one of them was Peter, she had seen his white hair. They saw that the car was gone from the driveway, that Tommy wasn't there.

She went into the house, locked the doors, pulled the drapes. She was shaking. "Stop it." She got the bottle of vodka from the cupboard, poured a stiff shot straight into a coffee cup. The liquor went down like water. She went upstairs and came back with a blanket wrapped around her. She was laughing, convulsively, low in her throat. How could she think she would be any safer if Tommy were here? She remembered a baseball bat in the closet. She got it. Nowhere was safe. She turned off the light. She went back with the bat and the bottle of vodka to the couch and sat down again, drinking. "Oh God," she said, "it's going to rain tomorrow." Her arm hurt where Tommy had broken it last winter. "Where are my friends?" she said crying. "What did I do with all my friends?"

To make matters worse, when she went to check the mail in the morning, in the box she found a tattered graying envelope without stamps. Inside was a picture from a magazine, of a *Playboy* centerfold who looked quite a bit like she did.

Chapter 4

The shed was unlocked. Peter saw a thin strip of light through the crack, but the shed was off limits, so he timidly knocked.

"Big Dan?"

"Entre nous," said his brother.

Peter stood staring at the strip of light.

"Come in, nerd. Open the door," said Big Dan.

Inside, the dark shed was partially illumined by a lamp from the house that Big Dan had rigged up in the area he was working in. Peter could make out his father's rusted tools, stacks of old wood, and a tall pair of skis leaning up against a wall hung with rain gear and fishing tackle. Next to the skis was a television set, and propped on the wood-piles were more TV's—six altogether. In the far corner was a brand-new yellow motor scooter. Men's suits hung over a sawhorse flanked by two stereo speakers. Around them were tennis racquets, basketballs, Reeboks, Adidas, Pumas and Keds. It was like Christmas in a TV movie. On the ground beside Big Dan was a big brass ashtray in which a long brown cigarette smoked. Big Dan was taking the back off a radio with a screwdriver.

"Police coming to get us, Big Dan?"

Big Dan took a drag off his cigarette, blew smoke rings into the shade of the lamp; they floated out the top of the shade, perfectly formed big gray doughnuts. He said, "Don't expect they will, if they haven't come by now."

"The lady didn't call the police?"

Big Dan didn't answer. He was thinking. Sacking the Brenner house now would be dangerous since the lady had seen, and probably identified them. Last night was foolish, but what the heck. Fuck it, he thought. A man was entitled to some fun in this life.

In the beginning he was cautious with the sacking, just taking food and necessities, a little cash. But lately he'd grown reckless, taking things he didn't need that people would miss—because he knew it was only a matter of time now anyway. Soon there'd be a slip-up, and someone would come and take them away. If his brothers were too dumb to see that, he wasn't. He couldn't protect them forever. Daddy was never coming back. That was consummately clear.

It would be wise, however, to employ a little restraint in regard to the Brenners—with the lady undoubtedly on the alert. But he thought he'd throw Sam permission for some window spying if that would make him happy; Sam fancied the lady, as Daddy would have put it. Old Daddy, the bastard, sure had some ways of putting things. What style Dan had he had gotten from Daddy, and once he was out of all this, off to the city where he belonged, he'd polish up his act. Get some new clothes, meet the right people, and maybe someday he'd run into the bastard, in a bar, or hanging out on the docks. They'd meet as men, equals, shake hands and have a talk.

Big Dan himself found the blonde old and wrung-out, although he could tell she was actually young; she gave him the spooks, how she tilted down her head and looked up with her eyes through her hair. Dan liked them innocent, fresh and young, so he could shape them. "You've got to make the woman, son," Daddy once said, his hands held out delicately, fluttering, as though he were modeling something from clouds. "You don't make the woman, create the woman that you want, she makes you." But Sam, having been seduced by a substitute teacher from Montauk in May, thought older women were the epitome of class. His two-day affair was the highlight of his young life, and though Dan was fairly certain that such an event was unlikely to recur, he did want to give Sam license to imagine it.

For Peter's sake, Big Dan had spent half the night in search of the old dog, Banjo. He was convinced now the dog must be dead. As second best, he thought he'd give his youngest brother a lesson in responsibility. He didn't count Peter's odds for survival in the world very high.

"This is the situation," he said. "Our independence is tenuous at best, after last night. What I want you to do is go back to the lady, apologize, do for her. Mow the lawn, pull the weeds, do chores around the house. Take her bike and get it fixed at the Shell on the highway. Tell her your mother died. That'll stir up her sympathy." Peter didn't know what his brother was talking about. He wanted Big Dan to blow smoke rings again through the lamp.

"And while you're at it, get some food. The canned stuff. She'll never know it's gone."

"Okay, Big Dan."

"I'm counting on you, Peter."

As for the guys, Big Dan felt it was time to get rid of them. All of Sam's friends hanging out made him and his brothers conspicuous. He'd have to tell them to get lost, and he'd better do it with a lot of effect. Tell them if they talked they were dead. Some trouble was coming, more trouble than just being taken to a home—he sensed it, palpable, eating at the edges of things. He would have to find ways to circumvent it.

Like China

Peter was still standing in the doorway, eyeing the loot with his mouth hanging open in that way he had, which made him look as though he had all the intelligence of a fish.

I'm sick of these kids, thought Big Dan, and with that he shoved Peter out of the shed, and kicked the door closed before Peter was clear. Peter, outside, gave a soft cry of surprise. Big Dan listened to him go away, then he lifted the crate he'd been sitting on—tamped down the soft dirt underneath it: two hundred. He thought he'd call Artie. Make it two-fifty.

Peter walked slowly, scraping his feet in the gravel. He wasn't riding his bike because he was afraid that the lady would ask for it back. The sky was all white. The sun was hiding, and Peter smelled rain. Past Harold's he gave a short whistle for Banjo but the dog didn't come. He thought he might stop around the corner and see if the rat-dog was home. He didn't want to go back to the lady's house. He didn't want to let Big Dan down, but he was afraid of her husband. Her husband would come back and she would tell him what happened. If her husband came back, Peter didn't want to be around.

Big Dan turned out the light and locked up the shed; put up his arms and cracked his knuckles. Damn Sam, the net was still on the line. Sam and his plans. His latest was to do a little netting, fresh fish for dinner, huh guys? Dan hated fish and besides, the net was full of holes. Rotted clean through. He pulled down the net, wadded the thing to a ball, and threw it over the fence into the woods just to get it out of sight. Rubbed his hands on his jeans. Just thinking of fish, he got a bad taste in his mouth.

Dan lit a Camel, then went to the side of the house to watch Harold. Harold was wearing his green suspenders and his weird-looking hat. As usual, he was working in his yard, raking away—at nothing, Dan thought. Trying to turn his small plot of land and his house, that no one ever saw, into some kind of a showplace. The house wasn't much, a simple white ranch with a dumb red roof. Pert looking. The house of a guy who didn't have much but made out like he did. That flag took the cake. When Weird Harold took it down each evening, he held that big flag as if it was gold. Harold knew Dan was watching him; Dan could tell by how Harold's shoulders were hunched, how he pushed at the grass with his rake in short angry spurts. What's he want? thought Dan.

Harold's house had stood empty for six solid months. Harold's sister and her husband used to live there before, but this year when they went to Miami for the winter, the sister died of a heart attack and the husband stayed down there. In June, Harold showed up, ten days after Daddy took off. Bad timing. Dan went over to pass off some lie about where his father was, and as far as he knew, Harold had bought it. Dan even thought he might strike up a friendship with the old guy, ask him how many Japs he had offed in the war. He'd even cleaned up the yard when Harold had pushed him, threatened him with that shit about the Department of Health, if there was such a thing. But ever since then, Harold ignored him, made out when he saw him like he was invisible or had a real bad smell.

"Hey, Mr. Meeversham!" Harold ignored him.

Dan went through the yard, crossed over the road.

"I'm on to you, boy," said Weird Harold. He picked up his rake and shook it at Dan. "Get away with that smoke! Don't you bring that damn secondary smoke in this yard."

Dan threw his butt in the road. "What's the trouble?" he asked. Harold kept holding him off with the rake, his eyes narrowed to furious slits in the shadow of his hat.

"Trash," said Weird Harold, "willful neglect. Your place is an eyesore, boy, a disgrace to the entire community." He stuck the rake back in the grass, started raking again with new vigor.

"Sir, we cleaned up the yard."

"You hauled it all around to the back of the house."

So what do you want, thought Dan, a landscaping job?

"That's just the first step," he told Harold.

"Bullshit, you know what I hate? Wise-ass kids. What else I hate is bonacker ways."

Dan felt his ears getting red.

"I told you," he said, "my father doesn't fish." He took a deep breath. "He's a traveling salesman, sir, ladies' hats, accessories, that kind of thing."

Harold set down his rake. "Don't give a hoot what he sells. I say a man lives like that over there cancels out the whole rest of his life. Where's your mother, boy?"

"Dead."

That should do it, thought Dan. He'd managed to look ever so slightly bereaved.

"Well," said Weird Harold, "we all got to go some time." He drew himself up, rocked back on his heels. "But you know what I say? While we're here on this earth we ought to take pride."

"My plan," said Dan, "is to clean the backyard. Then after that, me and my brothers are going to paint the house."

"Sounds good," said Harold.

Guy thought he owned the whole world. His old head was cocked to one side, his thin lips were pursed in righteous satisfaction.

"Let me tell you something, boy. If you come from trash it don't mean you've got to be it."

Trash, thought Dan, I'll tell you who's trash.

"You pull yourself up by your bootstraps, boy."

Do I have a choice?

"Looks like rain," said Harold. He looked up at the sky; but then he looked back. "You playing with me, boy?"

"No sir, I'm not." Dan gritted his teeth.

Harold walked right on up to him then, stuck a long knobby finger in his chest. "Well, boy, you better not. I told you once and I'll tell you again. Just neighborly like." The old loon smiled. "I want some improvement over there or you can expect a visit. Something official, don't think I won't do it." He looked up at his flag, looked back up at the sky, and went into the house.

Dan took a step onto the grass, lit a Camel, and blew a big cloud of secondary smoke. It wasn't too satisfying. He went back across the street and sat down on the stoop. The TV was blaring. Dan banged on the door. *"Turn down the TV."*

Sam poked out his head. "What's up?"

"Jesus, Sam, what're you wearing?"

"Calvin for Men. You don't like it?"

"Not much. Go in or come out."

Sam shut the front door and sat down on the stoop.

"Weird Harold," said Dan, "the guy's nuts."

"You talked to him?"

"Yeah. We've gotta paint the house."

"No way," said Sam. He took Big Dan's cigarette, sucked in a deep drag, coughed, and gave it back. "You know what Daddy would say, we don't hanker to threats. Nobody does like that to the Kramers."

That was true, thought Dan—bonacker, that was what got him, that was the word that made his blood boil. He sat watching the flag as it swayed in the breeze; Sam was watching it too.

"Let's get him," said Sam.

What the hell, thought Big Dan.

"Brainstorm, brainstorm!" said Sam. He jumped up from the stoop. "Oh wow, this is it." He bounced on his toes a few times, sat back down. "*The flag*, okay? We go in there tonight. We see A, where he sleeps, and B, where he keeps it. We take the garden shears, yeah? We unfold the flag and we shred it. Fold it back up." Sam was holding his stomach, he'd started laughing so hard. "He goes out in the morning to put up the flag, can ya see it? That ruined flag like a bunch of streamers, Harold pissed off and cryin' in the yard."

"Not bad," said Big Dan. "But too obvious."

Sam stopped laughing. "Then what?"

"Something subtle. Something, y'know, with a bit of finesse."

Sam looked deflated. "Like what?"

Big Dan didn't answer; he smiled, then took out his comb and gave it a run through his hair. "So, Sam," he said, "you like the blonde?"

Sam grinned. "I'm in love."

"You want my advice," said Big Dan. "Eighty-six the Calvin."

Katha lay on the deck wrapped in a sheet on a chaise lounge; she wore her shades though there was no sun. The cool air wafted over her face and ruffled the edges of the sheet. The phone rang inside but she didn't answer it. She'd shut her eyes for a while, then she'd open them, watch the gulls swirl in the sky through the lavender tint of her shades.

She had thought of calling the police, the Brenners, Peter's parents—but she did nothing. What happened last night was a childish prank that didn't call for any action. She basked in inaction. She drifted in and out of sleep, caressed by the motion of the air. The phone rang again—had it rung before?—and she didn't move.

When Peter crept up the driveway to the steps of the deck she didn't hear him. He said, "Mrs. Pinnell?" He'd been instructed to call her Katha but sensed that wouldn't be appropriate under the circumstances. Besides, her name confused him; he often slipped and called her Kathy. "Mrs. Pinnell?"

She sat up with a jolt, then she jumped to her feet and said, "What do you want?" Peter's head started hurting. He couldn't remember what Big Dan had told him to say. She was clutching the sheet around her, pulling her hair tight back from her face.

"How could you do such a thing?"

Peter didn't know; he looked down at his feet.

"I'm very disappointed in you, Peter."

"I know." He watched how his toe pushed through a little hole in his sneaker.

"Did you have any part in what I found in my mailbox?"

"Ma'am?" Peter thought hard, but his head was hurting.

"Well, did you?" she said.

"It was the other boys, bigger boys."

She let her hair go. "I thought so."

"I'm sorry, Kathy." He'd used the wrong name. "I'm sorry—" he couldn't think of it "—Mrs. Pinnell." He very much wanted to just run away. "I came to take the bike to the station, to fix it."

"Over there," she said, sitting back down. It was shoved under the slats of the deck where he'd put it. "What happened last night," she told him, "won't happen again."

"No, ma'am." He wheeled the bike off, listened as it thumped across the grass.

"Because if it does, I'll send you to jail."

She couldn't do that, Peter knew. He wasn't afraid. Big Dan said they couldn't put children in jail. They put children without parents in homes, and if he was in a home then Banjo couldn't find him. He had to be quiet and sly, like a cat. He knew how to be quiet, that was something he knew. When he brought the bike back he'd sneak into her kitchen and get Danny some food. He'd seen that under the sheet she had on a bikini, pink. He would tell that to Sam.

Katha felt like crying. Why? Because some little kid let her down? He didn't know any better. But God, it just made her so sad. She couldn't sleep anymore. She wanted the phone to ring again, so she could just lie here, not answering. Passive defiance. She kept thinking of something Tommy's mother had told her, before she'd informed her that marriage was sacred, that she had to have faith, that Tommy had always been good in his heart. She hadn't meant to confide in Theresa; she'd done it on the spur of the moment, at the time when she was beginning to be seriously frightened of the anger in Tommy, and of what it was doing to their lives.

"I'm an old woman," said Mrs. Pinnell, "you should bring me good news."

She stood tall and inviolate, her hair pitch black around her aged impassive face. Behind her, through the window, her son trimmed dead branches from trees at the back of her house in New Jersey. "It's not I've never liked you, Katha," she continued. "But I knew when you married my son you were wrong for him. *You're not enough of yourself* . . . But never mind. I don't understand American girls." Her son came in and she embraced him, then lapsed into Italian, which irritated Tommy as it always did. "My proud son," she said laughing. "He drops the *i* from Pinnelli and gets to be a big shot in New York City." Katha remembered feeling cold, and pulling the sleeves of her sweater down over her hands. She watched the leaves fall from the trees outside as Mrs. Pinnelli, feeling festive, opened a bottle of homemade wine.

She saw her own mother later that month, for the first time in a very long while. She knew her mother came into the city on Wednesday afternoons; she had a subscription to a series of matinée concerts at Carnegie Hall. So she waited outside the building for her mother one Wednesday in that bitterly cold late October. Her mother wore her fur hat and coat; she smelled of powder. She had on white gloves. Katha went with her mother to the Russian Tea Room where they had borscht and sherry. Her parents were going to Europe next month—since her father retired, they frequently traveled—and her mother talked of Vienna and Dubrovnik. She hadn't intended to say anything to her mother, but as they were leaving the restaurant, she took her mother's arm. Her mother withdrew, digging her hands in the pockets of her coat and remarking on the unseasonable weather. It wasn't anyone's fault. She'd been much closer to her father than to her mother as a child. When she looked to her mother, it was too late.

She remembered how later that day she'd gone down to the club, where she had an appointment to meet with an artist. Chinese Stand was known as an art bar; it was frequented by artists, and Tommy was something of a patron of the arts. She had studied art history in college, and she was in charge of buying for shows they hung in the club; sometimes she bartered with the artists, their work in exchange for a tab. But this was after the fire, when they weren't buying much art anymore. This artist insisted on seeing her, though, because he couldn't pay his rent. He told her a long sad story of years as a painter with little recognition, of his unending worries over money. He said that, alone, he'd raised two little girls.

He showed her three canvases, a triptych in brown and ocher oils, depicting what seemed to be stacks of reclining figures layered with crates of cattle. She was admiring and moved. But when she told him what she saw in the paintings—and of how they evoked a terrible still frozen silence—he said that his work was nonrepresentational, that there weren't any people in the paintings, or cattle, or crates; and for some reason, she didn't know why, she started to cry. He wore a white satin scarf around his throat that he gave to her saying, "Stop crying, you shouldn't be sad. No one so young and so beautiful has any reason to be sad." He said this impatiently, anxious to turn back the talk in his own direction. She saw condescension in his eyes, saw him looking at her as from a great height; and for his arrogance she gave him back his scarf, and told him she didn't have the money to help him with his rent, which was almost the truth. He went off broke, but satisfied that indeed the world was against him, that his pain and his work were far too profound ever to be understood.

Tommy said that she used her passivity as a weapon. He said that her air of abstraction and helplessness—what he termed her withdrawal from him—was as effectively hurtful as his temper was. His temper. It was so far past the point of temper. It was so far past the point of anything that had a name. But she hoped he was right that she hurt him, that somehow she'd pierced him, deep down.

She was refreshed now, her bones were water. She got up and stretched, went inside and wandered aimlessly through the rooms of the house. She left the sliding doors open to feel the breeze. The open translucent drapes swayed in the breeze, the chalky white air. And inside the house was relentlessly white, the walls, the ceiling, the furniture, as if planned that way to draw in the white from outside. She came down the stairs, trailing her hand along the white wall. In front of the couch was the sheet where she'd dropped it. She wrapped herself in it again, it was cool, and the air was cool. Closing her eyes, she whispered, "I wasn't always like this." She turned on the radio, an old song by the Platters. Michael, she thought, my first love. She felt sick. He'd had this song on a tape. She and Michael had turned out so bad that she dropped out of college, because she was ashamed—for what she had done to him. She was lost and confused. On the night they broke up Michael said she was crazy, said she lived under the impression that her beauty would get her whatever she wanted. She knew at the time she didn't believe that, had always felt quite the reverse, but—something in how he said it had convinced her that night it was so. When Tommy first kissed her she turned away her face. He turned it back gently, the tips of his fingers on her chin. She could still feel his lips, hear his voice: "You're so beautiful, look at you. God made you beautiful." God made her beautiful. Holding herself, she danced languorously with the breeze to the music.

Sam saw her dancing. He saw her lips move, saw her full breasts when she leaned down to pick up the sheet. Her blond hair blew softly over her face in the breeze. "My own," he said. "My true love." He was belly-down, flat-out in the tall grass beyond the deck. He wouldn't venture closer. He wouldn't take the chance of being caught at a window. What did Big Dan think he was? A voyeur? A pervert? He was learning finesse. With a little maneuvering and in the proper time, he was sure he'd get lucky. No more pictures in the mailbox; that had been dumb, kid's stuff.

Chapter 5

Katha thought it was sweet, how Peter was trying to make up for what he'd done. When he brought back the bike he also brought his brother, the one named Sam, and offered to clean up the house. At first she was taken aback by this suggestion, but Sam apologized so profusely, and seemed so desperate to please her—probably afraid of what his parents would do if she called them—that she said there might be a few chores they could help with. She told them her husband was gone for the rest of the week and that now was a good time to get the place in shape. It was, really; she hadn't had anyone in to clean all summer, and she herself hadn't done much in the house. And Sam said, "No charge." He had a large red bandana wrapped around his head. He looked ready to sweat.

She had the boys sweep and dust the downstairs rooms while she worked upstairs, stripping the bed and taking down the curtains to be washed. She found herself humming, reminded of what good therapy housework could be; of how nice it was to have people in the house. When she went back downstairs she found Sam at the sink, filling a lobster pot with steaming hot water and Mr. Clean. Peter had two heavy-duty steel brushes in his hands. They went into the living room, sloshing sudsy water from the pot, and started taking up the rugs. "Time to wash the floor!" sang Sam. The floor was polished oak.

"Uh, listen, guys," Katha said. "I think the floor looks pretty good." She said there was work outside to be done; some places on the deck needed sanding, there were weeds around the shrubs.

She stripped the beds in the downstairs rooms, put the sheets and the curtains in the washing machine, then she got on the bike to ride to town for some food, so she could make the boys lunch. They were skinny kids; they looked like they subsisted on Wonder bread. When she left, Peter was sitting cross-legged on the deck, peering up at a spot on the rail with intense concentration. Sam hovered over him, giving instructions.

She smiled to herself and took off, feeling wonderfully buoyant on the bike as it sailed through the heavy white air. She rode the mile into town, thinking of what she would buy, grabbing leaves from the elms that stood in elegant rows near the village.

As it wasn't a beach day, downtown East Hampton was crowded. People wore heavy sweaters, and slickers, though it hadn't rained yet. A long line fanned out from the front of the movies; people waited consuming huge dishes of ice cream or candy from tiny white bags. Others strolled along the sidewalks in twos, or in family groups of four or five— by the charming little shops painted white or soft muted red, some with hand-painted signs on delicate chains. They came out of Bookhampton with recent bestsellers and *The New York Times*. They looked so at ease, she thought, these handsome, affluent people, so relaxed that even the children exhibited an almost unnatural poise.

To Tommy, who'd grown up in Elizabeth, New Jersey—a depressed industrial town where the sky always simmered with reeking gray smoke—renting a house in this rich provincial place was a symbol he'd arrived. But to Katha, who grew up in Katonah in Westchester County, East Hampton was in that way a disappointment; she'd been surprised at how the artists, the musicians, the actors from the city—the supposedly unconventional people—fell all over themselves to vacation here, where everything so closely resembled her hometown. What a simplistic observation, she thought. How ignorant she had been when she thought that, how young.

It seemed a long time ago. She felt a stranger now here, as much of a stranger as she would feel in Katonah if she ever went back—she felt so out of place that it hurt. She started to fear she'd see someone she knew. After parking the bike, she ducked into a deli where she bought a few things without much consideration; picked up an *East Hampton Star,* threw it back on the rack.

She'd left her bike leaned against the wrought-iron railing that surrounded the patio of a fish restaurant she and Tommy used to go to. It was smack in the middle of Main Street and people were sitting at the tables, eating and drinking and watching the crowd moving by. Feeling exposed on both sides, she hung her bag over the handlebars, kicked up the bike stand and headed for the street.

At the light a car stopped beside her and a woman called, "Katha! Hello! I didn't know you were out this season." The woman put her white Saab in neutral and leaned toward the passenger window. She was in her mid-thirties, with bright yellow hair and a broad pretty face, lined white around the eyes from squinting in the sun. It was Claire Deyson, Ira's wife. Ira had been one of Tommy's partners in Stand, and in Gillorhan's, on the Upper West Side. She and Tommy used to spend a lot of time with the Deysons, even though Tommy didn't care much for Claire—but Katha liked Claire. All at once she remembered the ink spots on the pants she was wearing, that she hadn't washed her hair. She had on an old sweatshirt of Tommy's, and there was a tear at the neck. She'd forgotten her shades.

"How *are* you, Katha? Listen, I'll park the car and we'll chat a few minutes. Get a drink."

Katha felt nauseated. She went back to the sidewalk and curled herself up against the railing of the restaurant. She could just leave, take off on the bike and be gone by the time Claire found a space and got back. But she didn't. She waited, thinking of nothing and feeling progressively sicker. The crowd was surreal; the sound of the people and the cars was distorted, both loud and roaring, and dim, far away. She felt like she was tripping on hallucinogens.

"There you are! I got lucky and aggressive and nailed a space right at the corner." As Katha remembered, Claire had always been lucky and aggressive.

"Why don't you leave your bike here where you can watch it and we'll grab a table." Claire slammed her purse down over the railing to the closest table that had just been vacated on the patio, then she and Katha walked around to the entrance and back to the table and sat down.

Claire caught a waitress by the arm. "Oh, Irish coffee," she said. "Katha?"

"Nothing, thank you."

"Diet Coke? Water? Milk?"

"No."

"You sure?" Katha nodded. "So how've you been? What have you been doing? You should see the girls. Monica's going to be six feet tall, I swear. And Jeannie . . . Why haven't you called? I tried you a few times, I couldn't get you in."

"I don't know, Claire. It's been a bad year."

"Chinese Stand? Tommy hasn't lost it, has he?"

"No, nothing like that. But, it's, you know, a struggle."

Claire sighed, and looked apologetic. "We haven't been

by in such a long time." Katha shrugged, to put Claire at ease; a lot of people didn't come by. She'd noticed how, after the fire, the crowd at the club had subtly shifted until it was clear the allure, the particular magic of Stand had gone out of the place.

"We'll come down some night after Labor Day," said Claire. "I don't even attempt to get into the city when the kids are out of school. And when we're in the city, we don't ever seem to get downtown. I know, we should come by."

"That's all right, Claire. You know, whenever."

"How's Tommy's drinking?"

"What? Oh, all right." Katha laughed nervously. "He's cut it down. He was drinking too much."

"And what about you? Have you been working?"

"Working?"

"Modeling," Claire elaborated.

"No, no, I haven't been modeling lately."

"So what are you doing with yourself?"

"Pretty much I help Tommy. There's lots to do."

Katha watched Claire stir the coffee just put down in front of her; streams of it spilled down the sides of the glass. Claire scooped up a gob of whipped cream. "I saw one of your commercials on TV the other day," she said.

"Yes, that's an old one," said Katha. "It's been renewed. I get checks." She folded her hands like an anchor in her lap.

"Well, that's good . . ." Claire waved at someone she knew on the sidewalk. "Look, Katha," she said, in a tentative voice. "I've got to tell you. Ira's run into Tommy here and there, and he says he looks bad. Tired, too thin, really down."

"He's working too hard."

"Is he still doing coke?"

Katha laughed. "We can't afford coke."

That was true, they couldn't.

"I'm sorry," said Claire. "It's just that the last time we talked you said that was worrying you."

Katha didn't remember. "I did?"

She felt a twitch at the side of her mouth.

"You said . . ." Claire set down her spoon. ". . . when Tommy and Ira split up, Tommy acted as if he wanted to split up the friendship as well. But I hoped that wouldn't affect you and me."

Katha looked down at her hands. "It hasn't, there's just been—pressure. We've had all this pressure." She felt she might cry.

"You should come by the house, see the kids."

"Yes, I'd like that."

"This fall we should do the museums."

"Okay." She swallowed, and looked back at Claire.

"You all right?"

Katha smiled, pulled the sleeves of her sweatshirt down over her hands. "It's dumb," she said. "Lately I take things too hard." She shook back her hair. "Claire, I've got to go."

Claire studied her for a moment. "Well yeah, so do I. Know what I did?" She looked sheepish. "Left the darn car in a no-parking zone." Relieved, Katha laughed. Claire took a few sips from her drink. "Where are you this summer? Out at the Springs?" She threw up a hand for the check but the waitress raced by them. "This town," she said, rising, "is not what it used to be. Crowds, unbelievable." She left a five on the table. "I keep telling Ira we ought to put our place on the market, get something in Maine—in Maine we could buy an estate." They went out to the sidewalk. "Give me your number."

"I don't know it, I'll call you."

"You promise?"

"Say hi to Ira."

Katha watched as Claire turned and walked to her car; her walk was a sort of sashay, a long step then a swing of the purse that hung from her wrist. The crowd seemed to part as she passed. From the car she called, "Safe! I didn't get a ticket!"

Back at the house Katha made the boys lunch. She stood by the counter, watching them eat. She learned more about them: that their mother was dead, that, in Sam's words, their father was "out on the road, finding work." That explained the oldest brother's paternal attitude, and their wildness; these kids were largely without supervision. She didn't know how she felt about that. She'd had a normal upbringing, a privileged childhood, and look what had happened to her. Maybe, she thought, Sam and Peter were better off.

Sam said, for the third time, "This is the best sandwich I ever ate."

She laughed. "It's nothing special."

"You put something good on it, different, what is it?"

"Mayonnaise," she said. "I forgot the mustard."

"Good mayonnaise," said Sam.

Peter was quiet, sitting low in his chair. His enormous child's eyes moved from her face to Sam's. She had once wanted children. But she was too young when she married Tommy; it was dumb, but now she felt too old. One time, when Peter was mowing the lawn, the sky went all dark and a storm began. She had told him to stop, but he looked so distressed at this suggestion that she let him go ahead. She had watched him from the window as he pushed at the grass, while thunder sounded and rain began to fall.

Air fluttered in from outside. It was warmer, and it still hadn't rained. "I think I'll go to the beach," she said.

"What beach do you like?" asked Sam.

"Georgica, mostly."

"Me too." Sam dabbed at his mouth with the end of his red bandana. "Wish I had time for the beach, y'know, leisure. But I've got A, a trip to the bay, for dinner—I cook my own fish. Then B, I go home, clean the house. I like to keep up. Then C, cover business in the neighborhood."

"Wow," she said, "have another sandwich."

She went upstairs to change. When she came back Sam was gone, and Peter was mowing the lawn. As she was leaving the house the phone rang. But she was afraid it was Claire somehow, and let it ring.

The ocean was calm, a silvery color, the color of the sky, with a beautiful violet blur at the edge of the horizon. The smooth sand was cool, and the beach was empty for as far as she could see. She lay down on the beach and breathed with the ocean, licking the shore, caressing the land. She gave it her spirit. She slept.

A radio blared. Hip-hop music, rap. Katha stirred and, looking down the beach, saw a boy approaching. He carried a tremendous chrome box on his shoulder, a boom box, and as he got closer she saw it was Sam. He wore wraparound shades and a microscopic pair of blue bikini trunks. His cranelike legs were too long for his body; he looked like a white Watusi.

"May I join you?" said Sam.

He carried no towel, so Katha sat up and made room for him on the sheet that she used at the beach. She asked him to turn down the music.

"Prefer something else?" He fiddled with the dial. "Something along more classical lines?" She said that would be fine. "Thought I'd let things slide," Sam said. "Catch a few rays." He leaned back on the sheet, propped up on his elbows. Katha stayed where she was.

"There aren't many rays today," she said.

"They're diffused. That's how you get the deepest, darkest tan. The Bain de Soleil tan." The skin above his thin forearms, and below his neck, looked like the sun hadn't seen it for months. "It's a shame you're married," he said goodnaturedly.

For a second, startled, she thought, how could he know it's a shame? And then, still recovering from this flash of paranoia, she said, "I beg your pardon?"

"No criticism intended, Kathy."

"Katha."

"Oh. Peter calls you Kathy. I like Katha better. It suits you." He took off his shades. "As I was saying. I feel a person should take time before they marry. For example, me. I myself don't plan to get married until I'm very old. Twenty-five or twenty-six."

Yes, she thought, twenty-five was very old.

"Big Dan, my brother, he says a man should settle down as soon as he can. Then he won't be distracted from his life's purpose. Me, I believe the distractions *are* the purpose. Dan says I'm a dreamer." He polished his shades on the sheet, then he put them back on. "I basically follow the impulse of the moment."

"How old are you, Sam?" She thought he spoke well for his age. According to the thin line of hair on his lip, she figured his age at about fourteen.

"I won't lie to you, Katha. I'm recently sixteen. But a difficult life has matured me oh, far beyond my years."

"Do you mind my asking when your mother died?"

"It was Peter's mother died. Last summer. Mine and Big Dan's ran away before Peter was born. You might have noticed that me and Big Dan have the looks and the brains. That's from our mother. Except—excuse me, Katha— but our mother was a tramp. Peter's mother was a lady, like you. Except you have the looks and the brains to go with it."

She said, "Your brother's sweet, though. Peter."

"Yes," Sam agreed. "He's a piece of my heart."

Varley O'Connor

"I have two brothers," she told him. "But they're much older than I am and we're not very close." She hadn't thought about her brothers in a long time.

"I'm sure they're your great protectors," Sam said.

When Katha was twelve, her father was driving home from work one day and caught her in an embrace with a boy at the side of the road. She was promptly sent off to boarding school that following week, for the rest of seventh grade and half of eighth. Her brothers hadn't left home until college. They had been raised very differently from her. It struck her that that was the time, after boarding school, when she had begun to perceive her brothers as a unit, her parents as a unit, and herself as alone.

"Sam," she said, "I was hurt by that picture in my mailbox."

Sam turned a dark shade of pink and sat up. A full minute passed before he could speak. "I regret that, Katha. I told Big Dan not to do it, I pleaded with him." He shook his head sadly. "But, see, Big Dan has these pressures. He gets in a mood he does something like this, but doesn't mean it." Sam couldn't read Katha's face.

She said finally, "It won't happen again."

"No, ma'am. Sincerely."

She got up and took off her sweatshirt. "I'm going in for a swim. Come if you like." She started out and Sam followed. But he didn't swim, just splashed in the waves where the water was shallow. He'd never learned how to swim.

When they got out Katha said that she had to go home.

Sam took a chance. "Same time, same place? Tomorrow?"

She looked puzzled when he said that. "I'm not sure, Sam. It depends. I often come to the beach."

"If you do, I'll see you here." He decided not to wink.

He didn't know how he had done with her. One thing he knew was that women liked to feel in control. It may have

68

been good that the issue of the picture came up. It gave her the chance to put him in his place. Barbara had liked that, to put him in his place. Barbara couldn't hold a candle to Katha. Katha had a sweet suffering look about her face, like Peter's mother used to have. She wasn't hardened to the world; it got to her, she wasn't assured. With Katha he could talk. With Katha it would be more than physical. What was the physical part—a fly, a speck.

He hoped he'd made progress with her. On the whole, Sam concluded, things were looking up.

When Katha got home, the lawn was mowed and Peter had left. She was surprised to feel hungry. The ham and cheese she had bought at the deli were gone, but there was some bread left, and she remembered there was tuna in the pantry. When she looked it wasn't there. Funny, she thought, I could have sworn I had six or seven cans.

Just after midnight Big Dan and Sam were in the shed, putting black jackets on over their T-shirts. Sam was drunk on two beers and couldn't stop laughing.

"Can ya see it, Big Dan? I'll be up with the birds tomorrow to see it." Sam went into a spasm of laughter and rolled to the ground. "Hey man," he said, "where's the disc player?"

"How do I know?"

"I had it right here, by the tarp."

"Sam, what do you think, I keep inventory?"

This struck Sam as unbearably funny. "Ah shit," he said, laughing and holding his stomach, "we could open a store."

"You shouldn't drink," said Big Dan. "You lose control of yourself." Big Dan didn't drink. In his hands was a vinyl case that contained the guaranteed-surgically-sharp scissors that Peter's mother had sent away for from an ad on late-night TV. He took them out of the case and put the scissors in his pocket. "I'll bet he won't notice till he's missing six or seven," Dan said.

"I saw her today," said Sam, getting up from the ground.

"You wanna go?" said Big Dan.

"I think she likes me."

"You're nuts."

Big Dan would never be much of a friend, Sam thought. He was always either planning things or dreaming private dreams.

They went over to Harold's. All the lights were out.

"What if he keeps it in a drawer?" Sam said. "What if he sleeps with it under the pillow?" He started to laugh and clapped a hand across his mouth.

"The bedroom's in the back," said Big Dan. "Let's see if one of the front windows is open." A kitchen window was unlocked. Sam gave him a boost and Big Dan squeezed through. Sitting by the sink, he turned back to Sam. "You hear anything, make a big racket. I'll hide and you let him chase you into the woods."

"Right, got it."

"Take it easy."

"I'm easy, I'm easy."

Dan slid to the floor; shined his flashlight in an arc around the kitchen. "Check it out," he said under his breath. "It looks like a woman lives here." The kitchen was in perfect order. On all the appliances were form-fitting knitted covers, on the blender, the toaster, the microwave oven. Taped to the refrigerator were recipes and a Home*spun* from *Reader's Digest*. It said, "Having stocked up on sale carrots, one night for dinner I fixed carrot salad, stew with carrots and carrot cake. As we sat down to eat, my mother remarked, 'Sort of got carrot away, didn't you?'"

Dan said, "I might die laughing."

There was also a "Quotable Quote": "Faith is like radar, but only in heaven are the angels distinguished."

Like China

"Deep," said Big Dan. He ripped off July from a picture calendar and tossed it on the floor. He went into the living room. The first thing the beam of his flashlight hit was a gun rack holding three rifles. "Shit." His breath caught. "The old loon." He took the light off the guns and spun it over the room. Framed photographs crowded for room on end tables, the coffee table. There was one of Harold's sister who died in Florida. One was of a really ugly guy, Dan thought, with buck teeth, grinning at the camera to beat the band. Dan turned it face down on the table, thinking no one should have to look at that. Sure enough, some of the pictures were of guys in World War II uniforms.

Then the flashlight caught the flag, through a doorway in a smaller sitting room; it was resting on top of a TV cabinet like a centerpiece. When Dan went to the TV he could hear Harold breathing, long wheezy exhalations that whistled at the end. The bedroom was close, and the door must be open. He'd better be quiet.

He carefully undid the flag, memorizing the folds so he could put it back together. Then, after taking the scissors from his pocket, he cut out a single white star.

Chapter 6

"Where have you been?"

"Tommy. I've been here."

"You didn't answer the phone yesterday."

"I went to town on the bike. Then I was at the beach. Peter, you know? The little boy who mows the lawn. He was helping me clean up the house. We were cleaning the house, for when you get back." It was eleven o'clock in the morning and Tommy was drunk. "How's your mother?"

"I'll be back tonight."

"Oh. About what time?"

"I don't know what goddamn time. Six or seven."

"I'll be here."

"You sound like shit."

"I'm sorry."

"You're sorry." He hung up.

She ran up the stairs to the bedroom, took her wallet from her purse, but her damn hands were shaking so bad that when she opened the wallet all the cards and papers inside it flew out and scattered on the floor. She dropped the wallet and sat on the bed, staring at the papers with jotted-down phone numbers, theater tickets, business cards of people she'd forgotten. Pieces of her life.

Anyway, it wouldn't be there. She'd thrown it out. Even if it was there, what would she do? What would she say to the doctor? He would refer her to some crisis hotline or something when, after all, it wasn't that bad. It was that bad. What she needed was a friend, but what would she do with a friend. There was nothing she could say. There were some situations you were not to allow, you were not to get involved in, ever. Ever.

That's what you get for not playing by the rules, for playing with fire—what you get is the smell in your head. For life.

But were there indications, the doctor had said, before all the trouble, prior to the fire. She had said no, there were no indications. He always had a temper. He's naturally volatile. He's Italian, she joked. But his temper was never directed at me. No, there were no indications. I mean you could read indications of violence into anyone's behavior, couldn't you? Any man's. But if nothing ever happened then what would it be? Would it count then or wouldn't it?

What she wanted to say to the doctor was, look, don't go creeping around in my past, or in Tommy's—just tell me what to do, how to handle this thing. That's all I want to know, what to do. Because I don't have time, and because there's some love here, all right? Some love has gone on that you can't know anything about, the kind of love that can't be erased—so since you're the expert, just tell me what to do.

That's how she'd planned to be, brusque.

But instead she had just sat there, pulling the sleeves of her sweater down over her hands.

The doctor said, What are you doing with your sweater?

She was cold, but she said, I don't know, nervous habit.

What was Tommy's father like?

He hated him.

Revelation, insight. So what.

Where did you meet Tommy?

At Split, this rock 'n' roll club on East Thirty-third. He was one of the owners.

Tell me about it.

There's nothing to tell. Just me and my friend Maddie going to this place because her boyfriend was the drummer in the band. It was dark, it was hot. It was summer and the air-conditioning was broken. The band was so loud you could feel the vibrations up your legs from the floorboards. I remember there was this man in a dress who was dancing on the bar. And Maddie said, see that guy at the bar? And I said, the one dancing? And she said, no idiot, the one leaning. It was Tommy. He was beautiful. There was something so graceful about him. He had these thick-framed black glasses on, and a white dress shirt, and a tie, and I remember I said that he looked like a lawyer except that his jeans were faded and tight.

What happened?

When the place closed he had a drink with the band and I met him. He was very soft-spoken, and polite, but he didn't pay that much attention to me. The guitarist's brother was in some kind of trouble and Tommy was giving him advice.

Why was he giving him advice?

Tommy went to law school.

But never practiced?

No, he opened Split with a friend, and it went.

How did you get together?

I went back there two nights later because I wanted to see him. He remembered my name.

What was it about him?

Oh, it just seemed, he just seemed like the other part of myself. You know what I mean?

I think so. You say you're a model.
I used to be a model.
Successful?
Sometimes.
How did your husband feel about your career?
He was proud of me.
Ever jealous?
No, he knows I love him.
Do you still love him?
I don't know why I'm here.
Your husband broke your arm, Mrs. Pinnell.
He didn't really break it. He drinks too much, and one night I didn't want him to have another drink. The bottle was on the counter in the kitchen and I stood in front of it. He told me to get out of the way but I wouldn't, so he came at me, to push me out of the way, and I held up my arm and it got broken.
But he didn't break it.
He didn't mean to break it.
There was an incident—she hadn't told the doctor since she hadn't remembered it then—about two years after they were married. They had gone to a movie. She said some little thing, some stupid little thing that ticked Tommy off, and he started yelling at her on the sidewalk. She said, "Tommy, calm down, it's not such a big thing. I'm sorry, all right?" But he couldn't calm down. He kept yelling and yelling as if he couldn't stop. She stood weeping on the sidewalk as people passed by, as much from humiliation as from anything else. She said, "Please, don't do this here," and Tommy yelled, "You don't know these people, what the fuck is wrong with you?"
Everything. She had utterly failed to soothe her husband, to comfort him. When the anger came she seemed to draw it from him, no matter what she tried to do. And when it began to come frequently, when it was finally disconnected

from anything she had done directly, she shut herself off from it, kept a part of herself, deep inside, far away until it was over. She became calculating, her instincts as sharp as a deer's in the woods. For by then she wasn't dealing with temper, she was dealing with rage.

Tommy called it the blackness, the poison. It came into his eyes, and washed through his body like a storm, and then it would be gone. He suffered for it, and he tried to make it up to her later; though not so much anymore. It stayed with him longer now, sitting just below the surface. It built for days now, weeks, and when it came it was an explosion, a tempest, and behind it she couldn't see Tommy, the person. It destroyed him. It was as though something had split his spirit, and in the rift the darkness had gathered and conquered him. She couldn't find him. She didn't know where he had gone.

Someone knocked on the door downstairs and she leaped from the bed as if she'd been shot. She waited for the knocking to stop, and then she went slowly down the stairs. It was Peter. He stood on the deck, his face pressed urgently against the glass. When he saw her he started knocking again. She stood gazing at him; his nose was flattened and beneath it was a cloud of vapor from his breath.

She roused herself and opened the door.

He looked relieved. "Ma'am, I've come for more work on the house," he said.

"There isn't any more work on the house."

"Big Dan sent me."

"Your brother wields a lot of power in your family, doesn't he?"

Peter was obdurate; she let him in.

"Would you like something to drink? I was just going to have something." Peter shook his head no, and Katha poured some vodka into a cup. She said, "I don't feel well today." He stood in the middle of the room, staring at her.

Like China

"I guess we could put the sheets back on the beds." She'd slept on the couch again last night, wrapped in a bedspread.

"Have you found your dog?" she said, when they were through. She'd poured another vodka and made Peter sit down with her at the table.

"No, ma'am."

"I'm sorry. I had a dog once, when I was little. A beagle. It was real pretty. You know those velvet-brown eyes that they have? But it was high-tempered. It terrorized the neighborhood. Tearing up gardens, chewing people's lawn furniture. It ate one of my mother's satin pillows. Isn't that funny?" The drinks were going to her head. "Well, see, it's funny because my mother, she's got a thing for satin pillows." She put her face on her arms and laughed. "When I went to summer camp my parents gave it to a farm, where it would be happier." Actually, they had put the dog to sleep, but she didn't want to tell Peter that.

"Banjo," he said, "is happy with me."

"Oh, I know that. I'm sure he is." Poor little boy, he looked so sad. She was nine when she got home and found her dog gone. So she'd run away. It wasn't only the dog, she just thought it would be better if she left. She must have been pretty determined since she'd headed for Boston on a bus and had gotten as far as Springfield before she was caught. She'd been a fierce little kid.

She slugged back the vodka, then picked up her shades, which were lying on the table. "You know how I feel when I have on my shades?" she asked Peter. "Like I'm almost invisible." He looked perplexed. "Here, try it," she said. She gave him the shades and he put them on. "See what I mean? Don't you feel like I sort of can't see you?"

"I don't know," Peter said. "It looks dark." He got embarrassed and took the shades off.

"Where's your father?" she asked him.

He seemed to think very hard, his lips compressed. Then he said, "Sam said."

"I know, that he's out on the road?" Peter nodded. "But where?" Peter stared blankly at the shades he'd put down on the table. "I guess he doesn't tell you," she said.

"What should we do next?" Peter asked.

"I don't feel like more housecleaning, I feel—like going for a bike ride." She got up and put her cup in the sink. "Do you want to come? Come on, I'll help you look for Banjo."

Peter was glad that this time he had brought along his bike. Katha said she was happy to see it. She said she thought he lost it, then she said he could have it for good. Peter had forgotten that the bike wasn't already his. But now it was his.

He told her he'd looked everywhere for Banjo, so she said they would ride to the general store and put up a notice. This made Peter feel a new hope. After they'd put a sign in the window, with Peter's address and Katha's phone number on the bottom, she bought two Mountain Dews. They sat on a bench by the store and drank their Mountain Dews. Peter watched people getting in and out of cars, and he was happy, thinking how each one would learn that Banjo was missing.

"When your dad gets home," Katha said, "he can put an ad in the paper." Peter grinned hugely. "Do you miss your dad?"

"No." He thought of Banjo sleeping underneath his bed, about how when he was a puppy he was so small you could curl him up and fit him in a baseball cap. Sam said Peter's mother had given him Banjo for his birthday one time, but he didn't remember.

"I miss my dad," said Katha. "My father's a brilliant man. He loves beautiful things, books, and paintings, and furniture. He just doesn't do so well with people. People can't measure up to a book I suppose." She looked off up the highway. "See that road?" she said. "If I had any guts I'd get on this bike and I'd ride up that road. I'd even keep riding when I hit the expressway. I wouldn't stop in New York. I'd just keep riding. I'd settle down somewhere down south." When she and Tommy got married he told her to make up a list of what she wanted for the next fifty years. She'd put down "trips," so she'd gotten trips. She liked it down south—Tallahassee, New Orleans, Mobile. She could get lost in those places. Take a new name. She could really go anywhere she wanted to go.

"Down there," she said, "I'd get some kind of job, maybe in a diner. That's what I'd do if I had any guts."

"I couldn't go with you," said Peter. "Because if Banjo came home and I was gone, he couldn't find me."

She laughed and ruffled his hair. "That's okay, I'm not going anyway." She looked back at the road. "But if I did go, you'd want to come with me?"

Peter thought, sure he would, if Banjo came too.

"No," said Katha. "You'd have to stay here. You've got your brothers and your dad to think about. They'd feel bad if you left. Family is very important, Peter. You've got to remember that. I don't think that your father should have gone off like he did. There are jobs here in town, there . . ." She looked back at Peter. His eyes were shrouded over, but the rest of his face was in a thrall of concentration. "Peter?" she said. "What is it?" Then—watching his face—she thought of his house, of the desolate feeling she'd had on the day she had been there, of how Sam and Big Dan were guarding the house, and it came to her. "Peter. How long has your dad been gone? He's gone, isn't he? You and your brothers are living completely on your own."

Peter jumped up and dropped his Mountain Dew. "No!"

She said, "Peter, tell me."

"No." He was panicking. "If they find out they'll put us in homes, me and Sam and Big Dan. If Banjo came back I'd be gone." Now he'd done it, he'd told, the lady knew. Something pounded through his brain. He put his hand to his forehead and pressed to make it stop. He pressed and it pounded, harder and harder.

"Peter, stop it," she was saying. "Stop it, relax. Calm down." She had taken his arms and was making him sit on the bench. "It's all right, it's okay. It'll be okay." Her voice made the pounding stop. She put her arm around his shoulders. He liked it there, it was warm. He let it stay there.

She patted his shoulder; he was settling down. She tightened her arm around him, feeling his smallness, feeling him quiet. Thank God, for a second she'd thought that his eyes were about to pop out of his head. All his Mountain Dew had spilled onto the ground so she gave him the rest of hers to finish. She had to think. She thought if she hadn't been so self-involved she would have realized what was going on sooner. She'd have to do something, call the authorities, but who *were* the authorities, what would they do? She wasn't certain it was bad for the boys to be living on their own. With one mother who'd run off, another dead, and a father who'd deserted, how had these kids been any better off before than they were now? The oldest boy was sixteen anyway, maybe older, and Sam was mature for his age. They'd get along for a while. It was summer, there was no school.

She wasn't thinking clearly. If someone took them out of their environment now, when they were young, they might stand a chance for a normal, proper life. What was a normal, proper life? If her life had progressed the way it was supposed to, she and Tommy could have taken in the boys. She and Tommy.

"Peter, I won't tell," she said. She would give them until September. If no one else had turned them in by then she would have to. "I won't tell, Peter. I promise."

He believed her, trusted her. She had given him the bike and put a note in the window.

"But my husband's coming back tonight. So don't come around so often anymore. I won't tell, but if my husband knew I couldn't speak for him."

It was okay, Peter thought. He had told, but it was okay. Kathy had made it okay. He wished Kathy's husband wasn't ever coming back. He couldn't see why her husband hated her.

They got on their bikes to ride to the beach. The sun was attempting to break through the sky, through the leaves of the trees; the sky was pale blue. They cut across Hither and down Egypt Lane, and then walked through the trail by Hook Pond, where rushes, cattails and ferns fringed the water. In the reeds they discovered a nest made of grass. Katha knelt down and touched it; she told Peter that mallards had made it, and the one in the water, of sticks, she said was the swan's. The ducks lifted their tails, their heads down in the water, as they foraged for food. Getting close to the ocean, they saw a house had been razed; all that was left was the deep open pit of the basement. They stood at the edge of the pit, looking down.

"One time," said Katha, "when I was your age, I went for a walk with my brother and we stopped by this farm where my brother used to play—he was older than I was. The farm was deserted. There was a barn but the house was gone. There was just a big hole in the ground, like this. John said a man was buried down there, but I couldn't tell anyone, he said, because it was classified information. The man was buried alive. The government was using him for an experiment. They'd buried him at the bottom of the pit, providing him only with two plastic tubes, one for air so he could breathe, one for water and liquid food. At the end of two years they were going to dig him up to see if he survived."

"Did he?" said Peter.

"Oh no!" she said, laughing. "There was no man down

there. My brother was just teasing. No one would bury a person at the bottom of a pit."

They went on to the beach, and coming up to the dunes they saw Sam walking down by the surf. He carried his boom box again; he wore his blue trunks and his shades, and a great big straw hat. He spotted them and waved, started jogging to meet them.

"We put up a sign at the store!" called Peter, abandoning his bike and running to Sam.

"About what?" said Sam.

"Banjo," said Peter.

"That was very thoughtful of you," Sam said to Katha. "Hey, where's your suit? Mean rays today, huh?" The sun had just burst through the sky. Katha suddenly had to be alone. Sam's music was loud and the sun was too bright; the effect of the vodka was wearing off.

"I've got to go," she told Peter. "I've got things to do before my husband gets home. Nice seeing you, Sam." She left the beach, walking her bike to the parking lot, in the direction of the road.

"My luck," said Sam. He went rapidly away down the beach. Peter ran to get his bike, dragged it through the sand after Sam. "Sam, wait!"

Sam turned back, annoyed, and waited for Peter who was huffing and puffing with the bike. "Fuck it," Sam said. He turned off the music. "Here, nerd. You carry the radio, I'll take the bike."

"Going home?" said Peter.

"Yeah, mess around with the guys." Sam took off his hat and heaved a long sigh. "To be young is a curse," he told Peter. "It's something you've just got to get through until you're old enough for the good stuff."

Katha took her time going home. She rode a circuitous route through the roads on the ocean side, by the shingled

Like China

Victorians and moderns with glittering glass; she passed a strange house that looked a little like an igloo but more like a nuclear reactor. When she got to the highway she stopped, looked up at the sun, let it beat on her face. In back of her eyes there were diamonds. She laid the bike on the ground and sat down beneath a tree. Watched the cars whizzing by. People coming and going. Going. She didn't need a doctor, she needed a priest. She would kneel before the priest and say, Father, forgive me for I have sinned. I have sinned deeply, in my soul, or this wouldn't be happening. If only the sun would burn it away, burn away my sin. If the sun could make me pure again, take away what I have seen. I'm going to die, she thought. I think I'm going to die. She got up, the dazzling sun in her face. She picked up the bike. Then she turned, away from the sun and the highway. She got on the bike and rode home.

Big Dan had been jumpy all day. After his brothers had left in the morning, he screamed at the rest of the boys to get lost; then, every ten minutes or so, he lifted an edge of the newspapers taped to the windows, looked at Harold in his yard. Just before two o'clock, Artie came by and Dan sold him the compact disc player for eighty-five dollars. When he left, Dan went back to check Harold; he'd stayed where he was. Sam came in with Peter, bellowing, "Love, love, it's destroying me!" at the top of his lungs.

"Shut up," said Big Dan, "or I'll knock your head off."

"What's with you?"

"C'mere." Sam went to the window and looked out the slit with Big Dan; Harold was sitting in a chair on his lawn.

"So what?" said Sam.

"He's been there all day," said Big Dan. "Just sitting there, staring at the house."

"So what? I told ya, I watched him this morning and he put up the flag same as always and didn't even notice. You see that star we cut out, nerd?" Sam asked Peter. "Pretty funny, huh?"

Peter didn't appear to be listening. He was just standing there, dreamy-eyed. Big Dan thought he looked as pleased and as stupid as a piece of apple pie.

"You dumb jerks," Big Dan said. He checked the window again, then plopped down in the big easy chair that used to be his father's.

"Where's the guys?" asked Sam.

"Out! Out!" yelled Big Dan. "Which is where you two jerks are going too because I never get any peace in this house."

"Sure, Big Dan, sure," said Sam. "Come on, nerd, I'll give you a treat and take you over to Paul's. His uncle's a queen. Wait'll ya see." A queen? thought Peter. His uncle's a queen?

"Hey, Big Dan," said Sam. "You happen to locate that disc player yet?" He didn't get an answer.

"Big Dan?" said Peter. "Can we put an ad in the paper for Banjo?"

"You two," said Big Dan, "are the bane of my existence. Get gone, *comprende*?"

"The guy's senile," said Sam. "He's got no reason to be sitting out there, he's just sitting out there. What else has he got to do?"

"*Comprende?*" yelled Dan.

Harold wasn't senile, no way. Things were about to come down. The back door slammed shut. Bonacker, that was what did it. Damn bigot, thought Dan. He sank down in the chair, feeling the shape of his father—he could almost smell fish.

Even now, every year when the first frost came, Dan would wake up with the distinct unpleasant sensation of handling ice and fish in the packing house. He hadn't done it for years but still he could see himself standing next to

Like China

Daddy in the dawn, boxing those fish until his hands were numb and he was afraid he couldn't stand up any longer. He learned from Daddy to curse those fish, to curse a life where a man worked ten, twelve, eighteen hours a day and just ended up poor. "If I had any brains," Daddy said, "I'd get out of fishing, flush the damn saltwater out of my blood." But even later, when Daddy got busted, did time and lost his license—so he had to do road work, clerking, caretaking jobs, whatever he could get—even then he'd drive out to the beach every day in the morning, just to see the ocean. It didn't make sense. Dan went with him once, sat watching his father's gnarled, swollen fisherman's hands on the wheel, saw his face as he stared at the sea with a look that could only be love; saw him loving the thing that just about killed him. Missing the thing that turned on him time after time.

Dan stayed where he was, brooding and checking on Harold till daylight had started to fade. He saw Harold take down the flag and finally go into his house. He heard Peter and Sam and the rest of the guys out in back, trying to be quiet. Well good, he thought, it was good they were back. He waited a little while longer, for darkness to begin, then he got up to go out to the yard. Peter was sitting in the kitchen, drinking milk.

All of his hair had been shaved off his head.

"*Sam!*" Big Dan went to the door, threw it open. "Jesus," he said to Peter, "you look like an egg."

Sam came into the kitchen.

"What the fuck did you do to his head?" said Big Dan.

"Paul's uncle gave me a skinhead," said Peter. "Like Paul's."

"Nice move, Sam," said Big Dan.

"He wanted it, didn't you, nerd?"

"I don't know," said Peter.

"Who's in the yard?" asked Big Dan.

"Mike and Roger and Paul," said Sam.

"Go get Frankie and Ben," said Big Dan. "We've gotta get rid of the loot." He sat down by Peter and lit up a smoke. "That vacant shack out on Whippoorwill, that's where we'll take it. Well, go, Sam, I want this done fast."

"How come we've got to get rid of the loot?"

"What are you, Sam, mentally deficient? We get busted I don't want it around, you follow?"

"Who's getting busted? Man, this is *Harold, Weird Harold*." Big Dan was unmoved. Sam threw up his hands and went out the back door.

"Sam says Daddy's coming back," said Peter.

"No, Peter. Don't worry about it. You wanna help?"

"Yeah, Danny."

"We've got to go careful, back around behind the houses. Real quiet, okay?"

Even with eight boys working it took close to three hours to transport the loot from the shed to the shack out on Whippoorwill, near the north side of the bay; it was two miles away. When it was done, Big Dan told Sam and Paul to get rid of the loot in the house—there wasn't much. He told everyone else to get lost, forever, finito, don't ever come back.

Sam spat on the ground, shot Big Dan a glare.

"You got a problem?" Big Dan asked Sam.

Sam turned and went into the house after Paul, leaving Peter and Big Dan alone in the yard. "Take that bike back to the Brenners'," Big Dan told Peter.

"But it's mine."

"I don't want it here. You gonna take it or have I got to do it myself?"

"No, Danny, I'll do it." Peter knew better than to argue. He wanted to go over to Kathy's house anyway, to see how she was. But he wouldn't give the bike back. It was his. He'd hide it somewhere until Big Dan was out of his mood.

Like China

From his bike, on the way, he called Banjo but his heart wasn't in it. He was tired, and the breezes felt funny on his head. He reached up and touched the stubble. He didn't mind it. His hair was exactly like Paul's. Paul was thirteen, and strong. Sam said with the skinhead, he looked like Paul.

He parked his bike in the bushes at the foot of the dunes. Her husband was there so he'd have to be careful. He went down the last dune on his belly through the grass. The grass prickled his face.

The car wasn't there in the driveway. The glass doors were closed, but a light shone through the drawn curtains. Peter lay watching the curtains, translucent in the light. No one was there. Her husband had come in his car to take Kathy away. He took her to the beach and put her down in the waves. He took her to the pit and buried her for an experiment. Peter felt sick in his head. It was warm, and there were stars, but in his head there was Kathy and her husband and Banjo and Sam and Big Dan, all fighting, punching his brain.

Holding his head, he got up and recrossed the dunes, then he got on the bike and rode home. When he came around the corner of Rappaport Lane he remembered he was going to hide the bike, but he couldn't think where. He parked the bike behind the shed and sat down to think. But he was tired, it had been a long day, and soon he lay down by the bike on the ground and fell asleep.

When Peter went to take the bike back, Big Dan went for a walk to mull everything over. He walked through the woods, smoking Camels. His legs felt hollow. The eighty-five dollars he had gotten from Artie felt heavy in his pocket. He thought about how it would feel to be free. He thought about girls and nice clothes, and being free. At last he went home and buried the money in the dark empty shed, and then he felt better. He went into the house and found Paul in the kitchen, stacking canned food in a box.

"Skip the food," he told Paul. "Where's Sam?"

"He went over to Harold's."

"What do ya mean he went over to Harold's?"

Paul grinned. "He's shredding the flag."

"Go home, Paul," said Big Dan. "You hear me? Go home."

Dan dashed out the front door and across the road. The white house was dark. He went into a crouch to approach it. The kitchen window was yawning wide open; the curtain whipped out in the warm night breeze. Dan heard a voice— it was Harold's—and under cover of the noise he leaped up to the window, and in one single move he got in and over the sink to the floor. Harold's voice stopped. Dan crawled to the wall and followed it out to the doorway, where he could see, but dimly, into the living room and beyond, to where the TV and the flag were. There was a motion. A light flipped on. Harold, in pajamas and robe, had Sam backed up against the wall behind the TV. Harold's rifle was an inch from Sam's face.

Chapter 7

Dan sprang into the doorway, slapping the wall and yelling, *"Shoot me!"* He put up his hands and froze, waiting for the gun to explode.

Harold spun around, blinking through the darkness of the living room at Dan. In the light behind Harold, Sam was plastered to the wall, his face white and still, his eyes wide black holes. The curtain in the kitchen whipped in the breeze.

"You little SOB," said Harold. His sparse gray hair stood up like the feathers of a bird in a windstorm. "I've gotcha now. I've got two for the price of one." He cackled, the leathery crinkles of his face bunching up around his eyes. He moved in on Dan. "How's it feel, boy? How's it feel to look up a gun? New experience, huh, you little wiseass sonofabitch. Get over by the other one, move it!" He herded Dan to the wall behind the TV next to Sam, and stood grinning, holding them both with the gun.

Dan thought if the TV weren't in the way he'd dive for Harold's legs. The damn flag was on the TV. He heard Sam's breathing, quick and shallow.

"I'm gonna shoot off your kneecaps," said Harold. "The

other one, I'm gonna shoot off his ear. Just rewards. Invade a man's house, you take your just rewards." Harold raised the gun to his face, put his eye to the sights. "Who's first, you or him?"

Dan thought they were dead.

Harold lowered the gun. "In the kitchen," he said. "Step to, march!" The boys marched in single file to the kitchen, the gun in Dan's back. Sam took miniature, mincing steps. In the kitchen they stood in the dark, Dan and Sam with their backs to the refrigerator. Harold, with the gun in one arm, picked up the phone.

"Police," he said. "Reporting a robbery."

"Robbery of what?" yelled Dan.

"Breaking and entering!" Harold slammed down the phone and refocused the gun. "You think I won't shoot? Give me more lip, boy, come on, I'm hot for the trigger." Dan was silent. "What's it gonna be," Harold asked him, "blasted kneecaps or a trip to the juvie home?"

"Call 'em," said Dan. Now that he knew he would live, Dan's mind was working fast, darting out to the home for delinquents in Quogue, then to Daddy and to how he could get his hands around his throat and squeeze the life out of him. He pictured bars, and Peter alone in the house across the street. He saw Sam dead.

Harold called again, but he was put on hold. "Damn murder could be committed," he said, "before these jokers pick up the phone. Police? I've gotcha now, boy. Police? Hello, Sergeant. Harold Meeversham here, out at 444 Rappaport Lane. Caught a couple of hoodlums breaking into my house. I've got them subdued. You people want to come out here and get them or you want me to shoot 'em myself? That's right, 444. Just as soon," he said, hanging up. "Make the world a better place."

"They're on their way," he told Sam and Dan as if they

would be pleased. Then he smiled at Dan, cordially. "I've gotcha, boy. I've gotcha good."

Peter woke hearing sirens. Police, he thought, coming to get us. Police. He ran into the house to find Big Dan and Sam, but they were gone. Everyone was gone. He went to the windows and lifted the paper: three cop cars screeched to a halt in front of Harold's. The spinning top lights of the cars flashed over the road. The cops ran with their hands on their guns into Harold's. In a minute they came out with Big Dan and Sam. Peter lit out the back door. Leaving his bike, he scaled the back fence and ran through the woods.

He fell and then crouched, quaking, by a car on the other side of Rappaport. He scooted under the car on his back. He saw stars in the sky and the shapes that they made. He didn't hear sirens, just the breeze.

He kept lying under the car, waiting and trying to know when he would be safe. He needed his bike to make a getaway, but he couldn't go back. He kept trying to think where could he go in the morning when the people came out of their houses. He listened for cops in the woods but heard only the breeze.

Finally, he came out from the car. Then around behind the houses to the shack, on Whippoorwill, like Big Dan said. Peter remembered.

The breeze was cold, hitting black shadows back and forth across the lawns. But the dogs on chains didn't bark because he went quiet like a cat. Soon he heard chops on the bay, felt the wet on his face, and then Whippoorwill and the shack leaped out at his eyes in the darkness.

He opened the door and went in. It was dark. He bumped into the loot. He got to his knees and carefully felt for a place to sit down. He eased to the ground and began to lean back—his head hit something sharp, the radio Big Dan was fixing that day. Peter felt for the knob and turned it on. A song came: ka-boom, ka-boom, ka-boom boom boom. Peter settled back, holding his arms against the cold, and listened to the song. Ka-boom, ka-boom, ka-boom boom boom.

The thing to do, thought Katha, was to call the police. Tommy could be lying in a ditch somewhere at the side of the road, his head split open, the motor of the car still running while the life drained out of him. Drunk on the road, then dead on the road. Could be. She'd have to identify him.

She'd waited until four A.M. to call Chinese Stand, so when she called no one was there. Then she called the apartment and the phone rang and rang. Tommy never did this, something had happened. Unless he was setting her up by not showing, taunting her so that when he came she'd be one exposed nerve, ragged, pulsing and shining with fear.

She went back upstairs. She'd spent the night upstairs for as long as she could, then downstairs for as long as she could, then back upstairs. Soon it would be morning. The vodka was gone. Magazines and books lay in a path from the living room up to the bedroom, as well as a variety of shirts, sweaters, sweatshirts, and jackets. She kept getting cold and putting something on, and then getting hot and taking it off. The radio downstairs softly played static. She went back downstairs. She sat at the table and watched the glass doors. He would come through the doors.

"Hi, Tommy. I've been worried." No. She should go up to bed and pretend to be asleep. Feigning unconsciousness would give her time to detect what state he was in before she did anything. He might be okay, there was that to consider. He could show up okay. But the vodka was gone and he'd want some. Why'd she drink the vodka? She felt it bitter and rancid on her teeth, on her tongue. In the pit of her stomach it burned around a dull empty throb. To sleep. But her mind was wired, and at the tips of the wires lights sparkled, crackled, spread through the room. She shut her eyes but the lights were still there, more real than she was. She didn't feel real. She opened her eyes and felt herself divide, felt part of her rise from where she sat and float up to the ceiling; and from the ceiling she saw herself down at the table: her skin was so thin it was almost transparent. She was fading, a slow fade to black like the end of a movie. To cease, not to be. A blank, as if she had never existed. So simple, complete, easy, and sad, the saddest thing she'd ever seen. She got up and went to the doors, put her hands on the glass, saw the trees being tossed by the wind. Once you got hit a few times it wasn't so scary, it wasn't so scary to die. She felt a strange calm. She thought of the South, of Mobile, New Orleans. Of suicide trees. After two or three hundred years the great trees bend a branch to the ground, contracting diseases that spread upward, through the trunk. The branch has to be severed to save the tree. And there were dead forests, moss killing cypress. She remembered that moss is not a true parasite because it takes only water from its host; it kills indirectly by blocking the sunlight from the leaves of the tree.

But why can't you remember? she thought. Tommy. Remember us dancing. How we went to Vegas and drove out to the desert and were so drunk on love we got out of the car and danced. At the casino that night we dropped five thousand dollars. You said, you're my wife? I said I'm your wife, your life. Remember how the desert shone. How you kissed me so hard my lips bled. In the plane, on the way home there was a storm. We rose high above the clouds, clouds like tremendous black mountains, and a new moon appeared in a dark-blue sky that brought a flaming strip of sunset, flashes of lightning, and finally the clouds turning white and frothy. We flew over some town where, the pilot said, the sugar grew so fast and so thick that the land was like a paradise on earth. Just below us, under the sky, was a paradise on earth.

Tommy, she thought, by the time we rented this house I knew it was over. We came out to find a place late this year, in April. Afterwards, you were too drunk to drive back, so we stayed at the inn. We were over a garden, remember. I knew that I hated you. When you touched me that night I wanted to scream, I wanted my mouth to be gagged with the sheet. There was a crack in the window; in the morning a wasp flew in and circled my face. I opened the window, hoping the wasp would fly back out but it didn't, more flew in. Wasps filled the room. You were asleep. I shut the window, plugged the crack with a towel, and with one of your shoes I killed the wasps one by one, smashed them up against the wall when they lighted. When it was over I sat on the bed, your shoe in my hand, and watched some of the wasps, still twitching, dying on the floor.

The night before I'd dreamed I was walking, walking for days. I was hungry and tired. When I got home my key broke in the lock. I walked out on the pier—it was East Hampton or Montauk—and under my feet it was rotten. Black water seeped through the boards and they gave way. But the water got clear, and underneath it I was safe. I was in a huge underwater tourist vessel, safe, except every few minutes a shark drifted by. It didn't threaten or stalk, just drifted silently by in front of the window, every few minutes, like clockwork.

The phone rang. She jumped back from the doors.

Don't get it, don't get it. The phone rang again.

She went and picked up the phone. "Tommy?" She heard the hiss of his cigarette smoke. "Where are you?" He didn't answer. "What's wrong." She heard him breathing. Clutching the receiver, she hunched against the counter in the kitchen. "Don't. You know I can't stand it when you do this." The sound of his breathing, the hiss of the smoke.

Tears started sliding down her face. "Tommy, what did I do? Just say what I did." Didn't answer the phone yesterday, didn't say the right things, didn't tell the right lies. She thought she heard traffic in the background, a whirr through the wires. "Where are you?" He didn't answer— she carefully hung up the phone. Then she looked at it, thinking, now look what I did. Oh God, look what I did. She was shaking. She turned and looked back at the doors.

First, she thought, pick up the clothes. I'll pick up the clothes and the books and magazines. No, go upstairs for your purse and just leave. Where? Go up the stairs. Yes. Now take the purse and get a jacket, it's cold. Go down the stairs, go out the door. I have to leave a note. No, no note. I have to. Write, *Tommy, I've left you.* Nothing else? There's nothing else to say. Go out the door. Yes, but don't listen for the sound of the car in the driveway, walk. Walk to the ocean and walk along the beach. You have to walk a ways on the beach to get to a road that is safe, where he wouldn't be driving. Walk, just keep walking. Walk, it's getting light.

Two hours later, Katha emerged from the beach to a road she didn't know. Well, goddamnit to hell where am I, she thought. You motherfucker. She meant Tommy. All through the walk on the beach she thought, God, God, how can I do this to him? And now she was calling him motherfucker. He *was* a motherfucker. Motherfucker.

Headlights occasionally cut through the mist that rolled down the road, floating by like dreams in the morning. Her shoes were wet. In her purse were three expired credit cards, two that were charged up over the limit, and thirty-five dollars in cash. She'd left her checkbook on the bureau.

She'd decided she had to go to Claire's. But Claire lived in Southampton, and where was Southampton, which way? If she could get to a phone she'd call Claire to come get her— no, call a cab. Might as well blow the whole thirty-five in one shot. But after reflecting on this she decided it wasn't such a good idea, and there weren't any phones anywhere, so when the next car came by she stuck out her thumb. The car soared by and disappeared into the mist. Another came by, and another. Nobody stopped. This went on for half an hour, and with each car that passed she felt more dejected; this whole trip was becoming really grim. If no one would stop then she must look bad, crazy. She'd have to walk and she didn't know where and her shoes were leaking. She felt her bottom lip quiver but she said no, don't do it, don't cry. The one thing you can't do now is cry. That would be too much. Don't do it.

And in a few minutes, in a miraculous change of luck which she couldn't help but associate with the hard resolution she'd employed in not crying, a white Sirocco pulled up beside her and the door swung open.

The driver was a middle-aged black woman with hair about half an inch long, wearing tremendous pendulous earrings that were studded with rhinestones. "Come on, get in the car if you're coming," she said.

Katha murmured, "Thanks," and got in.

"Where are you going?"

"I don't know. I mean, I'm going to Southampton but I don't know where it is."

"The other direction. You in some kind of trouble?"

The car smelled like incense. "If it's in the other direction," said Katha, "you'd better pull over and let me back out. Thanks though for picking me up."

The woman kept driving. "I'm gonna pull over and let you get picked up by someone you shouldn't get picked up by? You some kind of damn fool, hitchhiking?"

"You're right," said Katha. "You can pull over. Now that I know where it is I'll just walk."

"Where are you going in Southampton?"

"To my friend's."

"Well good. Where's your friend live?" The woman did a U-turn and swung the car back into the mist in the other direction.

"I can't let you take me."

"You sure can. What's the address?" Katha told her, and they drove awhile in silence.

"Why are you doing this?" said Katha.

"Girl, you seem to be skating at the edge of a cliff for some reason. I'm afraid if somebody doesn't do *something* you'll skate right on off."

"I left my husband this morning."

"Oh. Bad scene?"

"Yeah, bad scene." This woman was out of the sixties, thought Katha, or out of some distant star in the solar system, sent by a beneficent force to rescue her. The car was like a capsule out in a misty white space, warm and womblike.

"I'm June," the woman said. "Who are you?"

"Katha."

"Did you leave him for good, Katha?"

"Yes."

"You scared?"

"Yes."

"You sad?"

"No."

June laughed and tapped a long wrapped fingernail on the wheel. "Mine took off on me a couple of years ago. I had three kids in school and no job and a big pile of bills, on *his* account. But I got along."

"What did you do?"

"Well, it took some time. I worked two jobs and hardly ever saw my kids. I got big as a house, because you know what I did to feel better? I'd come home from work and eat Oreos, a couple of packs a day. Yeah, Oreo cookies. Only thing in my bed was a bunch of crumbs. I see those damn

Oreo cookies in the store now I get sick. Eventually, though, I got thin again, started looking real good. Bought some new furniture and fixed up the house. The kids were happy too because before, when Bad News was around, there was tension in the house you could cut with a knife. That's *all* there was."

"You got a divorce?"

"Later I did, I didn't want one at first. Why I don't know. But one day, one sweet day he came walking in the door wanting back in the family. I looked at him and I thought about all those nights I sat in that big bed eating those cookies and praying he'd come back. I looked at him *hard,* and y'know? he didn't look so good. I said—ha!—I said look around you no-good something. Look at me and this house and those kids. We're doing fine without you, we're doing *better.* So he looks around. I was waiting, thinking he'd kick up a fuss. But he didn't. He just looked around, like I'd asked him to, and without a word he turned and went back out that door." June glanced at Katha, who was smiling. "It was a great, great day," June said.

"You're a brave person," said Katha.

"Nope," said June, "I came to my senses."

"My husband broke my arm," said Katha. "On my birthday."

"What for?"

Good question, thought Katha.

"Oh, I don't know," she told June, "Because I got born?"

"You should have done what I did. My husband came at me once and I said go ahead, go on and do it, because if you do I'll have a good excuse to wake you up some night and send you straight to hell."

"I probably should have," said Katha. "But in this situation—well, I'm pretty sure that my husband is sick, you know, emotionally, and I'm sure that in his right mind he would never have hurt me."

"Yeah, he sounds sick all right."

"And that's why I didn't think I should leave him, because it's not right to leave someone who's sick. But then I had to, to protect myself."

"I'd say you had to."

"I did the right thing?"

"You've got my vote for what it's worth."

"I thought I was dying," said Katha. "I still think I'm dying."

"You're too young and foolish to die. God looks after young fools. He sends down His angels to protect them. You've got two little angels on your shoulders."

"I'm not young."

"How old are you, Katha?"

"Twenty-five."

June laughed. "Twenty-five. That's so young it's *sinful*. You know what you're supposed to be doing when you're twenty-five? You're supposed to be *loving* yourself something *fierce*."

"I don't love myself."

"You better learn, it'll save you. This the street?"

"Yes." The sun had burned through the mist, and just down the road was Claire and Ira's. Katha was past the point of wondering what they would do when she appeared at the door, or whether she was doing the right thing by going there. There was nowhere else to go.

June stopped the car. "Good luck."

"I don't know how to thank you," said Katha.

"I wasn't in a hurry. Go in the house and sleep for two or three days, that's the first thing to do. Then go to the store and buy some packs of Oreos, Fig Newtons, whatever you like." Katha actually laughed, and shook June's long cool hand. Out of the car she thought, that was an angel. But there weren't any angels in the world, just people, all kinds of people.

She opened the gate to Claire's yard. Claire and Ira's house was several blocks from the beach, in a quiet green neighborhood where the houses were on big lots, private. Through the gate was the pool, the cabana, flowers, Claire's studio—she was a potter—and the back door. The house was two-storied, creamy white with mauve shutters. None of the curtains in the windows were open. No one was up yet. Katha felt like a criminal, prowling in the yard while Claire and her daughters slept peacefully inside. Ira wouldn't be there; it wasn't the weekend so he'd be in the city. Claire and the girls slept in the house, dreaming good dreams, while Ira, who loved them, worked in the city. They'd be happy when Ira came back. They were happy. What right had she to intrude with her troubles—her broken life, her bad marriage. It wasn't right. She didn't belong here, dragging her darkness, what she had become, to their door. She belonged with Tommy. She knew it and felt it with a flutter of sadness but also with the rightness of truth. She and Tommy were one, the same. She knew his face like the back of her hand. What happened was that when you knew someone like that you became them. Even what was bad in them you couldn't hate, or not for long, because it was too much like hating yourself. Someone's face was a landscape, and if you knew it well enough you belonged there, like it or not. It took you and without it, what would you be? It had seemed when she'd left at dawn that some part of her still belonged to other places, but standing there, staring at Claire and Ira's door, she knew it didn't.

Except she had to rest. She had to rest here until she could figure out what to do, where to go. God, he could be home now, seeing her note, knowing what she had done. What she had done. She was brave. She loved herself. She wanted to live.

She knocked, and Jeannie, a little girl of four wearing

green and red pajamas patterned with sailboats, opened the door, rubbing her eyes. She said, "Katha."

"Hi, Jeannie. How are you?"

"I was sleeping."

"I'm sorry. I have to see your mother. It's important."

"I should wake her up?"

"No, but if you let me in I'll wait for her. Would that be all right?"

Jeannie thought for a second, then turned and ran up the stairs calling, "Mom, Mom! It's Katha! She needs to see you, it's important!"

Katha stepped into the vestibule, closing the door behind her. She'd tracked in sand. She caught a glimpse of herself in the mirror that hung over the umbrella stand and quickly looked away from her tangled hair, her unnaturally bright eyes. She felt feverish. She pressed an icy hand against her burning cheek. She looked at her watch. Seven o'clock. In an hour it would be eight, then nine, ten. That's how it went. Claire had such a pretty house, neat, like her mother's. She could see one of Claire's ceramic bowls in the living room on a wicker table. It was glazed the color of a pearl.

Claire came quickly down the stairs, tying the belt of her terrycloth robe, which blanketed her from her neck to her feet. "Katha, what's wrong?"

"I'm sorry, Claire, I should have called." She felt the tears welling up in her eyes and now she couldn't stop them from coming. "I left Tommy," she said. "I just decided and I was hoping you'd let me stay here a few days. I'm sorry." She felt bad that Jeannie, standing at the top of the stairs, should see her weep.

"Of course you can," said Claire, coming to Katha and putting her big warm arm around her shoulders. "Come into the kitchen and we'll have a cup of tea. Jeannie, go play in your room, honey. I'm going to talk to Katha for a while." The little girl left obediently.

The kitchen was warm, old-fashioned, with a long wooden table, copper pots on the walls, and earthenware baskets of herbs on the windowsills. Claire put the water on, then sat with Katha at the table.

"I'm not in good shape," Katha told her.

"That's okay. You don't have to talk if you don't want to."

"I don't want Tommy to know where I am."

"He doesn't have to know. Where is he?"

"I don't know." The kettle whistled. Claire got up to get the tea and Katha said, "I'd like to go to sleep. Would you mind?"

"Here, drink this first." She gave Katha the cup, then left the room for a minute and came back with a pill that she put in Katha's hand. "It's Halcion, take it." She got her some water.

Katha took the pill and said, "I won't be here long, a few days. When's Ira coming back?"

"Tonight."

"Today's Friday?"

"Thursday."

Thursday. Katha looked at her watch, seven-ten.

"He'll be glad to have you," said Claire. "Come on, bring your tea and I'll put you upstairs in the guest room."

The stairs were carpeted in deep soft blue with a a grayish tone; the guest room was small, white and beige. Claire brought Katha a flannel nightgown with lace at the throat; the gown smelled like violets. Holding it, Katha sat down on the bed. "I tracked in sand," she said. "I was walking on the beach."

"That's okay, but take off your shoes. They're wet."

"How's Gillorhan's? I didn't ask the other day. It's doing well?"

Claire said, "Yes, pretty well."

"Chinese Stand is a bust. We're just about to lose it, and, Claire, we've got these debts, I can't tell you. I can't leave Tommy with all of the debts. I have to get a job—"

"Katha, honey, take off your shoes and your clothes and put on the nightgown. You're shivering."

Katha did as she was told. "I thought about going to my parents—"

"Why don't you go to sleep and think about all this later."

"Yes, I need to sleep. I haven't been sleeping." Katha stood up to take off her pants and the floor swayed. "I think the pill's working, Claire." She floated to bed and got under the covers.

"You want me to stay with you?" Claire asked, far away.

"No, I'm all right. I'm going to sleep." Claire melted into the wall and the door shut. Katha looked at her watch. Seven-twenty-five, seven-twenty-six. Seven-twenty-six in Southampton, New York. Thursday. Seven-twenty-six in East Hampton, in the Springs, and Tommy coming in and calling for her, and finding the note. She didn't care, she smelled violets, saw the faces of boys in the grass, shining in the moonlight. Angels, and June in the mist and how she was saved. The bed was deep and it held her, here in this house where there was light, where the walls were the soothing colors of tea and of cream. She was going to sleep, she was just about sleeping. On her shoulders there were angels cutting paths with their wings through the blackness of fire.

Chinks of light filtered through the uneven boards of the shack. So did the cold. There were lots of clothes among the loot and Peter found a jacket by one of the stereo speakers to put on. It went down past his knees but it was warm. His legs were skinny as a scarecrow's. He was hungry.

He was an outlaw. Outlaws went searching for food in the night, so the cops wouldn't get 'em. Weird Harold called the cops and the cops put handcuffs on Big Dan and Sam. Peter didn't want handcuffs. He would ride on the highway with Kathy to the South and get a job in a diner, that was what she said. But her husband came back, and anyway Banjo couldn't go, because he was dead. Some good Samaritan found him all smashed on the highway, took him out to the dump.

Peter took off his shoes and put on a pair of leather Pumas with green stripes. They made his feet look like boats. He got on the motor scooter and pretended to be riding, over the ocean and into the moon and bam! he hit a crater and dust flew, whoosh! in his eyes. He was blind. Poor Peter was blind. But he had on moon shoes and when he walked he went up into space and got burned on the sun but he survived and some men in a plane got him and took him back to earth saying, poor Peter, you were blind but now we can take off the bandages and look! He could see! The people were cheering. Hooray, hooray, and he got on the scooter and v-rooom! got Big Dan and Sam out of jail and v-rooom! got Paul, whose uncle was a queen, and v-rooom! they rode to Weird Harold's, shot him dead on the lawn. Weird Harold, dead on the lawn. Got to plant him, said Daddy. That makes the grass grow. It's the natural scheme of things, son. Look here, where your Mama is, see how the grass shoots up so fast because she was a fine good woman.

Peter got off the scooter. He couldn't ride anymore because he was so hungry his stomach was gone. He looked around. All of the loot was his, not Big Dan's and Sam's, it was his, Peter's. He opened a toolbox and fingered the tools. He took out a hammer and smashed the front of the radio that Big Dan had fixed. Then he felt bad because now he couldn't listen to the radio. He lay down on the ground and watched the chinks of light. It was warmer, there was dust flying in the light.

He could go out. He could keep low to the ground and no one would see. But he was afraid. Big Dan said they couldn't put children in jail. Were Big Dan and Sam children? Peter didn't know.

The day was long. Peter slept and dreamed of horses escaping from farms. They stamped their feet, kicking out fences, snorting and bellowing, stampeding children and houses and running through the streets, getting hit by cars. People picked up the horses in wagons, took them back to the farm but the horses were dead. They lay in the field and women came and put grass on them but the grass didn't grow. The grass only lay there in the sun with flies on all the dead horses and then it got dark.

Peter woke up and it was still the day. He wasn't hungry anymore, but his head was hurting. It hurt so bad that when the cops came he was glad. They were nice cops. They didn't have their guns out. One said, "Peter? Your brother sent us for you. Your brother Dan." He was a little cop, smaller than Sam, with rough hands. He asked if Peter was hungry and gave him a Three Musketeers. They were smiling in the cop car and they put on the siren but when Peter was scared they turned it off. They stopped at McDonald's on the way. Peter ate until his head felt better, and he never had to wear the handcuffs.

Part Two—In Transit

Chapter 8

Who ever heard of school in the summer? Peter had to get up at six-thirty in the morning for chores, make the bed, sweep. Then it was breakfast in a line and sitting next to that Toby, with freckles so thick you could barely see the white of his face, and teeth yellow and crooked like a bad fence. Taps his head and says cuckoo, cuckoo, rolling his eyes—always saying to go shave your skull, you've got five o'clock shadow. Peter would bite him again when the lights went out, this time hard.

After breakfast, school, after lunch, school. Fake school with only ten kids in the class, one Toby. The windows in the classroom were high, leaves brushing green against the glass. Then outside or the gym. Peter went outside. All around the playground were fields, then over the fields in the distance were houses. Peter's eyes held the houses so hard that Mrs. Daphne was right in front of him before he realized she was there. He looked up at her blocking the light.

"Hi there, Peter," she said. With a great breath and a thump, she sat down on the ground at his side. Mrs. Daphne was fat, but okay. She tried to get him to talk. "You know," she said, "it's been a week. I'm just a little bit tired of talking to myself when you and I get together, my friend."

Peter looked back at the houses. On top of the long gray house was a cloud so it looked like the house wore a cap.

"And today I'm embarrassed. Did you growl at Mr. Keene?"

Mr. Keene took Peter's arm in class, tried to make him stand up, and Peter was mad. People weren't even *supposed* to go to school in the summer; as far as Peter knew it was against the law.

"I tell everyone what a good kid you are and you don't back me up," said Mrs. Daphne. "Ah listen, I know it's tough, thrown in with strangers, you don't know what's going on. But today I've got some news. The news is, in case you're listening, that in, oh, about twenty minutes you'll be able to talk to your brothers on the phone."

Peter looked at Mrs. Daphne, at her big orange lips smiling.

"That interests you, doesn't it?" She started to touch him but then checked the impulse and withdrew her hand. "I've got to tell you that your brothers are in a lot of trouble. They were caught breaking into a house and that's serious. But you, sweetie, you've done nothing wrong. I want to keep impressing on you that you're here because we're concerned about you."

Mrs. Daphne talked and talked, but Peter didn't hear. The lid that kept pressing on his brain had come off; in his head he felt a wide open space where the air swished through. He dug at the earth with his hands in excitement. Sam, Big Dan on the phone. Sam, Big Dan.

"Your brothers are in what's called a youth house, Peter. They've got to stay there until the judge decides what to do about them. If he lets them off easy, and he may, he just may, we'll try to get them transferred over here, for a little while anyway. We'd like to see you boys together." She paused. "Peter? You know what a bribe is? This is a bribe. You'll talk to your brothers, but first you talk to me."

"Say what?"

"Well, well, the boy talks."

"I can talk."

"I hear. Don't get defensive. You hungry? You haven't exactly put on weight since you've been here." She reached into her blue leather bag and took out a sandwich wrapped in waxed paper. When Peter opened it he smelled eggs, but ate it anyway.

"You have any idea where your father could be? We know he's been gone for over a month," she added, "and we know it's not for work."

"Don't know," said Peter.

"Know why he left?"

Peter thought and said, "Stones around his neck."

"You kids?"

Peter nodded. "Stones around his neck."

"That's too bad."

Peter could see him clear as day, as if he were standing in the playground, tall as a tree, his belly sticking out.

"It was hard for your dad?"

"Daddy says there's the haves and have-nots. We're the have-nots. Daddy says the have-nots keep on having not." Peter tried a little smile on Mrs. Daphne. He felt good. He'd finished the sandwich and told her a bunch of stuff to keep her satisfied. He could almost figure out what was going on here. The whole place was like school except you never got out, and in school, Sam said, you had to keep them satisfied. Peter gave Mrs. Daphne a full-out smile for good measure.

"We'll talk more later," she said. "Come on."

Peter followed her across the playground and that Toby said, Yah! yah! yah! so Peter gave him the finger. They went into the main building and down the mud-green corridor to a glassed-in room with a desk and a phone. Mrs. Daphne put through the call, and Peter waited. He counted in his head to make the time go fast. Big Dan would be on the phone before he got to ten. Seven. Eight, eight.

"Okay, here you go," said Mrs. Daphne. "I'll be out in the hall."

"Big Dan?"

"No, nerd, it's Sam! How's it goin'? It's pretty good in here. Big Dan, y'know, he's got 'em all in line. I met a lot of guys, one guy named Wind, he's pretty cool. His name's Wind because he's so small if a wind came he'd blow away, know what I mean? Know why he's in here? Guess. Come on, guess."

"I don't know," said Peter.

Sam lowered his voice. "He stabbed a guy. Yeah, I'm not kidding. And oh, oh, guess what else? You'll never believe it. I'm in The Room, you know, we got this room, TV, Ping-Pong, hang out, mess around. And I'm looking at the TV and this woman comes on a commercial and I knew her, I knew her. It's Katha. Yeah, Katha, y'know? She turns out to be this big star on TV. Pretty cool. You have her number? I want to call her up. Huh, Peter? You got it? I am in love, love, love. Yeah."

Sam's voice got muffled and Peter heard shuffling sounds, then Big Dan saying get off the phone.

"Peter?"

"Sam sounds different."

"Sam has emotional problems. What are you doing over there?"

"What?"

"Behave, you hear me? Who'd you bite?"

"Toby. He put a frog in my bed."

"Sure, where'd he get a frog?"

"From a jar, Danny. He did. He got the frog from a jar

and he put it in my bed. So I bit him. Tonight I'm gonna bite him again."

"Well, don't bite him. You're not a dog or something. Jesus. You still miss your dog? I'll get you another dog, okay? What kind you want?"

"I don't need a dog, Danny."

"What kind you want?"

"I don't need one."

"You remember that night? Last time I saw you?"

"I saw the cops."

"Yeah? That night I took a walk, after we took care of that business we had to take care of. I was gonna keep walking, take off on my own because you guys can be a drag sometimes."

"Yeah, Danny, I'm a drag, I know it."

"But I couldn't go because we're blood, you and me and Sam, and we've got to stick together, right?"

"Right."

"And I didn't go because I didn't want to be like Daddy, just walk away. That's not the thing to do. I thought about it. So you be all right over there, you hang in because I'll *be there.* You don't have to be scared or stuff like that because I'll be there. Peter?"

"Yeah."

"Y'know?"

"When are you coming, Danny?"

"I'll be there. Any of the kids fool around you remember I'll be over there, okay?"

"Bye, Danny." Mrs. Daphne was knocking on the glass. "The kid Toby, that's his name?"

"Toby."

"Kick his ass he fools around. All right, later. Go ahead."

Peter listened to the click and then to the dial tone. Mrs. Daphne came in and said, "You look pleased. You had a nice talk?" Mr. Keene was with her. "Mr. Keene's going over to B building," she said. "Go on with him and get your dinner. I'll see you tomorrow."

He walked with his head down, hoping Mr. Keene wouldn't say anything, and he didn't. Everywhere you went around here someone went with you. Peter watched his sneakers and Mr. Keene's brown wingtips with flecks of white paint on one of the toes. Their shadows stretched way out in front of them, wavering over the dusty playground and up the steps of B building. Giants, thought Peter.

Mr. Keene let Peter off at the cafeteria line. That Toby was three kids up. Peter burrowed down his head so he wouldn't be seen, but he didn't have to because Toby was busy talking to the server behind the plastic partition and the food.

"Chicken?" said Toby. "Beef?"

"That's what I told you. Which do you want?"

"Neither." Toby had his glasses hanging off one ear. The doctor said he had to wear glasses but Toby didn't want to so whenever he could get away with it he hung his glasses off one ear. This made him look strange, and the glasses that way always looked like they were about to fall off, though they didn't. The whole effect made people uncomfortable.

"You don't want to eat?" said the server. She was a small thin woman with tufts of gray hair pushing out of her cap and sticking to her shiny forehead.

"I'm extremely hungry," said Toby, "but I can't stand chicken or beef."

"We've got potatoes," said the server, plunging a spoon into them and slapping a pile on a plate. "We've got beans." She put that on the plate. "And cornbread." She took the tongs and added two slices to the plate and put the plate up on the counter.

"I don't like your attitude," said Toby.

"Next," said the server.

"There's something wrong with these potatoes," said Toby.

"What's wrong with them?"

"Look, there's brown crud all around the edges."

"That's not crud, that's baked."

"That's not baked, that's rotten. You're trying to serve me rotten potatoes."

"You want me to call someone?" said the server.

"Give me a new plate, without potatoes."

"No. You don't want the potatoes, scrape them off yourself. You're holding up the line."

"You won't give me a new plate?"

"No. Get out of here."

"That's your last word?"

"Will you get out of here?"

Toby took the plate and said, "You're a worthless individual and a slave." He moved on.

"Every night I've got to be dealing with him," said the server.

When it was Peter's turn she said, "Chicken or beef?"

"I don't care," said Peter.

"Oh, give me a break, chicken or beef?"

Peter said, "That," and pointed at the chicken.

He walked with his tray between the long tables of kids, the noise hurting his head. Toby said, "Yah, yah, yah," when he saw Peter, but Peter sat down and ignored him.

"I'm wasting away," Toby said to the two girls about his own age, ten or eleven, who sat across from him. "I can't eat this mess they call food." He took his napkin from his lap and covered his plate with it. "Look." He pulled up his shirt and showed his ribs to the girls.

"Yuck," said one of the girls, but they both laughed.

"I wouldn't eat that if I were you," Toby said to them.

"I'm hungry," said one of the girls.

"You'll end up with ptomaine," said Toby. "Or botulism ... cancer. Don't say I didn't warn you." He curled his hand into a fist and showed it to Peter. "What's in here?"

Peter gave Toby a dirty look.

"No, there's something in here, a surprise. Wanna see?"

Peter shook his head.

"Suit yourself," Toby said. "Do you want to see?" he asked the girls. They said yeah so Toby uncurled his fist and held his open palm in front of them.

"It says something," said the girl with black bangs and a red shirt. "P, A, P, K. What's that mean?"

"Protected against Peter Kramer. Yah, yah, yah," he said to Peter. "Slimebag. Billiard head."

Peter put down his fork and just sat in his chair. They weren't allowed to get up until the night person from their dorm came to get them.

"I got something in the mail today," Toby said to the girls. "A piranha. You know what that is?"

"What?" said the girl with the bangs.

"A man-eating fish."

"There's no such thing."

"What about sharks?"

"Well, yeah, sharks."

"And piranhas too. They're small and they sell them in pet stores. They import them from South America. Down there they travel in schools and if a goat falls in the river they'll strip the flesh right off him. Their teeth are like razors."

"Ick, you've got one?" said the other girl, pulling at the neck of her purple T-shirt in disgust.

"Yes," said Toby, "and when I had one before I had to feed him raw hamburger meat. That's all he would eat. I'd toss that meat in the tank and get my hand out quick, let me tell you. That thing really went for it."

"I've never heard of that," said the girl with the bangs.

Like China

"Let me tell you what happened. The first one I had, I kept him in a tank in my room. And every Christmas when my grandmother came for a visit that's where she stayed. I slept on the couch. One night she gets up to go to the bathroom or something and she trips on the cord and the tank falls over. She turns on the light to see what happened and sees, aw, this cute little fish gasping and flapping on the floor. So she sets the tank upright and picks up the fish to put him back in. But my fish, he's hungry. Sinks his teeth in her hand, bites out a tasty chunk. She starts screaming her head off, blood's spurting all over the place. We all go running in and my dad flushes the piranha down the toilet and then we all get in the car and take my grandmother to the emergency room. The nurses say what happened? And my grandmother goes I got bit by a fish. Everybody cracked up. Five stitches.

"After she left I got another one. I had this friend, well, not a friend, this real pathetic kid who paid me three dollars a week to protect him. I invited him over. We're in my room. I said, see that fish? Pick him up. He didn't want to. I said, go on, he likes it, he likes to get picked up and pet on the head. He picks him up. Six stitches. My dad said no more piranhas."

"Put that fish in my bed," said Peter, "I'll kick your ass."

"Oh," said Toby, "I thought you were a mute."

"I thought he was a mute too," said the girl in the purple. "Or that he couldn't speak English."

"No," said Toby, "he's merely deranged." He took his glasses off his ear and put them on his face upside down. "What will you kick," he asked Peter, "when I put the little fishie in your bed?"

Peter scowled into his plate, and the girls were laughing their heads off. One of them got hiccups and kept laughing, and hiccupping, like an idiot, thought Peter. He counted silently, one, two, three, four, and when he looked up Ms.

Ryan was walking toward them with six other boys from Peter's dorm. Ms. Ryan was young and bossy and wore too much makeup. Her small green eyes were outlined in black, and in a few hours after she came on duty the black would smear below her eyes so she looked like a raccoon. But Peter was glad to see her, even gave her a wave.

"Hi there to you too, friendly," she said. "Toby, put your glasses back on your ear. Don't give yourself a strain." She turned to one of the boys, her pet, and gave him a flirty look. Peter and Toby fell in with the group.

"Everybody watching TV tonight," said Ms. Ryan, "except Toby?" On the way to the lounge they dropped Toby off at the library, where he read in the evening.

"He reads books," said one of the boys, "so he can sound smart."

"He reads books," said another, "for mean things to say."

"I read books," said Toby, "to exercise my mind, which is something you Neanderthals will never have to worry about. Catch ya later, Peter Pan."

Peter Pan. In the lounge, Peter couldn't concentrate on the TV. Kids kept talking. Even the lounge was like school. There were bulletin boards with kids' drawings on them and bright-colored posters of places no one ever saw except in books at school. The blinds were drawn over the windows. Peter thought, Big Dan will *be here,* and kick Toby's ass. Toby didn't really have that fish. What he could do was not sleep tonight, or sleep under the bed. But no, Big Dan would say that was like a dog. He couldn't bite Toby because that was like a dog. He had to kick Toby's ass, he fools around.

Toby was already in bed when Peter got back to the dorm. He had the covers pulled up to his chin with his freckled arms out, reading a book. Peter didn't see a tank. He looked under his bed, sneaked a peek under Toby's. Nothing. Toby was a liar. That's why he didn't say anything to Peter and kept reading his book. Still, Peter checked under his pillow; he picked it up and took off the case. He pulled the blanket all the way down, then yanked off the sheet. Nothing.

"What're you doing?" said Ms. Ryan. "Put the sheet back on the bed and get in it. You think there's bugs?"

Peter didn't care what she said. Next he felt with his hand all along the edges of the mattress, forgetting that if there was a fish under there he'd get bit. He quickly pulled back his hand, and lifted the mattress as high as he could.

"Peter, quit it!" said Ms. Ryan. She pushed the mattress back down and said, "Get in the bed. Go on, get in. You're weird tonight, you are really weird. Lose the book, Toby."

Peter waited for the lights to go out. Toby was a liar. Peter wished he could bite him, though. It wouldn't be a bite like a dog but like a fish. Six stitches. He heard Ms. Ryan's steps fade away in the dark. He counted, thinking that on twenty he'd bite—but on ten he heard Toby sit up in his bed. Peter sat up. Toby's feet hit the floor; his breathing got close, then his voice cut the dark, slow and mean, "Peter. Wanna see my fish?"

This is it, thought Peter. He leaped from the bed and knocked Toby to the floor, got on his chest. Toby yelled, "Help! Help!" He wouldn't fight. His legs were kicking but his hands stayed down at his sides. Peter pulled his hair with one hand, pressed the heel of his other hand hard in his face. He said, "Fight!" He pushed at Toby's face. Kids were yelling, the lights came on, and Ms. Ryan got Peter from behind and pulled him off Toby. "Fight," screamed Peter, "fight!" Tony was crawling off backward on his butt like a crab. "He attacked me!" he cried. "He's out of his mind!" Sissy, thought Peter. I'll get him. He thrashed against Ms. Ryan, kicked her in the shin. She cried out and let him go and he went charging after Toby. "Help, help!" Toby screamed. He scrambled under a bed on the other side of the room, but

Peter got under there, almost had him in a grip when some-body's arms pulled him out by the feet. It was Eugene, the aide. He made Peter stand up, and gave him a shake so that Peter stopped struggling. Toby was bawling under the bed. "Sissy," said Peter. Some kids laughed.

"Shut up," said Ms. Ryan. "Shut up, you kids." She limped over to Peter and Eugene. There was a run in her nylon where Peter had kicked her. "Think you're tough?" she said to Peter. "Get him out of here, Gene."

"Ah, come on," said Eugene. He had let Peter go, and Peter didn't try to get away. Eugene was young like Ms. Ryan, but nice—he had long greasy hair and a sweatshirt that said JUST SAY NO! One time he asked Peter to play a game of cards.

"I don't want him in this dorm," said Ms. Ryan. "He'll kill that other boy."

"I'll kill him," said Peter. "Kick his ass."

"Hear that?" said Ms. Ryan. "C'mon." She took Peter by the arm. "No one kicks ass in my dorm," she said. "*I* kick ass." She took Peter down the hall to a door that looked like a closet; he tried to hang back, and tripped on a gap in the tiles. He heard the sound of her keys; he looked up at her face, washed out in the light of the hall. She said something to him but Peter couldn't hear, he could just hear the sound of the key going into the door—the key turned, the door opened, she pushed him inside.

It was dark. He heard the key in the door from outside. He felt for the knob, tried to turn it—it was locked. He rattled the knob, he pulled at it, hit it, and the door wouldn't open. It was locked; it was dark, he couldn't see. The lid, it was pressing on his brain. He banged at the door, he reared back and threw himself against it. He dropped to the floor, holding his head, pushing at his head to make the lid stop. His head would explode. He lurched to his feet and tried to run, hit a wall, and he ran, for the door, to make it go down, make it stop—something caught at his feet. He tripped and fell and there was a crash: Peter froze. Something was in here. Something was wrapped around his ankle. He sat up and reached for the thing, a rope, a wire. He followed it back from his ankles to a lamp. He'd knocked down a lamp—and it worked. Peter blinked as it flickered to life.

He was in a room. There was a table the lamp should have been on, and a bed. On the bed was a blanket with cowboys on it. Over the bed was a picture of some guys on TV. Peter rubbed his head, and listened as his breathing slowed down. It was only a room, just a dumb room. He lay down on the cowboys. Across from him was the door and it was locked, but Big Dan would be here. Two times when Daddy put the stick through the doors to lock Peter in the shed, Big Dan let him out.

There was a window. He got up and opened the curtains. He was over the playground. There were lights and he could see the swings. He knew that beyond the swings were the fields and the houses, and farther than that was the ocean. He tried the handle of the window and it gave. In amazement he pushed at the glass and the window swung outward. The cool night air swept over his skin, seemed to push him with a swish up onto the ledge, and he sat there, his legs hanging out. He looked down; there was a roof.

He jumped down to the roof, then threw out his arms, wide like wings. He carefully walked to the edge of the roof and squatted, looked down. Bushes, pavement, swings, and then fields, he knew, and houses and the ocean. Couldn't jump, he thought. Too far. But the bushes looked soft as green pillows. He could smell them, reaching up to Peter on the roof. Way, way down. He was a bird on his perch, sleeping in the night. He made a few bird squawks then yawned, sleepy from the cool night air. He lay back on the roof. He liked it like this, sleeping out. He gazed at the giant black globe of the sky.

Chapter 9

Katha swam in Claire's pool in the mornings, and took long walks. She kept a bottle of vodka in her room. The week since she left Tommy seemed to her the longest week of her life, the emptiest, the strangest, the most confusing. Every night she dreamed of him. There were two types of dreams. In the first type he chased her, through city streets, the bowels of buildings, across the borders of foreign countries. Once when he caught her he carved his possession into her skin, just below the jawline on the right side. He used a small penknife. In the dreams he was calm, steady, determined; he saw through walls, time, thoughts, and she knew she could never escape from him, though still she tried.

In the other type of dream they were in love, glorious, tender, celestial, romantic love. His fingers slid over her skin like smoke. She woke sighing, touching her skin as if she were her own lover; and then she'd remember and be appalled. She woke like that one morning, love-kissed, light, and heard a car in the driveway downstairs. She knew it was Tommy. He'd come for her. She went to the window and saw a white van. It wasn't him.

Like China

Nothing felt real. The space around her had a different weight, dense as water. The flowers in the garden, the chlorine in the pool, the bread Claire baked in the kitchen—it all smelled too rich, too sharp. When she dropped a pen on the carpet, it crashed. Colors weren't pure. Green—she'd look at the grass—had red in it, gold, blues.

One day she went with Claire to a shopping center. In a crowded shoe store, they'd become separated. Katha looked around, bewildered. One minute Claire was there and the next she was gone. But then Katha spotted a passageway at the back of the store. She thought Claire must have gone through there and into some sort of an alcove. She approached it, but the passage was narrow and someone else was starting through from the other direction, a woman. Katha said excuse me, tried to pass around the woman on the right; the woman moved the same way. Katha moved left; so did the woman. Katha smiled and said look, you go left I'll go right. It didn't work. She was annoyed. She looked into the eyes of the clumsy woman—and her knees got weak. They were her eyes. There was no other woman. She'd been trying to walk through a full-length mirror.

A few minutes later she was sitting beside a large woman who was trying on a pair of patent leather T-straps. There was something about the woman's mass that attracted Katha: her broad shoulders, the hard black hair that sat on her head like a helmet, the girth of the hips. Katha looked at her feet. The shoes had narrow straps across the arch of the foot; these connected at the center to a vertical strap that met the toe of the shoe. Flesh bulged at the edges of the straps. The shoes weren't too small, she thought, something was wrong with their structure. The toes looked squished in there like a Chinese-wrapped foot. The heel was too slender. When the woman stood up all her weight would press forward and center on the ball of the foot. And Katha knew patent leather didn't breathe. The woman's feet would sweat, would swell. . . . Katha looked over the open boxes of shoes surrounding the poor imprisoned feet.

"If I were you," she said, "I'd take the leather pumps."

"I think I like the patent," said the woman. She stood, took a few wobbling steps. "Yes," she said in a dreamy voice, "I want a pair of patent leather shoes."

Katha and Claire sat on opposite couches in the living room, drinking brandy. A strong wind rattled the shutters outside. Ira had come in from the city two hours ago, just before nine, after a long and exhaustive drive. He said everyone seemed to be getting a jump on traffic this Thursday night. He thought Katha looked better; there was more color in her face than there had been last weekend.

They'd had a late dinner with the girls, Jeannie and Monica, then the girls went to bed. Ira had just gone into the phone in the kitchen, to try to reach Tommy at Chinese Stand.

"I still feel rotten having Ira do this," Katha said to Claire. Claire merely waved off the comment. She settled more deeply into the couch and closed her eyes, rubbed a finger over the lids. She's tired, thought Katha. Everyone in this house is tired. Even the walls are tired, from listening to me.

The two girls, of course, didn't know much about what had happened to Katha but they sensed that she was coming off something large, something their parents talked with her about in whispers late at night. They'd also been told not to bother Katha unless she seemed in the mood for them. Monica, especially, had been excited to learn that Katha was going to stay with them for a while. At fourteen, Monica was almost as tall as Katha, and thin; she wanted to model, she'd seen Katha's commercial on TV. But Katha didn't look like that person. She looked smaller, she didn't wear makeup, she jumped at loud noises, and the light beneath her door was always on.

They shouldn't know so much, Katha thought. No one should have to know so much. Claire and Ira weren't her family; until a week ago, she and Claire had never really been close. But Claire encouraged her to talk, and once she started talking she found she couldn't stop. She felt that her talk sucked the strength from the house, so that now it seemed to shudder defensively as the wind kept beating at the windows.

She watched Claire sip her brandy, then again close her eyes and lean back against the couch. Katha was awed by Claire's generosity. Claire and Ira weren't extraordinary people, they basically lived for themselves. With their house in the Hamptons, their apartment in the city and their daughters in good private schools, they were typical upper-middle-class New Yorkers, typically insular, Tommy would have said. They didn't patronize the arts, they didn't rush into burning buildings to rescue employees, they didn't challenge the Mafia; and Katha was reasonably certain Ira hadn't married Claire with the partial intention of making whole, for his own ego, an emotionally starved young girl from a cold and confusing family.

Yet when she showed up at their door, distraught and in pieces, they made room for her. Tommy, with all his seeming generosity, at least until the fire, was monstrously selfish compared with Ira; and compared with Claire, she had never made any kind of life for herself; in twenty-five years whatever shapeless qualities or needs she had that could have provided her with a direction and a steady course, she'd just thrown to the winds and let fall wherever they happened to go. At the center of her disorder was a void, and in the void there was Tommy, and then Tommy got sick.

After all the talk, this was all she knew. At least she expected that she would feel purged, and sometimes she did—but what she wanted was a *why*. If she could only know *why*, she thought she could look at her life and feel, know something other than exhaustion and dread. Except—except she wasn't alone anymore with what happened. Someone else knew, two other people in the world, and the world was still there. For that she wanted to kneel right now on the floor before Claire.

Ira came back. Katha watched as he folded his long rangy frame into a chair. She thought Ira had eyes like her father, heavily lidded brown eyes with lashes unusually long for a man. Her father used those eyes to get away with things, but Ira's were open and warm. In a way she talked more easily with Ira than with Claire.

"I don't know, Katha," he said. "He seems all right. He didn't say you were gone. I asked about you and he said you were fine. He said he'd be staying in the city for the rest of the summer."

Katha set her brandy on the coffee table in front of the couch. How like him, she thought, such containment. She could feel Claire, suddenly alert, carefully watching her. "But he sounds all right?" she asked Ira.

"As far as I could tell. You know, Tommy, he never says too much about himself, at least not to me."

"Or to anyone," said Katha. "Life of the party, everybody's friend. Tommy doesn't have any friends. Except me. God."

"Katha," said Claire, "you wanted to know if he's all right. He's all right."

"I just wish I could call him, just to say I'm okay." She stared at the brandy in her glass. "But I won't. I just hate this. I hate how I left. If I could have prepared him or something—but I had to leave then, the moment it hit me. That other time I tried to leave and I told him—he didn't get angry. Well, he got angry, then he said he understood only first we had to talk—*he* had to talk. I think it was nine when he began talking and in the morning, when we finally went to sleep, I didn't know why I ever wanted to leave in the first place." She picked up her glass. "Okay, I just talked myself out of calling him."

"Tommy should have been a lawyer," said Claire.

"I was more afraid of him talking to me than hitting me," said Katha. She evaded Claire's eyes; when she mentioned the violence, Claire's eyes got flinty. Ira's eyes just got sad.

"I feel bad about Tommy," said Ira. "I always liked Tommy."

"You did?" said Claire.

"Sure. Tommy's very—charming."

"Charming," said Claire.

"You know what I mean. He talked me into Stand. I didn't want in on Chinese Stand," he sad to Katha. "But Tommy wanted that place. He had it all laid out in his head. So I told him my money was in but that I was going to concentrate on Gillorhan's. Stand was his baby—well, that was a mistake. Tommy had the charm and the drive but he was never any good at business. He was too impatient. He opened Stand prematurely. After the fire—and I'm ashamed to admit it, Katha—when he wanted to buy me out of Stand I jumped at the offer. I should have discouraged him. I should have discouraged him from selling out of Gillorhan's and Split. But truthfully, I didn't think he would listen."

"He wouldn't have," said Katha.

"Something about Tommy," said Ira. "He has this enormous sense of self-protection. Whenever we disagreed on something he'd clam up. He'd get silent, walk away." Ira paused, thinking. "You know what it was. He gave me the impression that if I disagreed with him I was attacking him on a personal level."

"*Yes,*" said Katha, leaning forward, excitedly. "He can't

stand to be crossed, he can't *stand* it, he gets crazy! If you say he's wrong about something he reacts like you've betrayed him, I mean wounded him ultimately."

Katha looked from Ira to Claire and flushed. Claire was listening with a detached expression, more than that, with a cynical look, as if this discussion of Tommy's character was entirely beside the point. Katha read this look as a judgment, as if after what Tommy had done he was unworthy of the usual consideration given to the motives of normal human beings.

Katha looked back at Ira. "That's what makes this so hard," she said to him. "Tommy really believes now that everyone's betrayed him. And then I leave, I don't even tell him. I'm just gone." She felt Claire's eyes. "Claire," she said, "what is it."

"You want me to tell you?"

"Yes, I do." Katha wished she were up in her room, alone. She wished it would rain. The wind just went on, but the rain wouldn't come.

"I don't like to see you so consistently absorbed in Tommy. I think you should be thinking of yourself and not Tommy."

"I do think of myself," said Katha. "I think of myself so much that my head hurts."

"I don't think you do," said Claire. "Which makes me think you might go back to him."

"Claire," said Ira, interceding, "she's not going back. Still, he's her husband. She can't turn off her feelings in a week."

"In my opinion," said Claire, "she's been emotionally withdrawing from Tommy for nearly two years. She just didn't have the strength to leave until now."

"Yes and no," said Ira.

Katha felt like a specimen, slit open and spread on an examining table under harsh lights. Example: the heart.

Like China

Type: victim of abuse. Interesting case, societally urgent. Notice, the heart is not red, it is blue. Deprivation of oxygen, also cut the supply to the brain. Limited motor reflex—her hands were shaking. Why do they shake? she thought, now, when it's over, *why do they shake?* Because I am afraid, I am more afraid.

"I'd like to get my things," she said. "You don't have to come with me, Claire."

"Of course I'll come with you."

"I'll come too," said Ira.

"No you won't," Claire told him. "You get to bed."

The wind pushed at the windows, the windowpanes vibrated softly. Ira said, "Maybe you should go tomorrow."

"For all we know he could be back tomorrow." Claire finished her brandy and stood. "What do we need, Katha, a suitcase, a couple of large handbags?" Katha nodded and Claire started out of the room to get them.

"If the rain gets bad," Ira called after her, "pull over to the side of the road until it lets up."

"Yes, Papa," Claire called back.

Katha picked up her glass; her hands had stopped shaking. "It'll be nice to have my clothes," she said to Ira. "I don't look too hot in Monica's."

"Even Monica doesn't look good in Monica's clothes," he said. Monica favored fluorescent colors. "My daughter, the stop sign."

"You and Claire are nice together. I like how you take care of each other."

Ira smiled. "She's stubborn. Be sure she pulls over if she should."

"You look terribly tired."

"Nah, get me out on my boat in the morning I'll be a new person. Would you like to come? So far it's just me and Jeannie."

"Oh, I don't know. I'll see how I feel."

"You should come."

"Ira? What caused the fire?"

She immediately knew she'd made him uncomfortable; he put his hands to his face, then drew them back over his head through his thinning brown hair. "I mean," she said, "what's your opinion?"

Ira brought his hands to his knees, and then looked at her. "I was never approached for a payoff, Katha. I told you, Tommy was there more than I was. I was uptown. But Tommy was good with that type. I think he would either have paid them or adroitly put them off. They liked Tommy, I always thought. I never bought it was arson."

"So what was it? The stove?"

He regarded her steadily. "It had to be the stove because the day Stand opened I went over early to check things and I didn't like the looks of some of the equipment, in the kitchen particularly. I was upset. I asked Tommy why the hell he cut corners in the kitchen." Ira stopped, abruptly. "I don't know, Katha. I might have been wrong." He looked away from her, and she followed his eyes up to Claire, who stood, watching them, from the stairs.

"You want to go?" she asked Katha.

Claire seemed tense, bitter, for some reason angry with Ira; he sighed, and then gave her a look that said don't.

"I really don't know," he told Katha. But it didn't go away—something taut was in the air between Ira and Claire, as if something important hadn't been said. But then Claire started down with the bags, and Katha decided Claire's anger referred to Ira saying he might have been wrong.

"Katha, where is the light switch? I can't see anything."

"Just a sec." Katha got the suitcase inside, then reached around Claire and turned on the light.

"It's freezing in here." Claire pulled the collar of her

sweater up close to her face, then glanced back at Katha who was standing stock-still, just inside the door. Claire moved into the room and turned on the lamps. "Why's it so cold? Oh, here's the thermostat, I'll give us some heat. Listen to the ocean, it's going mad. I didn't know you were so close to the ocean. Katha?"

"He picked up my clothes. I had . . . and there were books." The note was gone. "Claire? It feels like he's here."

"Let's just get your things and leave. Maybe we can beat the rain. It's strange it hasn't rained yet. Where's your clothes, upstairs?" She took the suitcase from Katha and began to go up.

Katha went into the kitchen. She peered into the refrigerator and then opened all the cupboards.

"What are you doing?" called Claire.

"Everything's here. He's coming back."

"So? Will you come on?"

Katha opened the drawer by the sink and found three pink candles which she put in the deep pocket of her jacket. There was a strong smell of vodka in the air. Under the sink were two empty bottles in the trash. There has to be an unopened bottle around here somewhere, she thought. She found one behind the trash and took it, since the vodka she kept in her room at Claire's was almost gone. Isn't it funny, she thought, that now I know why Tommy drinks. Vodka turns down the voices, overspreads the harsh colors of the world with a lovely blanket of gauze, so the world's Chinese Stand. She picked up the corkscrew that was out on the counter and put it in her pocket with the candles. Souvenirs, she thought.

"Katha?" called Claire.

Katha put the bottle of vodka by the door and went upstairs.

The bedroom windows were open, the light by the bed was on. Claire closed the windows, dimming the sound of the ocean. "Everything would have been soaked by morning," she said. "He could have closed the windows."

Katha was looking through the bureau drawers; all but two of them were empty. She opened the closet. "Where are my clothes?" she said to Claire. "Some of his are here but mine are gone." She went out to the hall and checked the closet where she kept dresses and jackets. "Nothing," she said. "I don't believe this." She stared at the empty closet for a moment, and then brushing by Claire, who'd come out to the hall, she went back in the bedroom. She opened the suitcase on the bed and started tossing in Tommy's clothes from the drawers and then from the closet.

"What are you doing?" said Claire.

"I need something to wear. I've got exactly twelve dollars and fifty-three cents. What do you think I can get for that?" Tommy's shirts—all white shirts, all he ever wore were white shirts—smelled of bleach and smoke. She began to fold and stack them more neatly in the suitcase.

"I told you I'd lend you some money," said Claire.

"I don't know when I'll be able to pay you back. What do you think he did with them, threw them out, burned them, what?"

"He was probably upset."

First he's the scourge of the earth, thought Katha, now he's probably upset—her hands paused in midair. The shirt she was holding transformed from something familiar and kind to an unrecognizable object; she let it drop. She turned away from Claire because she thought she would cry, then she saw that her checkbook was gone from the top of the bureau. She had expected that.

"I was willing to give up the apartment," she said. "Everything *in* the apartment, but God, I thought I'd have my clothes anyway."

"It doesn't matter," said Claire. "You'll be getting more

money from the commercial soon. You can buy clothes with that."

"But I need that to—to get started or something."

"Katha, slow down. It's been a week. I told you, stay with us until we close up the house after Labor Day. Rest for a while, take your time."

Katha felt weightless, like the wind would reach through the windows and carry her off. She felt like a child, a waif. She felt ashamed. "Claire," she said, turning back, "what will I do?"

"What will you do?"

"What will I do now?"

"Oh, well, what do you want to do?"

"I don't know, get on a ship and sail around the world." Good idea. "Join the circus." She laughed. Freak show.

"You've got your career."

"What career?"

"Your modeling."

"No I haven't. I threw it away. And anyway, I never wanted to be a model. I just did it because—I don't know why I did it. I wanted to do something with art. What I'd really like to do is to go back to school."

"So go back to school," said Claire. "You're free now, you can do anything you want."

"Yes," said Katha, breathing deeply, "I'm free." She looked down at the bed, which looked suddenly huge; beside it on the table was an ashtray overflowing with cigarette butts. She thought of him lying there, smoking, alone.

"I'll take one of these bags," she told Claire, "for my stuff in the bathroom—if it's still there."

"I'll put away his clothes," Claire said gently.

In the bathroom—her hand raised to slide aside the mirrored panel that concealed the shelves—Katha looked at herself. She thought if she did want to model, now she had the right look: the gaunt, tubercular look. The I've-been-to-hell-and-back look. The dark shadowed eyes. Her eyes were so dark they looked black instead of blue. Black holes. Tunnels.

Melvin, that little creep of a photographer who kept calling her for sessions though he didn't like her look, her style. He got off on asking how come she had hips, and breasts—no no *wrong,* he would say, and go striding away across the studio, flinging back his hair from his too-low forehead, swinging his too-long simian arms in disgust. Then he'd dash back as if inspired, and in a voice edged with danger—she'd heard him say once at a party, that's how I get them to listen—he'd say, *Don't give it to me, Katha, keep it.* Keep it back. We're talking aloof, we're talking disdain. We're talking New York, New York Ice. They can't have it, babe, they can't get you. You look into the eye and it's a dare, try to touch me. I can do that—he grabbed her arm—and you don't flinch. You're a rock, the ice queen, untainted, incorruptible, you have *been there.*

Yeah I've been there, she thought. What a charming career, really soul-expanding. She slid the mirror aside, and there were her cosmetics, her shampoo, just as she'd left them. They looked so normal sitting there. Keeping her eyes off his things, his razor, shaving cream, a bottle of aftershave she'd bought him for his birthday last month, she quickly transferred all that was hers into the bag. She heard Claire on the landing, slid back the mirror, went with Claire down the stairs.

Then it started to rain. It smashed at the roof, at the windows. She stopped with Claire at the foot of the stairs for a moment, feeling it. It was like the last flood.

"We'll have to wait," she said. She put down her bag and went to look out the glass that faced the deck; she pulled aside the drapes.

"Damn, we almost made it," said Claire, coming up beside her.

Their voices sounded hollow and empty under the rain.

"Your things were in the bathroom?" said Claire.

"Yes." She thought of Peter, mowing the lawn in the rain. She reached down and picked up the bottle. "Want a drink?"

"Oh sure, why not."

Katha went to the kitchen for glasses, then she and Claire sat on the couch, drinking and facing the rain. It kept coming, driving.

"You okay?" said Claire.

"Yes, well no. I don't know what I am. Sometimes I think—" She thought she shouldn't say this. "Sometimes I think there's something wrong with me, intrinsically."

"Honey, you've just been through hell," said Claire, "of course there's something wrong with you."

"No, there is something, apart from all this, from Tommy—there's something about me that isn't right. Something wrong like at the bottom of my being." Slightly rocking, she stared at the rain.

"Tommy fucked with your brain."

"No, before that, or why did I stay? Why was I with him? I should have left. It's like I wanted it, like I wanted to be punished, or why? Claire, no matter what happened I was never afraid, not really. When it was bad I was just always thinking, what am I doing here, how did I get here?" That was it, always.

"Bad luck," said Claire.

"Oh please."

"I mean it. You were what when you met Tommy, nineteen? Who knows anything when they're nineteen?"

Katha wished she were more like Claire, able to see things so simply and conveniently. She wanted to believe what

Claire said, that it was bad luck. When she was younger she used to latch on to a phrase someone said, or read a line in a book that put her world in order for a while. That didn't happen anymore. Secrets seemed frozen on the tips of tongues.

"When I was nineteen," she said, "he was so, I don't know, like the world unfolding. His stillness. His face. I used to like to sit at the bar, at Split. It was so loud it was quiet. I'd light up a joint or a cigarette, and sit there knowing everything. And everything was good. I didn't need anything then, except just to sit all night at my boyfriend's bar."

Back at Claire's, the rain dripped, half-heartedly. "Come on, rain," she said. She wanted it to pound like before. She poured some more vodka into the cup she kept in her room, then she took Tommy's shirt from the bag. She'd told Claire she forgot something upstairs, and she'd gotten the shirt. She took off her clothes and put it on. As Ira said, he was her husband, she couldn't get over him in a week.

She emptied the rest of her things onto the top of the dresser, and then set it all upright in a line. No, there was more. She got the clothes she'd worn when she left and draped them around the cosmetics like a still life, then she sat on the bed and looked at it all.

"What they call," she said, "stripped down."

There was nothing to do, she couldn't sleep.

She got up and took the Renoir print, the one of the girl with the bow in her hair and the watering can, off the wall and put it in the back of the closet. She had one like that when she was young. Renoir was a sap. Claire lacked a bit of taste in certain areas, was a bit provincial, one might say. Katha set down the cup and took a swig from the bottle. Don't trash Claire, she thought. But what it is—she doesn't know me. No one here knows me.

Like China

She heard steps in the hall, Jeannie or Monica. They'd think oh there's the sicko staying up all night again.

Now Tommy, Tommy was at Chinese Stand, leaning up against the bar, talking to someone like nothing was wrong. He wasn't bereft, incapacitated, drunk. Well, he was drunk. Certainly. But he wouldn't collapse, he never collapsed. He didn't know what that was. No matter what, he went on. He never doubted himself, not really; he never considered that perhaps there was something deeply wrong with him, something about him that brought all this on. He could rant and rave, even weep, but then it was over. He was right with himself. He would die that way. Shoot him full of bullets but his hand would curl over his rightness, freeze it, protect it in a fist, a death lock. She could see him in the cold hard ground, his hands in fists, holding his rightness. His entitlement. It was a miracle, it was brilliant, it was pathetic.

She wanted to talk to her mother. But it was after midnight. So tough, she thought. She's my mother, she should want to talk to me. I'm her child, in need. She put her jacket on over Tommy's shirt in case Claire should wake up and see her in the kitchen where the phone was. Eased quietly out of the room.

Heard her mother's voice. "Mom? It's Katha . . . No, nothing's wrong . . . Tommy's fine, he's in the city. I'm at my friend Claire's. I got lonely at the house . . . How are you . . . You are? to Norway? That's wonderful . . . Tell me about it. . . ."

She didn't listen to what her mother said, she absorbed the lilting rhythms of her mother's voice. She thought her own thoughts of Norway, where everyone was blond, a land clean and bright, under snow.

Chapter 10

When Peter woke up on the roof that morning Mrs. Daphne was there. She said, come on kiddo, let's go back to the dorm. She said fighting wasn't the way to get things solved, but Peter knew she was wrong because Ms. Ryan got yelled at and Toby never bothered him ever again. He tried to be Peter's friend. He tried even harder when Big Dan and Sam were sent to the center three days after the fight. Sam said he and Big Dan were Toby's ideal. Toby tried to hang out with the brothers in the playground, he stopped reading nights and went to the lounge where Peter and Sam and Big Dan watched TV.

The kid's cracked, Sam said, a perpetual liar. For instance, Toby never had a piranha or a grandmother, or even a family. That's what everyone said. He made that stuff up. Now he went around saying that he once had two brothers who were killed in a flood. Mostly, Sam said, Toby wanted to be tough.

Peter was tough, Big Dan had him in training. They did laps around the playground and worked out in the gym. Sam wasn't interested in this. Sam said tough was in the money. Sam had learned three-card monte in the youth house and already in the week he'd been here he'd won twenty-five dollars off kids. Yesterday he won a gold watch and chain off Eugene, the aide.

It was August now, and still Peter was in school. Mr. Keene was saying some boring stuff about the president. The president looked like a guy with money, Peter thought, he had that kind of face. There was a poster of him hanging next to the chalkboard. Tonight they were all supposed to watch him on TV.

"Peter Kramer."

Peter stood up.

"When is our next presidential election?"

"What?"

"What is our presidential term?"

Peter looked up at the sun that blazed against the window just above his head. Far off he could hear someone calling, and cars; music playing maybe in a house far away.

"What is the name of our current president?"

A girl laughed, a new girl with bunches of braids all over her head, and Peter gave her the hard-guy look. This involved a total relaxation of his face, a studied stillness, a heavy hot look from his eyes. He felt the stillness wash over the girl until she dropped her eyes to the book on her desk. He held the side of her head a moment longer with his eyes.

Sam said now they were hard guys. Institutions, Sam said, were the breeding grounds for society's outcasts. Big Dan said to Sam, you think you're at a party? You think you're the star of some lame TV show? Me, said Big Dan, this place drives me nuts. You, said Sam, you've got about a hundred and eighty percent hostility and maladjustment. Big Dan said go flip your cards, and tell it to the shrink. Sam liked the shrink, Big Dan hated the shrink, and Peter didn't care. Sam stayed up all night, under the covers, practicing cards.

"Peter," said Mr. Keene, "are you on this planet with us?"

"Yes," said Peter politely. "Earth."

The new girl, and then the other kids, cracked up. Toby laughed loudest. He had a high-pitched laugh that sounded like heee-haw, which made everyone start laughing more. Toby had his glasses hanging off his ear. Peter turned and grinned at everybody. Mr. Keene said, "Can we please settle down?"

Mrs. Daphne poked her head in the door and said, "Can I have Peter Kramer, Doug?"

"Sure," said Mr. Keene—he pitched a piece of chalk at the wastebasket—"you can *have* Peter Kramer. Class, take a miss with the noise, okay?"

"I'm sorry," said Mrs. Daphne, "he has a visitor."

"You guys *shut up*," said Mr. Keene. "Go ahead, Peter."

"Catch ya later, Mr. Keene," said Peter as he passed.

"You," said Mr. Keene, "Peter. You're off free time this afternoon. Come back here when you're through with your visit. We'll go over the government of the planet earth."

"Okay," said Peter. "See ya then."

The kids were laughing behind him again as he and Mrs. Daphne walked off down the hall. She looked mad. "What did you do?" she said.

"Nothing."

"Uh-huh."

"Who's visiting me?"

"A neighbor. Someone named Katha."

Katha. Peter got tight inside. He felt strong, like a power that he had was pulling things from outside to in here where he was. It brought Big Dan and Sam and now Katha was here, someone he never even thought of too much, except when Sam talked about her during commercials, or when Ms. Ryan turned out the lights. He couldn't see her in his mind but he could see the sky flying when they rode together on their bikes. He saw her house. He never thought he would see her again

Like China

Mrs. Daphne opened the door to the lounge. Katha stood up.

"I'll be right back," said Mrs. Daphne.

"Hi." She looked different. Her eyes were sharper. She wore a pink dress and her hair was pulled back and caught at her neck with a clip. Peter didn't know what else to do so he walked up to her and put out his hand. She gave him a shake. "How are you?" she said.

"Pretty good," Peter said. They sat side by side in the chairs against the window.

"You got a haircut," she said.

"It's a skinhead," said Peter. "I'm growing it out."

"Yeah, I think you look better with it long . . . You look thin. Did you get taller?"

"Probably." He watched her hands playing with the clasp of her purse. "How are you?"

"Good." She laughed. "You couldn't have grown in two weeks. But, I guess, it seems longer than that." She tucked a strand of hair behind her ear. "I went by your house and you weren't there." She opened her purse and took out her wallet. "I owed you some money. Can you have it? I mean, I don't know what the rules are here."

"We have a store," Peter said.

She smiled. "That's nice. Well, here you go. You earned it."

Peter put the money in his pocket. Words were forming in his mind of things he had to tell her, things he had thought about before.

But then the door opened, and Sam came in.

"So hey hi!" said Sam. "This is utterly amazing."

"Hi, Sam," Katha said. She seemed happy to see him. Peter knew that Sam loved her, but Big Dan said Sam had no hope in this direction. Sam came over and stood in front of them, nodding and grinning so his face scrunched all up and his eyes disappeared.

"Too cool," he said. "How'd ya know we were here? Oh

God," he said, before she could answer, "you know we got busted?"

"I found out. I went by your house and your neighbor told me."

"Harold," said Peter.

"He has a flag?" said Katha.

"Yeah," said Sam. "Ah, man. It's all a big misunderstanding, Katha, I want you to know that. Mind if I sit down? See, this guy Harold, the guy is some kind of youth hater I think. We weren't breaking into his house, though that was what he said. It was more like a practical joke and the guy, I don't know, he took the whole thing serious. So he turns us in and then later they find out about our dad. See our dad, he split, y'know, like at the beginning of the summer. It's tragic, y'know? What we were doing, we tried to get by."

"I'm sorry," said Katha.

"Hey, don't worry about it," said Sam. "These things happen, like I try to tell Big Dan. I myself try to make the most of any particular situation, y'know, ya gotta deal with things that come along in life. It's a road, y'know, an illusion. Life. Peter's learning this good, but our brother, man, he's depressed. Like kinda off his head or something. I mean, this is what I worry about."

"You can't really blame him for being depressed," said Katha.

"He's not depressed," said Peter.

"Oh hey!" said Sam. He jumped up and knocked his fist against his thigh. "I saw you on TV, on this commercial, right? Am I right?"

"I guess so," said Katha, smiling, but rolling her eyes.

"Hey, it's high-quality stuff," said Sam. "I mean it. It's this one for, y'know, oven cleaner, right? You've got this thing on your head. A scarf, and you're looking in the oven with this sad expression. The camera's at the back of the oven, right?" He turned to Peter. "That's how they do it.

They cut out the back of the oven for the camera. Then at the end," he said to Katha, "the oven's clean and you're happy so you whip off the scarf. You did that part good."

Katha laughed and said, "Thank you, Sam. I felt a little silly."

"Hey," said Sam, "you musta made some big bucks. Electronic media, man, that's where it's at." He sat back down. "You saw Harold, huh?" He shook his head. "Harold, man."

"He did seem sort of strange," said Katha.

"Green suspenders?" said Sam.

"Green," said Katha. "Lime green."

"The guy's eccentric, right?" said Sam.

"We call him Weird Harold," said Peter.

Katha laughed, put a hand to her mouth. "I shouldn't laugh. None of this is funny, but, you know that flag he has? Well, when I was talking to him I looked up and noticed that one of the stars was missing. So I mentioned it, just casually, and he, well, he went into sort of a—frenzy. He pulled down the flag, he went storming into the house. I didn't know what happened."

Sam was holding his stomach he was laughing so hard. "Peter, Peter," he said, "funny or what?"

"Yes, Sam," said Peter. "Pretty funny." Peter remembered Sam had mentioned this before, but he still didn't know what Sam was laughing about. There were a lot of times he didn't know what Sam was laughing about.

"The guy's obsessed," said Sam. "He knew where we were?"

"No, I made a lot of calls and found out."

"Wow," said Sam, "you're a thoughtful and supportive person, Katha."

It seemed to Peter anything that you needed to know, you could find out on the phone. Big Dan said this was true, he said the whole world was connected by telephone wires. Peter felt that his mind was like that, thoughts shooting out in a million directions, pulling things in and sending things out. If he could concentrate completely, get his mind on one wire, the right one, and keep it there, he felt he could go anywhere.

Mrs. Daphne was back. "I'm sorry, guys," she said, "we need the lounge for a class. This isn't a regular visiting day," she told Katha.

"I'll come again," Katha said, rising.

"You will?" said Sam. "Fantastic. But oh, we may not be here."

"I'll let her know where you are," said Mrs. Daphne.

"We're getting foster parents," said Peter.

"That's great," said Katha. "I think that'll turn out to be really great."

"I'm open to it," said Sam. "It could be rich people or something."

They shook hands in the hall. Peter felt tight and happy inside, but as he was walking away with Sam he turned back, something rushing in his head, and called, "Kathy?" She stopped. That wasn't her name, he knew it wasn't. He ran to where she was. His face burned.

"Bye," he said. Her face swam above him.

"Hey," she said, "can I have a hug?"

"I don't care." She put her arms around him and her arms felt good, warm. He felt the softness of her chest against his face. Out of the corner of his eye he saw Mrs. Daphne move off to get a drink at the fountain.

"Kathy," he said, "if your husband hurts you again, then kill him."

"What?"

"Kill him," said Peter.

For a moment her face got very cold, and Peter was afraid. But then she knelt down, putting her hands on his arms. She looked like herself. Her face was flushed at the edges of her hair. "What's gotten into you," she said, "to say a thing like that?"

"I don't know." He looked down, his face hot.

"Listen." She let him go and opened her purse, took out a gum wrapper and a pen. "I'm giving you my number. If there's anything you need I want you to call me, okay?"

"Okay." He put the wrapper in his pocket.

She straightened. "That's the number of my girlfriend's where I'm staying. I'm—I'm not with my husband anymore." She stepped back. "See ya."

Peter caught up with Sam. "Man," said Sam, "I coulda used a hug too. You're lucky you're just a young kid. God, she's so pretty I could just about cry."

Peter didn't tell Sam he had her number.

There was a plaque on Sylvia Daphne's desk that said, ACT AS IF AND YOU WILL BE. She offered Katha a cigarette, then lit her own when Katha said no. "Sure you're not a relative?" she said, shooting out smoke. "I can't find a relative. No-one, no-where." She opened a box she had on her desk, peered inside. "Peanut brittle?" she said.

"No thanks," said Katha.

Mrs. Daphne closed the box and shoved it in a drawer. "I think it's stale anyway." The room was close and they were both perspiring lightly.

"So what happens now?" said Katha. "I appreciate your talking to me about it. There's not much I can do but—"

"These kids need a friend," said Mrs. Daphne, smiling. "You're a nice friend. Damn, I wish they'd fix the air-conditioning. This is a good place but, typically, we don't have enough money. Same song everywhere, not enough money." She sucked in smoke.

"What's happening now," she told Katha, "is we've kept the boys here about as long as we can. Ordinarily, they would have been put right into temporary foster homes.

But, with three brothers, we like to keep them together if we can. In this case that's impossible outside of here. We've got two teenaged kids on probation. Peter's easier to place, but with Sam and Dan, uh-uh, that's hard. I kept hoping an aunt, a second cousin, someone might turn up. No one did." She crushed out her cigarette in the ashtray. "We've got something now that may turn out permanent for Peter, and something for Sam and Dan too. But separate, unfortunately."

She suddenly stiffened, her eyes leaving Katha's, and stood.

"What can I do for you, Dan," she said sharply.

Katha turned and saw Big Dan just outside the glass door. He pushed the door inward and leaned against the frame, holding the door with his foot. He took Katha in slowly, tucked the tips of his fingers into the front pockets of his jeans, then he looked at Mrs. Daphne.

"I couldn't remember," he said to Mrs. Daphne, "if Mr. Sabartine comes today or tomorrow."

"Tomorrow," she said. "You know that."

He looked at her vaguely. "Yeah, I forgot."

Watching him, Katha felt the same way that she had when she encountered him earlier this summer—something about him was much older than a boy of sixteen, something heavy and insistent, just under control, in how he stood, in his eyes. She felt the intense self-awareness of his body, and rather than saying hello as she wanted to, she turned away.

"Tomorrow," repeated Mrs. Daphne.

"Tomorrow," said Dan.

"Where are you supposed to be?" she asked him.

"Outside."

"Yes, outside, not lurking around my office for the third time this week."

"I'm *drawn* here," he said. "By the truth."

Mrs. Daphne sighed deeply. "You heard what I said."

Like China

"Yeah, since I happened to be *lurking*, I heard what you said."

Reflexively, she picked up her package of cigarettes, dropped it back on the desk. "I was going to tell you later today, Dan," she said. "You know I never keep things from you. It'll be a week anyway before it happens. I'll keep you posted."

"You do that." He looked at Katha again, then he kicked the door gently and started to leave.

"You mind if we wait a few days to tell Peter and Sam?" said Mrs. Daphne.

"Your call," said Big Dan.

Mrs. Daphne lit a cigarette, sank back in her chair. "I just told him I'd *try* to keep them together. Well dandy, I feel like shit." She touched a folder by her right hand. "It's Peter I'm worried about. Kids are so stoic, but you can't help thinking—how much can they take?" She picked up the folder, set it back down. "I got the psychologist's report yesterday. He asks Peter who's his best friend, Peter tells him Big Dan. He asks who is the person you most admire—kids that age say Rambo, or Michael J. Fox. Peter tells him Big Dan."

"I couldn't handle your job," said Katha.

"I should have gone into psychology. At least there you can make a good living." She smoked, contemplatively, wiped her brow with the back of her hand. "Sabartine," she said, "the probation officer. He told me he's forty and still paying off school."

Katha took off her shoes because they hurt, and walked in her bare feet through the parking lot. The heat of the blacktop curled up around her ankles.

She got in Claire's Saab and rested her head for a moment against the steering wheel. The car had been in the shade and the coolness of the wheel soothed her face. She put her hand to her neck, then brought it down, rubbing her shoulders.

Peter didn't know about Tommy, she thought. Not really. But kids had intuitions. She wondered again about her motives for coming here, whether she should have. She decided she should have, if only for something to do.

She started the car, thinking how easy it would be to drive past Southampton, through town, veer right around the pond and the windmill, and then to the Springs. She wouldn't turn in her old road. She'd go beyond it, park down another street, then simply sit in the car until she felt better, until the hard, lonely ache that came over her three days ago, replacing anxiety and fear and all of the other wild, swinging emotions she'd had since she left—she'd just sit in the car until it went away. She thought maybe she'd do that, or maybe, if she could stand it, she'd go back to Claire's.

Big surprise, thought Dan. Really, in his whole life, he had never been surprised. He was in a corral, that was what it was like: the whole place was enclosed with a chain-link fence; three gray brick buildings, ugly and squat as three toads, made a horseshoe around the anemic-looking dirt that marked off the playground. Most people sat around talking, a few of the smaller kids ran or jumped rope.

He stood by the one tree in the whole goddamn place. A little ways off, Sam was doing cards on a newspaper spread on the one patch of grass; a couple of girls and Toby sat watching. Dan watched a girl who was sitting at the bottom of the slide with her head bent forward, combing her hair. She looked like Marie, this really nice girl he had liked in ninth grade: the girl flipped up her hair and leaned back, her hair slick and as bright as the light slanting over the slide. He had gone to Marie's one time late in the day, like now, when the sun was low and hot on his back. She came out on the porch to greet him and stood there, shielding her eyes from the sun, her reddish-brown hair like a pool flowing over her shoulders. He'd bought her a book, for graduation, by an author they'd studied in school; "Whatcha got, Danny?" she asked. He had stopped at the edge of the lawn and thought, nothing. I have got nothing. It wasn't the book, or how pretty she was or the rich-person's house where she lived, but he knew he had nothing—the girl who'd been combing her hair was draped on the slide, her hair spilling over the sides. He thought of Daddy, at home in his chair, stinking of beer; Peter's mother, supine on the couch, so constantly sick and so still she was like a sick bloom that had grown from the couch.

He had to do something. He crossed his arms over his chest, pressed his back to the trunk of the tree, watching the girl on the slide.

"Hey, Sam," he called.

"Later," said Sam, with a wink, to the girls who'd been watching him play. "Get lost," he told Toby, and Toby drifted off. Sam gathered up his cards and came over to Dan.

"You get busted with those cards," said Big Dan, "don't come crying to me."

"They don't know I do it for money," said Sam, "you think I'm a jerk? Check out Toby." Toby was twenty yards off, lazily moving an unoccupied swing back and forth by the chain. Really what he was doing was watching Big Dan and Sam. "I'm sick of him hanging around," said Sam.

"He's attracted to you," said Big Dan. "He reminds me of you. Bullshit nonstop."

"Fuck you," said Sam. He put two of the cards in the palm of his hand, his palm down; he threw one of the cards, picked it up, put it back flat in his palm and threw it again. "You shoulda come and seen Katha," he said. "Man, she looked hot. And guess what, she went over to Harold's—"

he dropped the cards. "Shit." He picked up the cards and looked at Big Dan. "What's with you?"

"Nothing." The girl who'd been combing her hair went inside. "I sold some of the loot."

"What d'ya mean?" said Sam.

"I sold some of the loot and the money is buried in the shed."

"God, how much?"

"Wanna keep your voice down?" said Big Dan. He beckoned with his head for Sam to come closer. "A couple hundred dollars. We've gotta go get it."

"Fuckin' A we've gotta get it," said Sam—then his mouth fell open and in an incredulous voice he said, *"Man, you sold the compact disc player."*

"So what? I didn't, would you have it now?"

"I *loved* that compact disc player," said Sam. He shoved the cards in his pocket, crossed his arms over his chest like Big Dan and glared out at the playground, sulking. "You coulda told me," he said. "I feel betrayed."

"Knock it off. We go get it we split it, equally, you and me. We've got to go soon."

"You gonna run?"

"Fuck no, I've grown really fond of this place."

"If you do, I'm not going with you. This place is okay. My future looks good."

"I just gotta get out for a night."

"Yeah, well I want my share of the cash." Sam shot his brother a put-upon look, then after a pause he said, "Eugene. The guy's kinda dim if ya know what I mean. He's enamored with my cards. He thinks he can win back his watch and his chain. We're supposed to start playing at night. I think I can figure out a way to get his keys."

"We need a cover when we're gone," said Big Dan.

"The nerd," said Sam.

"Nah, I don't wanna tell Peter." Big Dan looked around,

he patted the pocket of his T-shirt as if he had cigarettes there, then for the first time in nearly three weeks, he almost smiled. "Hey, Toby," he called, "ya wanna c'mere?"

Toby jumped back from the swing, so excited he knocked off his glasses. He left them where they were in the dirt and came running to Big Dan and Sam.

Peter walked with Mr. Keene across the playground at dinnertime. He felt like skipping. The playground was empty but filled with hot sun; summer light, August light that seems always as if it will last forever. Peter walked slowly, filled with the light, thinking the dark would never come. Peter felt like the light.

Chapter 11

The trees were gold. Soon, on the beach, the froth of the waves would be lit with phosphorescence, would absorb the last light, and the skin of the people in the sand would turn rose, and gold like the trees, and soft like the clouds, trailing color as they moved.

Katha pulled the cord above her head and released the white door of Claire's garage. She stood in the driveway for a moment, watching the trees and thinking, I did it. For another day I did it. I didn't go back. He could be there in the house or in the city or dead and I am here.

Her legs felt heavy, aching, as she opened the gate to the backyard. A bar was set up by the pool. On the grass a long table was covered with a light blue cloth edged with eyelets. At the center of the table were yellow roses, irises, baby's breath. Claire and Ira were having a party tonight. Katha had forgotten.

The house smelled of baking. "Claire?"

"In the kitchen! How'd it go?"

There were no other voices in the house.

"Where's Ira?" Katha called.

"At the beach with the girls. They were getting in the way. I told them to scram."

Two huge sheets of pastry were cooling on racks in the kitchen.

"What are these?" Katha asked.

"Ah, for my masterpiece." Claire was at the sink washing pans, wearing a long red kimono over a bikini. There was flour in her hair. "Napoleon. I got it from the chef at Anthony's. Remember Anthony's?"

"Oh yes." An Italian restaurant on the Upper East Side. Very chi-chi, filled with celebrities. Too many mirrors, too many people drinking San Pellegrino instead of red wine.

"My assistants," said Claire, "who will be Monica and Jeannie, bring the pastry to the table when coffee is served. They also bring me my stainless steel bowl. In it I mix the sugar and cream until it's stiff. I spread it on one sheet of pastry, then top the layer with the other sheet. I slice it, *voilà!* my guests are amazed."

"Then you soak it with brandy," said Katha, "and set it on fire."

"Well no," said Claire, a bit uncertainly. She shut off the water, took a towel to dry her hands. "The thing with napoleon is you want to keep it light." Turning to Katha, she smiled. "It's like biting into heaven. What's wrong?"

"Wrong, with me? What could be wrong?" Katha tossed her purse on the table and dropped into a chair. "Sorry, I'm just tired. I'm not used to driving." Her skin felt gritty and hot.

"You saw the boy, and his brothers?"

She felt more than a little ridiculous; as if her own life weren't troubled enough, she had to go forming relationships with abandoned children. Then tell Claire, too enthusiastically, she was sure, with too much concern. She should never have told her, but she'd been so worried when the boys were gone, more worried than she should have been, but still—and that Harold person had startled her, frightened her, jumping out of the bushes like he did. How he'd looked at her too, it gave her the creeps. He'd demanded her name and address, to verify her residence in the neighborhood, he said, before he could release information. If he came by the house, though, Tommy would have to deal with him, she wouldn't. Stop it, she thought. I think every man in the world is out to get me, is looking at me.

"You're busy," she told Claire. "We'll talk later."

"No, dinner's all cold in the fridge. Ira's grilling swordfish. I just have to take a shower." Claire crossed her arms and leaned against the counter.

"It's just that the boys are being split up, you know, they're going to be placed in separate homes."

"That's sad."

"Yes, and I thought, I don't know, I sort of wished I had a place, a home. I could get it certified the social worker said, and take them in for a while."

"Katha, be serious."

"What?" Katha laughed because it was *Claire* who was serious. She couldn't believe how Claire misread her at times. "Just dreaming," she said. "Feeling silly and wistful." But she got up from the table feeling hurt, thinking of all that marvelous psychic energy that was said to exist between women.

"You're still joining us, aren't you?" said Claire.

"No. I'm too tired."

"Honey, you've got to start doing things that will make you feel good." Call me honey once more, Katha thought, and I'll scream. And who says a party will make me feel good? Strangers. People looking at me. What would you tell them about me?

"I have things to do," she said. "Some friends I've been meaning to call."

"In New York?"

"That's where my friends live. In New York."

"You think that's wise?" Claire moved away from the window, toward Katha. "They could tell Tommy where you are, or they could tell you things about Tommy that would bother you—"

"Claire, I can't avoid that forever! I mean, I'll be back in the city eventually, I'll see him eventually, I'll have to."

"You're moving back to the city?"

"*Yes, I am.*"

"Why?"

"Why, because that's where everything is, my friends, my—" Feeling tears in her eyes, Katha blinked several times, then unclipped her hair and let it fall down around her shoulders and against the sides of her face. "Where do you think I should go, Claire? I mean, if I were fourteen years old we could find me a foster home."

"Katha—"

"No no, it's okay. Really. Tommy got six years of my life, he got my clothes, the apartment. It's only right he should get the whole city of New York. It's an ugly city anyway. I was never happy there. I can't remember ever being happy there." Tears spilled over her face, she let her hair fall forward. "It's not the city, it was never the city. I have to lie down. I'm so tired, I don't know why, I just have to lie down."

"Katha, I'm sorry."

"It's okay, I just have to lie down. I did want to come to your party, I'm sorry, I have to lie down." She didn't hear Claire follow as she left the kitchen and moved through the blur of the living room. Going up the stairs, she heard Ira and Jeannie and Monica coming home; she rushed into her room and shut the door. She heard their voices, then their laughter.

*　　*　　*

When she woke up it was dark. At first she didn't know where she was, but then she remembered the argument with Claire. Damn, she thought, I didn't want to do that. She thought about Peter. Kill him, he said. She thought of Big Dan—I'm *drawn* here, he said, by the *truth*. He was too young to say something like that, though you had to be young to think you could get at the truth about anything, especially yourself. The older you got, she thought, the less you knew really. It seemed as though your actions had less and less to do with what happened to you. You'd think you were doing things that were right for yourself, but then later you'd find out those things were all wrong. You could go to sleep with someone, and wake up with someone else. People changed. They turned in the dark.

She reached under the bed for the bottle of vodka and the glass she kept there. She poured some and took a few sips, then went with the glass to the window, drawn by the voices outside. The guests were drinking too. They hadn't sat down to dinner yet; she hadn't slept long. Ira stood by the barbecue grilling fish. Two women stood near him. Yuppies, she thought. All of them yuppies with nicely settled lives. One of the women, the one with the short black hair badly permed, was a therapist. Talk therapist, specialized in addictions. In college, Katha had taken a course in Gestalt; she thought there seemed to be something in that. But nobody talked of Gestalt anymore. The other woman, in the Anne Klein suit, was in real estate. No, they were both in real estate, she decided—I ought to go down, ask about an apartment. They'd find me a cute little studio on Avenue B for two grand a month.

The man in bermuda shorts by the pool was a broker, perhaps an investment banker. He talked intently with Monica. He and his wife—who couldn't be here tonight because she needed the time to catch up on work—wanted children, a daughter, but they were waiting for their schedules to clear. The guy in the shorts was forty, forty-one. The two swains who sat at the table with Claire lived more on the fringe, but did well. Mr. Dap with the wavy tan hair was an actor, there had to be an actor, an actor on soaps. The swarthy type managed restaurants. Out of all the people here only two were a couple. Anne Klein and the one who managed restaurants. Cheers.

Katha drained the glass and went back to the bottle for another. I ought to go down, she thought, all they're missing is a model. You're having a party you had to have models— pretty ladies for scenery, and a joke. If you were a model people assumed you led an exotic and glamorous life, or they assumed you were stupid, which was often the case.

She sat down on the floor, her legs stretched straight out in front of her. The hem of her pink dress was smudged with grease where she'd caught it in the car door this afternoon. On her knee was a scab, just like a little kid's, from where she fell while chasing Jeannie by the pool the other day. Just below the scab was a crescent-shaped scar as long as a finger, still several shades darker than the skin on the rest of her leg. The scar would never go away. The scar came from a burn when Tommy pushed her against a hot oven while the oven door was open.

Pretty lady, beautiful. Sweetness. Loveliness. Bella. Carissima. Darling. Saint. My love. My life. Light. Soul. Heart. My wife. My girlfriend. My friend. My pal. My partner. Pony. Devil. Dangerous. Kady. Kady, like your father used to call you before there was me. Before there was me you were nothing, were you? You were waiting for me, weren't you? Say how you want me, baby. Baby. Say how you want it. Bitch. Whore. Puttana. Slut. Madonna. Mama. Mama.

"God damn you to hell," she said. She got up and turned on the lamp on the dresser. She took her address book from her purse and opened it to A. Abernathy, Selena. West Fifty-fifth Street. Selena and Rose. They liked to dance at the Duchess, before it changed hands. They walked with their arms draped around each other. Lovers. Selena was a blonde but she dyed her hair brown and said it changed her life. My looks are no longer over the edge, she told Katha. Still, they would always be beautiful women, Selena and Rose. They were high-fashion models, tall and slim as young trees. Selena liked to shock. She and Rose walked in twilight through Washington Square to the Duchess, arms draped, and men behind them saying, what a waste. This bothered Rose. But Selena would laugh, drop her hand to Rose's ass, say come along my little snake. Sick, said the men, sick and disgusting.

Katha lived for a time with Selena and Rose. They kept rats as pets. She went with them one rainy morning to Coliseum Books. Rose was sullen and sad. Shape up, Selena told her. She pinched Rose's arm. She pushed Rose hard against a table of reviewer's copies.

Katha closed the address book. The smell of fish outside was strong, tantalizing. She went to the bathroom and turned on the bath. She took off her dress and sat at the edge of the tub. How long have I been lonely? she thought. Two years, maybe more. She looked at her arm, surprised it wasn't withered. The skin was smooth, lightly tanned, young. Her fingernails were bitten to the quick. Dried flecks of blood dotted the cuticles. She loved her hands, because they were strong; she used to take care of them. She grew out the nails one time, very long. Her agent sent her up for a spot to model rings, but the advertiser said that her knuckles were too big. She was glad.

She got in the water and the water turned gray. She closed her eyes against the steam. Kady. Once she was Kady and Kady could fly. Richard and John had come home from college. She was six. Her brothers took her out back to where the ground sloped down to a ravine. A thick rope with a loop at the end was tied to a tree at the top of the slope. Kady knew what it was, a Tarzan rope. Richard and John had one when they were children. Now they'd made one for her. You sat in the loop and you hung on tight and you swung way out, above the ravine.

Her brothers were laughing. The autumn air pushed at her body. She settled down lower in the loop, hooking her knees around it, and then she let go, her hair flying, the world upside down. Her brothers were laughing, she threw out her arms. The leaves at the top of the world started spinning, so beautiful, flying, so her legs got weak, and released, and she wasn't afraid, she was falling, falling softly through the air.

Hidden under the leaves was a broken toy truck, red and rusty, metal. She hit a jagged edge when she fell. It cut her face. She screamed from the shock but the cut didn't hurt.

Her father came and wrapped her in a blanket. He carried her to the car saying, Kady, why do you do these things? *Why do you do these things? All day she ran so fast and so long that by night she lay in her bed her legs burning and stiff until she went to her father in his bed and he rubbed her sore legs as she cried and she wanted his hands all night on her legs.* Kady, why do you do these things? Daddy, I was flying. The cut didn't hurt. The blood was warm. The blanket was warm.

Her father was worried about her cut face. In the emergency room, he demanded a plastic surgeon for the stitches, because it was her face. The cut was by her ear, but still it was her face. They waited and waited for a surgeon to come until the cut began to hurt, to throb, and her father snapped be quiet, it's your face. The nurse gave her a shot and she slept, dreaming of her face as though it belonged to someone else.

Katha rose from the tub, feeling frail. With the towel she felt the bones that stood out between her breasts. She'd bought three new dresses, all pink. One pink was as dark as the color of dusk. Pink is your color, her mother used to say. Pink was womanish, fey; her mother never wore it. She went back to her room and put on a pair of jeans and a charcoal gray sweatshirt. Then she went down to the party.

They'd finished dinner. Netted candles and the spill from the lights around the pool lit them sitting at the table. The tops of the trees beyond the hedges swayed gently. She stood on the steps, taking sips from her glass of vodka. She liked watching the scene at a distance, hearing the murmur of the voices without any words.

"Katha, hi!" called Claire. "Come meet everyone. Ira, put some fish on the grill for Katha, will you?"

Katha sat at the end of the table by the actor; she didn't get his name. He nodded to her and the swarthy type across from him raised his snifter of brandy, saying, "Greetings, greetings, greetings. Salutations." Then he turned back to Anne Klein and said, "No, you're missing the point." This convinced Katha that she was his wife.

"Talk to Lenny, Katha," said Claire. "He's incredibly glum tonight." Then Lenny was the actor. He stared silently into a cup of coffee while the others drank and bubbled with after-dinner high spirits. Monica left, with some friends.

Jeannie was peeking at Katha from behind her mother's chair. Katha said, "Boo!" and Jeannie raced around the table, then back behind her mother. She was ready for bed. Her pajamas said MECHANIC on the back, and were patterned, appropriately, with mechanic's tools.

"Jeannie," said Katha, "can I see you for a minute?"

"What?" said Jeannie. Her head popped out and she squealed, then disappeared.

"I want to tell you something."

"What?" said Jeannie, invisible.

"Go on," said Claire, "you big tease. Go see Katha before

you die of anticipation." Jeannie came slowly around the
table, her head tilted down, her fist by her mouth with the
pinkie pointed up in that coy way she had with adults.
"What?" she said again to Katha.

"Well, come here."

"What?" said Jeannie, coming closer.

"I like your tools."

"Oh!" said Jeannie, snapped out of her act. She ran her
hands down her pajamas. "Yeah, I got wrenches and look,
all this stuff. An' I got one with cars. I got Jags and Mer-
cedes—an' I got music! Pianos and drums and—*Mom!*
what's that one I like?"

"Trumpets," called Claire.

"Trumpets!" said Jeannie. She collapsed on the grass.
"You like trumpets, Katha?"

"Oh yeah. I'm mad for trumpets."

"You can't be *mad* for trumpets. If you're *mad* then
you're angry."

"That's true," said Katha.

"Dad's got a disc with trumpets and I dance all night
long. Mom makes me go to bed but I keep dancing. See,
look, I'm on my back but I'm dancing." Jeannie's feet
kicked and tapped in the air. Her dark little head flailed
back and forth. "I dance all night long. I never go to sleep."

"You must be tired in the morning."

"Never," said Jeannie, "I have *unbelievable* energy."

"No kidding," said Claire. "You want to dance up to
bed?"

"Okay." Jeannie sprang up from the grass and danced
and hopped into the house with Claire, snapping her fingers.

"How many drinks did Jeannie have?" said Anne Klein.

Ira laughed, and on his way back from the barbecue with
Katha's fish he said, "You know what we used to do when
she was little? This is rotten. We sometimes put whiskey in
her bottle to knock her out."

"You didn't," said Anne Klein.

Ira shrugged. "It was the only way we could get any sleep. But she's a dynamite kid. Happy all the time." He put pasta salad on Katha's plate and passed her what was left of the French bread. "Monica," he said, "was born sad. She had existential angst by the time she was two."

"An oldest child," said Anne Klein.

"Partly that," said her husband. "But as soon as you're a parent you begin to see how predetermined in character all of us are."

"I don't buy that," said the woman with the perm, who'd been busy eating a second piece of napoleon. "That's simply fashion. We swing too far with the behaviorists and then everybody's saying oh no it's not the environment it's all in the genes. You want to try and tell me psychosis is nothing but chemicals? No way José, we *choose* to go mad."

"I like these large leaps you make in split seconds," said Anne Klein's husband.

"All I'm saying," said the woman with the perm, "is that it's all perception and perception is fashion, don't kid yourself. And politics, which is fashion as well. When we feel especially powerless we all start saying there's nothing we can do. We become instant fatalists. But it always swings back."

Katha stopped paying attention to the talk and focused on her food. She was so hungry she had to concentrate to keep from eating too fast. She heard Bob Marley come on from inside the house, and then Claire rejoined her guests at the table.

"I'm sorry there's no more corn," Claire said to her.

"I ate it all," said the woman with the perm. "You can't get decent corn on the cob in the city, I don't care what anyone says. Not even at Balducci's."

Everything in the Hamptons, Katha thought, was compared to the city by New Yorkers. You couldn't get *this* in the city, you couldn't see something like *that* in the city—like an ocean. To New Yorkers, the ocean was an amazing phenomenon. Since it didn't exist in the city it was amazing. She thought this feeling suddenly fond of the woman with the perm, and of the city too.

"Why is everything so boring?" said Lenny the actor. "Why is everyone so boring?" Katha thought he was referring to Claire and Ira's guests and this didn't make her like him. She rather liked Claire and Ira's guests; they hadn't asked her any questions.

"Uptown is downtown," said Lenny. "Downtown is uptown."

"You mean the same?" said Katha. "Oh, I don't think so." She glanced at him briefly from under her hair. He looked like a lot of actors she knew; he looked better from a distance than he did up close. Up close his features were almost caricatures of regularity.

"You live downtown?" Lenny asked. Katha nodded. "I could tell," Lenny said. Katha wondered how he could tell if uptown was downtown.

"You're hungry," said Lenny.

"Very." But he made her self-conscious and she picked at her food.

"You out here every summer?"

"Five years."

"I think I've seen you at Bobby Van's."

"You might have. Not this year."

Lenny ignored this. "What do you do?"

Well, Katha thought, in general I'm having a nervous breakdown but at this particular moment I'm feeling sort of chipper. Or I was. "Nothing," she said.

"That's original."

Why did Claire want me to talk to this person? she thought.

"I'm getting a divorce," Lenny said. "I just decided. My

wife has wanted one for months but I wouldn't give in. I think I'll give in."

Nice of you, Katha thought. "I think I'll get a drink."

"Yeah, me too."

Great. He followed her over to the bar.

"When I met my wife," Lenny said, "I had a lot of things going. I had a role on a soap, an apartment off Fifth in the Sixties. Lately, I've been thinking that since things changed and then she wanted a divorce, I shouldn't really blame her. Because what I've got now, it's not what she bought into."

"I hate that," said Katha. Lenny had his body turned so that it would be awkward to go past him and back to the table; giving up, she stayed where she was. She looked at her reflection in the water of the pool. "I hate that expression. Bought into. Whatever happened to love? And loyalty?"

"You're a romantic," said Lenny.

"No, I'm not. I just think when you marry someone, you shouldn't go running at the first sign of adversity."

"Adversity is ugly," Lenny said.

Katha stared at the pool.

"You're not married?" Lenny asked.

"I'm separated," said Katha.

Lenny laughed. "Whatever happened to love? And loyalty?"

"You're assuming I'm at fault?"

"Someone's at fault."

"You don't know my situation."

"So what's your situation?"

"Maybe I'd prefer not to talk about it."

"Your choice," said Lenny. He had his legs deliberately planted to block her from passing, Katha thought. "You're very nervous," he said. "How come you're so nervous?"

"I'm not nervous."

"Yes, you are. Do I make you nervous?"

"Why should you?" Then she thought, I've heard this before.

"Relax," said Lenny.

"Don't tell me to relax," she said evenly. "Or do you enjoy putting people on the defensive?"

"Are you on the defensive?" said Lenny, smiling.

"Excuse me." She stepped over his foot to go back to the table.

"Katha, right?" He maneuvered to stop her again.

She'd lost patience. "Look, I don't know what you want. To talk about your wife, to get laid, but I'm just not interested. Sorry." She moved to get by.

His voice stopped her. "I know you," he said.

Something caught in her throat; but then she thought, they play it like this because it works. This was just the next step, the next assault. After making her nervous by saying she was nervous he would claim he could see, beneath her facade, who she was. His reading of her would be mean or too sweet, depending on his mood. What he wanted was reaction.

"You're Katha Pinnell. You're married to Tommy Pinnell. I've seen you at Stand."

"You could have said that before."

"I remembered you from Stand but you didn't know me. You offended my delicate sensibilities."

"Well, I didn't mean to." She didn't know if he was kidding or if he was actually offended. She also didn't know why she should care.

"I always admired you at Stand," he said. "That's why I started talking to you. Then you said you were separated."

"I am, Lenny." She used his name to soften what she had said earlier, the uncharacteristically crude remark about getting laid. "And the separation is recent. So can you please just try to back off?"

"Sure, I understand. You know what happened to Tommy?"

Her eyes locked on Lenny's too-regular features. Something bad had been coming all through this conversation: she had felt it, though she couldn't get a sense of what it was.

"I guess you don't know," he said. "Maybe you don't want to know."

"No, what?" *Say it fast.*

"Well, he got busted, for some blow I think I heard. But he's out on bail, and Tommy's well connected so I wouldn't worry about it if I were you." Lenny looked vaguely embarrassed.

For a moment, she had thought Tommy was dead. But Lenny wouldn't have told her like that. Lenny was a jerk but he didn't seem cruel, and if Tommy was dead Claire and Ira would have told her.

"I used to do coke," Lenny said. "But it gets to be a drag."

"I think I'll go back to the table."

"You want another drink?"

"Thank you." She gave him her glass. "Vodka." Just go away.

The talk at the table was real estate now. She didn't want to hear it. She gathered up some plates and headed for the house. "I'll help," said Claire, and she followed.

"Was Lenny being a jerk?" Claire whispered.

"You could say that." Claire opened the outer door, Katha kicked the screen open.

"Sorry," said Claire. "He's not usually such a bad guy."

Katha laughed. "I'd like to see him on a good day."

"I'm glad you're not upset."

"No, there's—" They said in unison, "There's a lot of jerks out there," and together they laughed.

Keep it light, Katha thought. Act calm because there is

nothing else to do. She found a paper bag in the kitchen for the fish bones.

"We're going to Melon's for a drink," said Claire. "Ira said he'll stay with Jeannie. You up for that?"

"No, I'll stay with Jeannie. But do me a favor, take Lenny, okay?"

Claire scowled. "Do I have to?"

Claire looks beautiful tonight, Katha thought. Her white cotton dress was soft and cool, and her bearing was regal. Katha felt envy wash through her as she looked at Claire, envy of her friend's smooth, ordered life; she quickly submerged the feeling with gratitude.

"Forgive me for being so touchy today," she said.

"Don't apologize," said Claire.

"I just want you to know how much I appreciate you, and Ira. I love you and Ira." She felt tears in her eyes. "I love Jeannie and Monica. I love your house—" Damn, she was being effusive. She laughed and said, "Although your taste in actors is questionable."

"Yeah yeah," said Claire. "I'll get the rest of the stuff from outside so he won't be able to accost you. You'd better watch it," she said as she left the kitchen. "You're beginning to look shamefully pretty again."

Watch it, Katha repeated to herself. This is where you could slip. He's in trouble, bad trouble. But if he is, she answered back, it is not my concern. Nothing that happens to him now has any more to do with me. I left, I had to. What if he dies? Then he will be dead, she thought. He will simply be dead. No, I shouldn't think that. I should never allow myself to think like that. I don't want that. I don't want to be like him. That is not what I want.

She rinsed the plates she'd brought in, then filled the sink with soapy water. She welcomed the distraction of Claire, and then Ira, bringing in the rest of the dishes.

Then they were gone and there was only the sound of her hands in the water, the click of a glass as she set it out to dry, and the sounds she imagined Jeannie making upstairs in her sleep; a sigh, dancing feet in a dream.

Every so often she looked at the clock on the wall. It was nearly eleven. Friday night. Max would get off at eleven and then he could talk. He often stayed around for several hours to come down from his shift. Max tended bar at Chinese Stand. She and Max got along, and he would tell her what happened without telling Tommy she had called if she asked him not to. Lenny could have been wrong. He could have heard a rumor. People had always loved to talk about Tommy.

Katha, she thought, if you need to talk to someone so badly, call your mother. By the time you've talked to her you may find you don't need to call Stand. Put it off and you may lose the urge.

But I shouldn't call my mother, she thought. What did my mother ever do but remind me of everything I'm not?

Self-pity, I *hate* that.

Then she thought, so I want some information, is that wrong? She let the water drain out of the sink and then went to the phone. I'm making a mountain out of this. Claire's got me convinced that the slightest bit of contact will turn me to stone.

"Chinese Stand." The rush of noise in the background made Katha feel strangely comforted; it was familiar. Then she felt exiled.

"Hang on for a minute," the bartender said—it was a voice she didn't know—"I got tequila monsters at the enda the bar. Hey gents, lick it outa the glass I'm on the phone. Yeah, Stand."

"Is Max there?"

"Yeah—where's Max? Ya know where's Max? Max left."

"Oh, is Tommy there?"

"Who's this?"

"A friend of Tommy's—Sally."

"Yeah Tommy's not here."

"Can you tell me when he'll be back?"

"Uh—this Sally?"

"Sally."

"Tommy's in Jersey. He'll be back a few days. His mother died, y'know. You wanna leave a message?

Huh?"

"No, no message."

Katha hung up the phone.

Theresa was dead. Theresa died.

Katha picked up a wine glass and threw it at the wall. "You died!" she shouted. "You had to die *now*!" Her shoulders convulsed; she was weeping, she sank to the floor. She held herself, thinking, I live in the dark, I will never be released, it's too late.

She suddenly calmed. She said, "I am hysterical." She got up and picked up the shards of glass, felt their sharpness bring her back to her senses. She swept up the rest. She listened for Jeannie but her shouting had not awakened the child. She looked toward the window. She listened to the trees. She pictured them swathed in the black of the night. "You were a mean old woman," she said.

She called Jersey. Tommy's sister, Angela, answered the phone.

"Angie, it's Katha."

"Surprise."

"I'm so sorry."

"You coming or what?"

"I don't know, Angie, I'm—"

"He's not good if you care. He's out."

"How are you?"

"How should I be, Katha? My mother is dead."

"Oh, Angie . . ."

"The funeral's day after tomorrow."

"I'm—"

"If you're interested."

Angela was crying.

"Katha, please come."

When Katha got off the phone she was numb. That soon changed. Because she was so terribly afraid of being alone, she went up to Jeannie's room, and she sat with the child for what seemed a long time.

Chapter 12

"New York," Sam said, "is the place to be."

"I've been to New York," said Toby. "What happened is I went there with my class on this field trip, right? We were going to the Metropolitan Museum but I, personally, was more interested in the Museum of Natural History because there they've got this enormous whale suspended on strings."

"Suspended on strings?" Sam said. "What am I hearing here?"

"Yes," said Toby, "it's suspended on strings. In the air."

"Don't tell me this," said Sam. "They've got a whale on strings?"

"It's a model," said Toby. "A life-size model of a whale."

"Oh. That's what I thought you meant. So what?" Sam gave Toby a disgusted look. "As I was saying, New York's the place to be. It's the land of opportunity. For one thing it's got a lot of rich people. For another thing it's got a lot of poor people."

"Living side by side," said Toby. "Mansions and slums."

"I'm talking here, huh? I want a running commentary I'll

let you know." Sam took a breath. "So there's the rich and the poor, and then there's guys like me. Guys with imagination."

"Like con men?" said Toby, excitedly.

"Did I say that?" said Sam. "Did you hear me say that? Can you keep your mouth shut long enough to hear someone impart some valuable information? Stuff that could help you get ahead in your future? Man, you could use it, you know what I mean?"

"Knock it off," said Big Dan.

Big Dan was thinking, Peter knew. He appeared to be gazing at the girls who sat at the bottom of the bleachers screaming at the guys playing basketball, but really he was thinking; Peter could tell. Big Dan wasn't depressed, like Sam said, he was thinking.

There was something going on. Peter knew it last night when Toby had dinner with them, and this morning at breakfast and now, when Big Dan let Toby hang out at the top of bleachers with the brothers in the gym. Peter hated that Toby.

"Guys with imagination," Sam went on, "they slide into the gap between the rich and the poor and then, my man, they can make some big scores. Beyond that too, there's the women. Beautiful women. Thousands and thousands of beautiful women. Go out in the streets you can pick 'em like flowers because, I'm telling you, these women are desperate. The main reason for this is that most of the guys in the city are gay."

"Why is that?" said Toby.

"Cement," said Sam.

"Cement?"

"Yeah, there's too much cement. These guys lose touch with their animal instincts." Sam stretched, luxuriating in his male expansiveness. Then he resumed his usual posture, elbows on knees, back slumped, head dangling from the stem of his neck.

"What I'd like to get into," he said to Toby, "is film. Some kind of media. This woman I know, she's in commercials. She said she'd get me a job when I'm out of school."

"Commercials," said Toby. "That interests me too."

Sam looked at Toby in disbelief. "You can't do that."

"Why not?"

"For that you need flair. Could you honestly tell me— like, right now say you had to write me a résumé. Could *you* put down flair as one of your primary traits?"

"I'm only eleven," said Toby, defeated.

"Face it man," said Sam, "things like flair generally surface in a person at a very young age."

Big Dan stood up. "Where to?" said Sam.

"The head," said Big Dan. "I need your permission?"

"I'll come," said Peter. "I've got to go too."

Peter thought Big Dan might get mad but he didn't; then when they got to the guy at the door who handed out the hall passes, Big Dan said, "Playground."

"Outside?" Peter said to Big Dan.

"Yeah, you want to hit the head first?"

"No, Sam and Toby were getting on my nerves."

Big Dan smiled.

"I hate Toby," said Peter.

"I wouldn't kiss him on the lips."

Just before they got to the Exit sign, Big Dan slipped in a door off the hall and beckoned Peter to follow. Inside was a storage room stacked up with boxes, nearly dark except for the light coming through the small, dust-coated window. Big Dan rummaged in a box and took out some Camels, propped open the window and lit up a smoke. "Shit," he said. "Saturday."

"No school," said Peter. "I hate Toby," he said again.

"I need him for something. Forget it, okay?"

"But Sam knows." It was obvious.

Big Dan didn't say anything.

Peter watched a shadow, like a curtain, move across Big Dan's face; he stood in profile to Peter, half-turned to the window. "I know things, Danny," said Peter. "There are things that I know. I can think things." He wasn't saying it right.

"Yeah, like what?"

"I can think a thing, and I can make it happen. Sometimes I can stop things from happening."

"I used to do that," said Big Dan.

"Sam thinks he can but he can't."

"Sam's bullshit. You know that?"

"Yeah, Danny."

"You know not to listen to Sam?"

"Yeah, Danny, I listen to you."

"You listen to yourself."

"Okay." When Big Dan sat down on a box, Peter did too. "I wonder where we're going," said Peter. He was thinking about the new foster parents but as soon as he said it he was sorry he did; Big Dan looked away.

"Sam's jive," said Big Dan. "The youth house? That place was a pit, and Sam couldn't see it. You never want to be in a place like that, Peter."

"Sam talks a lot."

"Yeah, and doesn't think. Like Daddy."

Then Big Dan did something he seldom ever did: He looked at Peter directly, and hard. "You've got to spend your time thinking," he said. "There's all these things out there you can think, y'know? What you do is you run your thoughts over these things, all these things—like a search-light, until something takes. The thing that you want."

"You pull it in," said Peter.

"You *choose*," said Big Dan. "You don't have to be like

Sam or like Daddy or like anyone is what I'm telling you. And, Peter, yeah, you've got to be tough, but you don't have to talk tough or act tough. You've got to be it."

"I kicked Toby's ass."

"Yeah, right, when it comes down to it but—you remember those things Daddy did?"

Peter looked at his sneakers.

"You know what I mean, you remember—that's bullshit. Daddy's bullshit, Sam's bullshit, I'm bullshit, you don't have to be, yeah?"

"You're not bullshit, Danny."

Big Dan was silent. "I'm responding," he said finally, "to that crap Sam's been cramming in your head." His cigarette was out; he lit another. Peter watched Big Dan's eyes in the flare of the match; his straight nose, his hair, which was longer now, with the clump further down on his forehead; his mouth, soft and curved at the corners. He blew a big cloud of smoke. "You know why we're in here?" he asked.

"The cops," said Peter. "Weird Harold."

"No, Daddy's why we're in here, Peter, Daddy. That piece of *dirt* who was supposed to be your father. That's why you're in here."

Peter got a pressure in his head.

"You think that's a man? You think your father was a man? That's not a man, Peter." Peter's head was hurting. "How many times did he lock you in the shed?" said Big Dan. "How was he with your mother? What kind of a man hits a woman? Peter. Take your hands off your face." Peter brought his hands down.

"I don't want to make you feel bad," said Big Dan. "I just want you to know that's not the way to be. It's not right. Those things Daddy did, that's got nothing to do with a man." Big Dan leaned his elbows on his knees. "I went for it, Jesus," he said. "I bought it worse than Sam.

"When I was a kid he took me out to see the mako—that

picture he always used to carry in his wallet. Out at the Point, me and Daddy standing next to that thousand-pound shark. That's a man, y'know, that's how I always used to see him in my mind." Big Dan wasn't looking at Peter anymore. "He'd been to the city a couple of times. He married a woman from the city, my mother. He talked a good line. Shit, he talked a good line—he thought he was some kind of philosopher." Big Dan took a drag off his cigarette. "He had a jive line for everything, he thought he had everything down, he had *nothing* down.

"The only thing he could do, all he knew anything about, was fishing, and he couldn't even do that by the time you were born. He gets busted for, shit, this small time—he's carrying a couple pounds of grass on the boat because he's got these big plans. These big plans, he can't even keep his own wife. So she's a tramp, and I have to hear it all my life, my mother is a tramp."

Big Dan got quiet, so suddenly still it appeared he didn't breathe. "Sometimes," he said, "I think I could stop talking for the rest of my life." He looked back up. He looked at Peter very gently, as if it were difficult to see him or as if he had never seen him before. "You remember your mother, don't you?"

"Yeah, Danny."

"She was all right."

"I know it, Danny."

"She loved you."

"I know."

"I gotta get out." Big Dan went to the window, pressed his hands against the wall at either side of the panes. Peter saw the muscles in his neck and across his shoulders straining; then they relaxed. "Sam's okay," he said. "I'm not telling you to hate him or anything like that. You can love him, I love him. Just don't try to *be* like Sam."

"I don't have to be like Sam," said Peter. "I don't even

want to be like Sam. You know that lady Katha, Danny, she came to see me? She gave me her number and she didn't give it to Sam."

"She's got taste."

"I can call her if I want to."

Peter's voice felt empty in his head. Big Dan was there but he wasn't; Peter felt alone. "She's my friend," he said.

Even outside it was quiet. Big Dan was in the room but out the window, past the houses and the fields and the ocean, to a place far away that Peter couldn't see.

"That youth house, Peter. I'd never go back there."

"You don't have to, Danny." Peter stayed very still, thinking if he could be still enough, good enough, Big Dan would come back.

Big Dan turned from the window. "You want to go outside?"

Outside, Big Dan watched his brother. He had the kid running laps around the playground. That odd little kid with the loaf-shaped head, he ran good. He put himself into it. Dan usually ran with Peter but today he couldn't do it, he felt as though something had drained all the strength from his body. He wasn't even thinking; he didn't want to think. He couldn't think. All of the plans he had made were suddenly lost and could never be found. Something was over.

Sitting in the dirt, he leaned his head against the fence. He felt the fence and nothing else. Nothing but the fence. A fence around nothing.

He tried to see behind his eyes what Mrs. Daphne had said was his future. A man and a woman who would act as his parents. A home. A fresh start, Mrs. Daphne had said. It'll be good, she told him last night. Peaceful for a change. But it was no use. He tried, but he just couldn't see it.

Katha packed the new clothes she had bought and put on what she wore when she left Tommy—faded black jeans, a yellow T-shirt, the blue-gray windbreaker, still smelling salty from her walk on the beach. Traveling clothes. Nothing nice to get messed up.

She pulled back her hair and clipped it in place, then put on new shades with dark lenses, black frames. She liked how she looked; she thought she looked anonymous but faintly tough. She stared at the mirror, feeling detached.

"You know where you're going," she said.

Yes, and what was the difference.

In the dawn she had made her decision—to go. It wasn't even Tommy anymore, he was such a small part of it. It was mostly just to go, to let go. Letting go was so beautiful; all of the tension and the trying stopped—her eyes had relaxed, and she almost slept. It all became simple and clear—not clear, translucent. In her mind she saw Tommy and herself and she just saw two people who had loved each other but couldn't get along, and it just seemed so sad. Then she thought about how he might go to jail and how that would be, and she thought even after all the bad things he had done he didn't deserve that. He'd always tried. He had always tried but he could never get it right. He never would. She'd always known that about him, known the hurt, the defeat he struggled with. No one knew it like she did, and she was the only one who could—sometimes—make the hurt go away. Tommy said life was hard but that dying was easy.

From outside came the steady splash of water; Claire was swimming laps. She would tell Claire, then she'd walk to the train. She left the sleeping house that was a dream and emerged into the shifting, weak light of the morning. She set down her bag and sat in a chair by the pool.

Claire swam to the edge. "What's up?"

"Tommy's mother died. Please don't tell me not to go."

Claire pulled herself up from the water, took her robe from the chair beside Katha. A voice called, "Mo-om?"

Plaintive, Monica's voice. She appeared on the stoop in a floor-length black satin nightgown looking very much fourteen years old as well as imminently, achingly forty. She was clutching her stomach.

"Well, what is it?" said Claire. Snapped Claire.

"God, Mom, it's my stomach. That pain I've been having in my stomach is terrible today. I can hardly breathe."

"What do you want me to do? Call an ambulance?" Claire waited for an answer. "Tell me then, do you feel like you're dying?"

Monica looked daggers at her mother. "My worst doubts," she said, "are constantly confirmed. No one in this family cares anything for me." She turned with imperious dignity, and limped into the house.

"Hang on," Claire said to Katha.

"I'm fine," said Katha. "I'm not in a hurry."

Claire went into the house.

Katha closed her eyes. The world, all of it was passing, passing faster than anyone could see. You had merely to, gently, close your eyes.

"Katha? Have some coffee."

Katha took the cup and when she had a sip the hot liquid was a jolt through her veins. "How's Monica?"

"She'll survive." Claire sat down, dressed, with a towel slung over her shoulders, the steam from her cup pushing up at the air. "I won't tell you what to do," she said first. "But there's something you should know." She stared straight ahead, at the empty white chairs on the opposite side of the pool. "I should have told you before, but Ira didn't want me to—Katha, Tommy arranged that fire. It wasn't an accident. Tommy effectively killed those people."

Claire's voice seemed to be coming through a tunnel.

Katha spoke automatically, "How do you know?"

"I don't know for sure, but Ira's almost certain." Claire paused. "I'm telling you," she said, "because I can't stand your image of Tommy as this magnanimous, suffering man"— she was lingering over the words—"tormented by the deaths of two people he struggled to save. He may not have meant for those people to die, but if it hadn't been for him, there never would have been a fire."

"I don't believe you."

"Just listen." Claire put down her cup, turned her chair to face Katha. "Remember when Tommy came in with us on Gillorhan's?" She waited for Katha to nod. "He was straining economically even then. I don't know why, he always threw money around. I think he's always done a lot of cocaine." Katha looked away. "How did he get Split in the first place?" said Claire. "He was in law school then, he tended bar on the side. Where did the money come from?"

"I don't know." Katha glanced at the lawn, at the house.

"How could you think that Tommy would refuse to pay off the Mafia? How could you believe he was ever that innocent?"

Katha said nothing. She saw the sun starting to ease through the trees; the house, the line of the hedges, she thought, looked foreign, far away.

"This is what Ira believes," said Claire, "and so do I. Tommy's been a borderline front man for crooks since even before he met you. He's in deep and in debt to a lot of unsavory people. He may have had some small shares of his own in the clubs at one time, but he went much too far when he had to have Stand. Once he got Stand, he couldn't juggle it all anymore, so someone who wanted the business offered him an out with the fire—Ira says this is done. Insurance recouped a few of Tommy's losses and there was a transfer of power. They gave him the money to buy the others out. But at this point he has nothing, Tommy's nothing but a cover. All he has are commitments to people you wouldn't want to meet in an alley after six o'clock at night." Claire sat back in her chair.

Like China

"What's your ultimate point?" said Katha. Women fighting, women struggling, she thought, were as silly as women who did nothing at all. She set down her coffee, started pulling the sleeves of her jacket down over her hands.

"Don't you know?" said Claire. "How much trouble he's in, who exactly he is—what sort of person you're so determined to throw yourself away on, can't you see? What Tommy has done comes from greed, not good intentions, and some sort of crazy desperation you should never have been near."

"But I was." She couldn't absorb this. "Even if some of what you're saying is true, he's my husband. His mother is dead."

"Katha, how long has he been hurting you?"

No, don't do this. "I told you, two years."

"No, over three years ago there was a party at Stand, for that artist's daughter—you know who I mean. I was there, with Ira. You were late from a shoot. Tommy kept watching the door, he downed Absolut as if it was water. When you came in, he took you by the collar and shook you, and then he took you down to the office. I don't know what he said or did there, but you were gone a long time. When you came back you'd been crying, you sat in a corner all night. I saw this, Katha, even though later I forgot."

"He didn't hurt me then."

"It was the *way* he did it. And shortly afterwards, you stopped your modeling, yes?"

"Which I never should have done with all the debts."

"You feel implicated on level after level. Could you have covered the debts? Were they your responsibility? And even with the best of intentions, how were you equipped at the age of nineteen or twenty to deal with all the problems Tommy had? Look me in the eye and tell me, too, that Tommy had nothing to do with your stopping your career."

"I didn't want my career."

"Yes, but then you did nothing except be with Tommy, am I right?" Claire waited. "Since that's how he wanted it, am I correct? It was always how he wanted it, wasn't it?"

"This is complex," said Katha. "This is much more complex than you're making it."

"But I don't understand what you're doing!" cried Claire. "Even if Tommy was the mayor of New York, he beats you, Katha—you can't go back to someone who beats you."

"That's an inaccurate word, and I'm not going back. I am going to a funeral." She spoke stridently, so her voice wouldn't shake. "Tommy's not—I'm not a fool. I know what he's done, but I also know the good part of him." She sounded crazy, she knew it. "When I met him, you know what I loved? How we could talk. We could talk about everything. I was—I had this rotten love affair in college, with one of my teachers. He was married and I didn't know it, and when I found out I was—shattered. I can't explain it, but I felt so unworthy of—anything. I met Tommy and he got me over those feelings. Sometimes he would hold me all night, he made me laugh—" Her voice was shaking, her hands were shaking. "And I still can't see how he could be that person I loved and this—other person. He's not evil, Claire, he is sick."

Claire softened her voice. "I don't think that's the issue, whether he's sick—and I know you loved him, but, Katha, you just can't go back."

"I can't stay here."

"Why can't you?"

"I don't belong here, Claire." All she could feel was the shaking of her hands. She gripped the arms of the chair. "I'm nothing but trouble."

"Oh, no." Claire leaned forward. "You have some troubles, but *you're* not trouble." Katha turned away her face. "You never let me too close," said Claire. "You start but then you always pull away. Why must you be so alone with this?"

All Katha could feel, almost hear, was the shaking of her hands. Tears welled in her eyes but she had on her shades.

"I think you can't accept help," said Claire, "because you associate caring with hurt. For a long time you loved someone who betrayed you over and over. I know—well, I don't, but I can imagine what that must have been like, what it's still like. No wonder you can't trust anything. You couldn't trust anything in your own home."

No, I couldn't, thought Katha.

"You're always tired now because you could never rest."

I could never rest, I could never.

"You have this enormous capacity for caring, Katha. How you feel about those three boys, that's—it's wonderful. How you are with Jeannie and Monica. But all that was misplaced with Tommy. You care about people, but does Tommy?"

Hearing this hurt Katha, physically. Claire was pushing at something under the shame, something Katha didn't want to know, not now, not yet—and she wasn't that good, not as good as Claire said.

She regained her composure; or rather, she froze. "He could go to jail," she said. "Lenny told me—"

"He told me he told you."

"You knew?"

Claire nodded. "I won't say what I think about that."

"I have to go back."

"Katha, *why?*"

She felt calm, incredibly calm. "Just for a few days," she said slowly, "not for Tommy but for me. There are things I have to know. It was too unresolved when I left."

"Under normal circumstances," said Claire, "I might agree. But these are not normal circumstances."

"For me they are, Claire. This has all been my life for six years and I'll always have to live with what happened. I need to understand it, I need to see him. I need to look at him."

"He could kill you."

"Theoretically, Ira could kill you."

"No," said Claire, "not even theoretically."

Katha kept her gaze steady. Claire took the wet towel from her shoulders and held it for a moment, watching Katha. "Does everything look that bleak to you?" she said. "It won't always. It will take time, but life can be good. I swear to you it can."

Katha smiled. "Someday I'll meet someone like Ira? Make ceramic pots and napoleons, have a few kids?"

"You sound like Tommy."

"How?"

"Hopeless, hard."

"I have to go, Claire."

"What will you accomplish? Even if he doesn't hurt you."

"He won't hurt me."

"You're making a mistake. You're underestimating the hold he has over you."

"He *doesn't*," said Katha. "No more." She couldn't sit. She got up and walked to the pool, then walked back. "You said you wouldn't tell me what to do."

"All right." Claire stood. "I'll drive you to the station."

"You don't have to."

"I want to, but tell me—about the fire. Did you ever suspect he had something to do with it?"

"No." Maybe something had told her, in a voice she couldn't hear.

"Now do you believe it?"

She was calm, very calm. She reached down and picked up her bag. "Yes, I do."

Part Three—Tommy

Chapter 13

The train got in at Penn Station at two o'clock in the afternoon. As she rode up the escalator, she unclipped her hair and let it fall like a veil around her face; zipped her jacket up to the neck. She stood with her bag in one hand, the other in a fist, her eyes forward, never meeting other eyes—eyes that darted, scoping for space.

Hey, mama, you are a planet and I am your satellite.

Tell me your name and I'll put you in a song. I pluck the stars from the sky and I make you a bracelet.

The voice went through her like a ripple of heat, then diminished in the sound of the station. Her jeans were wet through with perspiration and stuck to her thighs.

She stopped in the concourse: food smells from the stores, and people brushing by. Feeling dizzy, she leaned for a moment against the dirty wall, then rejoined the steady stream of walkers.

She found an information desk and got directions to a window where she purchased her ticket for the train to Elizabeth, New Jersey, that was leaving in an hour. She took a seat near a shoeshine stand, put her bag in her lap, closed her eyes. I'm going back, she thought. She heard Tommy's voice in her head and felt the flesh tighten over her face. She opened her eyes. Voices echoed in the terminal. A bag lady asked for a dollar; Katha gave it to her. The woman tucked the money in a green velvet pouch that hung from the yarn she wore around her waist like a belt. Then as she walked away, she winked—Katha thought she did, and felt taken. She sighed, and got up. She felt like a mark, it was better to move.

She wandered over to a clump of blue pay phones, wondering who she could call. She decided on Peter; he might try to call her at Claire's while she wasn't there—Claire was right, you had to care about people, since nobody cared about anybody anymore. Peter was alone in the world, or nearly. She was alone. She spread out her change and her address book on the Plexiglas counter and put through her call; waited while Peter was summoned to the phone. At the next phone a woman said, "I don't care if he's in conference, I told you, this is an emergency." Katha slipped her foot from her shoe and touched it to the smooth marble floor for a moment.

"Hello?"

"Peter, it's Katha."

"Hello." He had his mouth too close to the receiver.

"Guess where I am? I'm in New York."

"So am I," said Peter.

"No, in the city."

". . . why?"

"Oh, I have some business here. I wanted to let you know I'll be back on Monday, I mean at that number I gave you."

"Okay."

"And I thought maybe, once you're settled in your new home and everything, we could do something—go to the zoo or whatever."

"Okay . . . can we go to the city?"

"I don't know, maybe we can."

"I'd like to go to the city," said Peter.

". . . is anything new?"

"Sam wants to go in films."

Katha looked up at the clock. "What do you think you'll do when you grow up?" she said.

"Be an astronaut."

"You know what? If we go to the city together we can see the planetarium. It feels just like space."

"In the city?"

"Yes. Peter, I have to go. Take care of yourself. Don't be nervous. Everything's going to be all right . . . Peter?" He'd already hung up.

"You through with the phone?" The voice startled her. She spun around to get away from the phone and knocked into the briefcase of the man who'd been waiting. "Oh sorry," she said. Then again she saw the woman she'd given the dollar to, walking by her toward the information desk; she wore a knitted cap and a hard, lascivious grin. But this was a different woman, younger, hardly older than Katha herself; and she wasn't grinning she was squinting, as if even the fluorescent light of the concourse hurt her eyes. Who was she before? Katha thought. Her weathered face was permanently chapped, already deeply seamed at the corners of her eyes. Her shoulders slumped like inverted wings.

Katha looked up at the clock. She felt shrunken by the monstrous space of the concourse. She decided to go to the platform and wait, and she followed the signs to the suburban trains: Elizabeth, Philadelphia, Washington, D.C. . . . She remembered a story she'd read once about a lonely man who was obsessed by a beautiful and mysterious woman. Watching her apartment from across the street, as he did every day, he saw her come out with a suitcase and then hail a cab. He tracked her to the airport, bought a ticket to where she was going, to Paris. In Paris she bought another ticket, to Lebanon, and he followed. From Lebanon they went to Rome, Martinique, Boston, London, Hong Kong; so on and on they circled the world. In the airports and planes he was always just slightly behind her.

She entered number 10 to the smell of damp wood and warm steel. She looked at her watch, then leaned against a pole, feeling calmer in what felt more like an enclosure than the concourse had.

She thought she heard someone call her name; jerked her head to the left, to the right—no one. She squeezed her eyes shut, then opened them wide. Don't think of him, she thought. Or think of him split. In two. Think of this: his thick silence on the phone that night, his theft of her clothes—not outbursts of passion but a slow, and almost—enjoyed kind of torture, a mocking display of—hatred, for who she was. A deep well of poison, an invisible source. She clutched the handle of her bag.

Her list of his attributes—of his charms, his small acts of courage and love—this she held, through repetition, as a talisman against who he'd become. His grief for the people he had killed—for the people he had *killed,* and this *unbearable grief* as his excuse for how he hurt her—she had believed it. She pressed herself close against the pole; heard the whine of the train in the distance.

This person, this shadow, my husband, she thought, I've never known who he was. I've never understood his intentions, his beliefs, known the web of his mind. I've never known what was genuine, what was an invention, and yet I said yes, I said yes. A pulse throbbed in her throat. I endowed him with love. I let him teach me who he was as if I had no eyes. I let him teach me what was true and what was right and *nothing* was right. It was lies, fine lies.

But how could he, she thought, have justified, rationalized such a thing to himself as the fire?

Or the fights, horrible fights like the one with the knife and the times he threatened to throw me out the window, or strangle me, or the fists raised to my face or smashed mirrors, paintings, walls, or grabbing me, hard, by my shirt, spewing hate in my face while I cried with fear, and despair because I couldn't understand—

The train was pulling in.

—and when it was over he said, well, we must have needed the release, it's too bad it had to happen like that but when people are under pressure they hurt each other, and she hated him, then he would change and see her hate and he would hurt and she couldn't bear to see his hurt so that she would feel guilty and pretend that she wanted to stay when she didn't, and she would comfort him—

The train stopped.

He *planned* the fire, he had *killed* those people, he said it, Katha, I killed them, but she didn't want to hear, to know, and the paintings, after the fire, the colors looked like they were bleeding . . .

The door slid open.

A few other people had collected on the platform. Not many, it was Saturday. Katha walked through the door of the train and took a seat by the window. She hadn't slept last night; she was exhausted. She resisted the temptation to close her eyes. She didn't want to sleep but to think. She felt she would never sleep again. She sat up straight and looked down at her hands in her lap; they were steady. She wanted to see him, to look at him.

She could almost hear him say: this is how the world *works,* I didn't invent it; this from his fine lawyer's mind, in reference to certain "adjustments," as he said. This pertaining to business and to such things as the "hard real world," and to how you had to accept the game and then play it. She could hear him say, this is how people *are,* not always such a pretty sight, Katha, but "part of the package." This stemming, of course, from his keen perceptions of human behavior. So he was exonerated. Beginning with all the little deaths.

Yet even Tommy wasn't such a good liar. Even Tommy couldn't really take the lie. Claire was wrong, he did suffer. The booze, the drugs—Claire didn't know, it was more than cocaine. He did so many pills that Katha didn't look at the labels anymore. She didn't want to know. What she knew was more to hold back, for if she didn't hold back she was in danger.

He did the booze and the coke and the pills to keep going, he said, not even to feel good, not now. He did it, she knew, to keep pushing alive a thing he once dreamed, of a place for the weary to go, to get away—to where they could sit in laconic half-silence that was stiller than the music and the cool dreamy motions in the dark, and affect their ironic redemptions, nothing mattered, ever would, ever did. The smoke of their cigarettes drifted up to the ceiling; hovered there, like small spirits, floating just above the world.

She had seen his remorse. She saw it sometimes when he hurt her, before he had the presence of mind to cover remorse with excuses and the language of his lies. He bought her gifts, books from Rizzoli, flowers, silk blouses, at which she stared with her glazed, empty eyes. Then, steeling herself, she would look up at him and for a moment they would meet in the complicity of knowledge, knowledge of the deadness of the gifts, of their union, and of glamor itself, and she would see, she would know, his anguish—of something else, something deeper and unknowable, something with roots that went far far down.

She knew now, she knew finally, that it was over, that he wouldn't change: to change, he would have to lie down and crawl out of his skin.

It was hot on the playground. The winds had shifted, stilling the breeze that sometimes brought a pleasant relief to

Like China

Quogue in the summer. Big Dan leaned up against the fence; so did Sam on one side of Big Dan, and Toby on the other.

Big Dan had Peter running laps again. The kid had complained, and taunted Sam with his call from the woman those two always made such a fuss about, but there was business to discuss; and besides, thought Big Dan, the kid was looking good. His legs looked spindly. He could maybe have a body someday. His hair was growing back.

"So how much do I get?" said Toby. He had his right hip thrust slightly up, in imitation of Big Dan, with his hand tucked in the top of his pocket. Dan noticed this and changed his position.

"Twenty-five," said Sam; he watched Peter, still annoyed.

"Thirty," said Toby.

Sam glared at him. "You spend your whole life trying to win a popularity contest, Tooby-tone, or what?"

"Knock it off," said Big Dan. "Twenty-five," he told Toby.

"We have to do it Monday," said Toby, "when Ms. Ryan's back on shift. I know how to put her in the palm of my hand. One time I told her this story about how I ate twenty consecutive hamburgers in a contest and made the front page of the *Post*." Sam spat. "She was impressed," said Toby.

"What I'm thinking," said Sam, "is we can go out through the room Ryan locked Peter in. See, Peter remembered the key to the room had a stripe of red paint on it. I'm playing cards with Eugene last night and I look on his key ring—no key with red stripe. But then he gets intense, we're doing poker, and he puts all the stuff from his pockets on the table, his change and a couple spare keys. One's got a red stripe. Cool, or what? I can get it, no problem."

"I bet they got the window locked now," said Big Dan.

"So we bust it," said Sam.

Big Dan frowned. "Yeah . . . I got us a ride."

"Yeah, who?" said Sam.

"Guy who bought the loot, guy Artie."

"Kid Artie?" said Sam. "Man, some choice."

"I'm not gonna open a business with him," said Big Dan. "We need a ride to the neighborhood. With a face like yours in the dark, you think I can hitch?"

Sam let this slide. "It's cool, it's cool. Artie's a mama's boy," he said to Toby. "Rich kid. His dad owns like half of Westhampton or something, and *nobody* likes Westhampton."

Toby giggled. "Oh yeah," he said, "right."

"It's hard to believe," said Sam to Big Dan, "that you sold that damn dweeb my compact disc player."

Peter bounced off the chain-link fence across from Big Dan and Sam and Toby, trying to run and keep his eye on the three of them at the same time; he got back his stride.

"On the way back from the lounge," said Big Dan. "That's when we slip out. You do your thing," he said to Toby.

"Yeah," said Toby, "right." He grinned at Big Dan.

"What're ya gonna do?" said Big Dan.

"Okay, it's lights out," said Toby. "I'm sick, I am sick as a dog with these mega stomach cramps. I'm crying, I'm *writhing* on the floor—"

"Don't writhe," said Big Dan. "I don't know, you can moan if you want." I must be nuts, he thought, this kid's a damn head case.

"So I moan," said Toby. "It's like I've got botulism, or possibly appendicitis. I've got to look up what side the appendix is on. This distracts her. I get her out of the dorm to the bathroom and all, but sooner or later she'll know you guys are gone and so then I go into where you actually are."

"Where we actually are?" said Big Dan. He was getting miffed. The kid Toby was overexcited; his eyes glittered brightly, as though he was high on something. "Where are we, actually?" Big Dan asked him.

"I haven't decided," said Toby, grinning. "But it'll be something she'll go for big time. Count on me."

"Shit, count on you," said Sam. "You're a fuckin'—"

"Shut up, Sam," said Big Dan. He put a hand on Toby's shoulder. "Toby, this is serious, huh? This is my ass. This is my brother's ass, you understand?"

"My brother asked you a question," said Sam.

"Shut up, Sam," said Big Dan. "Toby, you understand?"

Toby's grin quivered. "I've got them written down," he said. "Like six different stories. I just haven't decided which one is the best."

"No," said Big Dan. "No stories. Something that sounds like the truth, capisce?"

"I do that all the time," said Toby. "Me and my brothers, like you guys, y'know, we used to—"

"You don't have any brothers," said Big Dan. "You never had any brothers. Your brothers didn't die in a flood."

Toby's head dropped; he felt for his glasses, but they were gone and yet to be replaced.

"Yeah, that's bullshit," said Sam.

"If you don't want to do this, Toby," said Big Dan, "you don't have to. No problem."

"I *want* to," said Toby. He looked up at Big Dan, glanced at Sam. "I want to and I can."

Big Dan looked up at the sky. He was sick of the whole damn thing. Peter dashed by, red in the face; Dan watched him for a moment, then looked back at Toby. "Okay, this is it," he said. "This is what you say. You listening?" Toby's head jiggled fast, as if it was set on a spring. "You say it how I say it and you say it for real."

Sam took his new lighter from his pocket, the lighter that used to be Eugene's, the aide's, and gave it a flick.

*   *   *

Peter ran, fueled by fury, his eyes blurred with sweat. *There was something going on.* His brothers thought he was dumb, a kid to send running. But he wasn't dumb because he *knew* things, knew the world was connected, like telephone wires, so that, any second, you might know a new thing. He looked up at the soaring telephone poles, rising high above the fence, and saw the sun glinting on the wires. Big Dan was far away, Sam was bullshit, but Peter wasn't dumb. Maybe Big Dan was starting a gang.

Peter didn't care. He was going to the city—unlike Sam. He tasted the word, "planetarium," as he ran. It sounded like aquarium. A giant glass tank. Filled with outer space. Maybe guys went up in rockets, trapped the space, and brought it back to earth. It figured they had things in the city like that. Or else the guys poured the space down through tubes that led to other guys, in airplanes, in the blue sky. Those guys would fly the space back down to the city. If he was one of those guys in the planes he'd let out a little space, on the way back, and bob in the space like a cork, defying gravity.

He got a cramp in his side. He staggered a few more steps, then looked across the playground at Big Dan, who was giving him a sign to come back. He would watch Big Dan, he would listen. He would find out what Big Dan didn't want him to know.

Katha took a cab from the station to the house in Elizabeth. She felt beat but alert, though the town never failed to put a pall on her mood. It seemed to exist to dampen dreams, to infect the mind with oppression: a town of faded rust colors, stained browns and grays, overheated and choked with the smoke from its outmoded industries, running on coal. The city was fringed with modern buildings, but at its center lurked blocks of abandoned brick buildings, gutted and forlorn but stubbornly standing. Trains roared persistently above, and on the waterfront, edged with short steep beaches, rotting black piers jutted hopelessly out at the water, proclaiming a town passed by and forgotten, an angry town, traumatized by decline.

Katha remembered thinking once how strange it seemed that Tommy, a man of such striking and even refined good looks, had grown up in this place—a foolish thought. What drove him was always the need to get out. She knew, of course, he had never escaped. When he came back to New York after visits with his mother he carried the town like a fever.

She rolled the window of the cab up tighter. Smoke stung her eyes and the smell of it lingered at the back of her mouth.

They pulled into a maple-lined street of old and yet hopeful small homes: brick flats, a few nondescript whitish frame houses with short square front yards; homes of second- and third-generation Italians, some Spanish; hardworking people. The limp, browning grass in their yards was well trimmed.

In Tommy's front yard was a stake, planted deep in the lawn, with the letters of the family name carved vertically into the smooth yellow wood. Tommy's father had made it years ago. A single light burned in the window of the house. She didn't see Tommy's car—a black Lancia that was his car, never hers—on the street or in the driveway. Still, she approached the house hesitantly, although that came as much from habit as from anything she was feeling at the moment. She had never fit in here, never felt comfortable with Tommy's family. Outwardly demonstrative and accepting of her, they nevertheless exuded a message of exclusion, seemed to hint that their closeness was, for a stranger, impenetrable. Angela, Tommy's sister, was kinder than her mother. Yet she kept her distance in silences, and in looks.

When she knocked at the door, even knowing Tommy most likely wasn't there, she felt a surge of excitement—fear—no, it was excitement. *Even now,* she thought. Then she felt fear. Dismissing it, she thought, she hoped, her excitement came from her decision to see, to know, but that suddenly seemed a delusion, a hoax on herself. She shivered as she waited on the step in the warm purple dusk.

The porchlight came on.

Tommy's Uncle Joe pulled in the door and wrapped her in his big bearish arms. He pulled back and said, "Katha," holding her arms and looking at her face. "Katha," he said to the others in the living room, without turning his head. One by one they came and greeted her, Joe's wife Minna, the other uncles, Nick, Michael, and Mario, and Patricia, a teenager, Nick's youngest daughter.

All of them except Joe and Minna had been just about to leave, so after the hugs and condolences, Katha said she'd see them in the morning and went on, with Joe and Minna, into the house.

The front room was clean, and dark, but for the light of one lamp, and it smelled of Angela's cigarette. Angela sat in the only upholstered chair in the room, her feet up on a footstool, smoking a Virginia Slim.

"She came," said Minna, proudly, as she settled herself beside Joe on the floral-patterned couch. The couch crinkled as they sat; it was covered with plastic, and seldom used. They sat uncomfortably in their formal clothes, looking anxious to finish what had no doubt been a long and unpleasant day. Joe rubbed his grizzled head, patted Minna on the knee. "I said she'd come," he assured her.

Angela smoked.

Katha stood at bay in the center of the room. At last she brightly said, "Hi," to her sister-in-law, and took a seat on one of the folding chairs that were set up for the others who had left. The air-conditioning had a wet, old-rag smell. She waited for some cue from Angela, but it still didn't come. Tommy's sister simply smoked, her long brown eyes narrowed against her exhalations. She'd lost weight, which sharpened her prominent, almost masculine brow, and her skin had a waxy shine that suggested the complexion of a woman many years past her age, thirty-three. Her dark curly hair was loose around her shoulders. She put out her cigarette and then folded her hands beneath her breasts.

"Something to drink?" said Minna. "Katha, have some nice wine. You come in from the city, on the train? You're tired." Minna was already up and bustling toward the kitchen. Minna was a wiry woman who looked like she'd never enjoyed relaxing a moment in her life.

"Thank you," said Katha, "but—"

"It's Mama's," said Angela. "Have some."

"All right." Katha smiled, but then let the smile fade.

Minna vanished. "We'll miss her," said Joe. "She looks good, Katha, real good. She was a beautiful woman the day she died. I sent my girls with Minna to help Angie. Tommy got here—what Friday? Yeah, Friday, yesterday."

"A nice glass of wine," Minna said. "He came yesterday, Joe."

"Came breezing in," said Angela, "as per usual, king of the world. I do the dirty work, as per usual, then the king appears."

"Don't talk that way about your brother," said Joe.

"Uncle Joe, she died on Wednesday." Angela's voice was almost a whine, a child's protest to a father. Tommy and Angela's father had died twenty years ago, and Joe and the other uncles, their father's brothers, had since exerted a paternal influence.

"He has a business," said Joe. "He and Katha, they're having some problems." He said this lightly, without presumption; Joe was a good and cautious man.

"What problems could they possibly have?" said Angela.

"Tell me, and don't I have a job? I don't have an apartment on the other side of town I haven't been to for the last three months? I clean up after Mama day and night," she said to Katha, "and the king, he comes when it's convenient. And Mama, who's she want to see? Tommy. She gets up and out of the bed when Tommy comes, she's like a miracle better." Angela looked away from Katha. "It's nothing new."

"Aw, Angie," said Minna. "Your mama loved you."

"Why should she?" said Angela. "I didn't bring her flowers, sing her songs, sweep her off to the city for a fancy lunch—I did what *had* to be done and for that you're not thanked." She looked back at Katha, studied her. "For you, you don't look good," she said. "He's no good either . . . What's wrong with you?"

Katha felt herself blush, and shifted her eyes from Angela's frank gaze.

"Drink your wine, Katha," said Minna. "Angie don't feel good."

"No, Minna, I don't." Angela rose with difficulty; Katha was surprised—it never failed—at how tall she was, as tall as her mother had been, and nearly as tall as Tommy was. "I'm going to bed," she said. There seemed to be a touch of apology in her eyes, but then she added, "Now he's over there with her, he won't leave. His grief is better, bigger, he won't leave with the rest of the family."

"He has to leave when they close," said Minna, practical.

"I'm going to bed," said Angela, leaving. "All I'm doing is going to bed."

The old air-conditioner whirred. For Minna's benefit, Katha took a sip of wine; it was cold, red and harsh.

"It's hard on her," said Joe, "with no family of her own. She's not a strong girl." Katha had always perceived Tommy's sister as strong, she still did.

"We're gonna go, Katha, huh Joe?" said Minna. "We've

got the funeral in the morning. Tommy should be home soon."

Joe rose and again embraced Katha. Minna kissed her cheeks. Katha walked with them to the door, almost loving them, wishing illogically but fervently for an instant that Tommy had been their son, and Angela their daughter. She watched them walk to their car, an old Buick; Joe opened the door for Minna, then took her arm gently as she got in the car. They waved and were gone.

Katha stood staring out the screen door at the darkening sky. She'd forgotten to ask Joe and Minna what time the funeral parlor closed. She looked at her watch; it was nearly eight-thirty. Nothing to be done, she thought. She walked listlessly back to the living room, and then she heard someone humming. She stood still and listened. It was outside—no, it came from the back of the house. She went through the kitchen to the hall where the bedrooms were; it was Angela crying, not sobbing, but softly, a refrain.

Katha went to the door. "Angie?"

"Yeah, all right."

She was in her mother's room, lying on the wide bed beside a lamp with a shade covered with withering lace. Above the bed hung a crucifix, casting a long narrow shadow on the wall. The small space was cramped, overwhelmed by the size of the bed, a chest, a trunk stacked with clothes. The window was draped, the room—from the light diffused by the maroon-colored shade, the reds of the fabrics, the browns of the wood—was the color of blood.

"Can I get you something?"

"Sit with me."

Katha took a sewing box from a chair at the foot of the bed and sat down. Angela's arm was flung over her eyes. She pushed herself up on the pillows, and rested her head against the headboard. "I can't sleep."

"It's early yet."

Angela gazed at Katha as she had before; first studiously, and then frankly. "You're always so nice," she said. "How come?"

Katha lifted her shoulders. "I'm not, especially."

"It's not so easy in the city these days," said Angela, "is it?"

"No," said Katha. "Though I doubt it ever was."

"It's not easy here."

"No, I know it isn't."

One side of Angela's mouth cracked a smile. "Things you find yourself saying at times like these." She sighed. "Mean things about your brother."

"That's all right," said Katha. "He can be like that."

"Can he?" Angela's eyes fixed on Katha again, with penetration. "I get suspicious I see him just from when we were children—but he's different now. Something I see is he's very, very nervous."

"Yes." Katha looked at her hands. The room was very hot; the air-conditioning puffed ineffectually from the living room. "Angie? He's hardly ever talked about his childhood. I've always found that—a bit odd." She kept her voice light.

"He likes to be the silent type," said Angela, twinging her voice with disdain. "Most of them do. I love my brother." She sat up more, took a tissue from next to the lamp on the bedstand, dabbed with it at her eyes and her forehead. "He was so handsome, always was. My brother. Those long eyelashes, all that *straight* black hair. Papa called him the injun." Angela frowned, then brightened. "Smart? My brother was so smart he was called the little prince. Oh yes. Now I call him the king." She nodded to herself.

"I couldn't stand it, his smartness. I was missing school all the time, on account of the rheumatic heart. Then they sent me to the nuns. But my brother, even though I hated him because he was everything I wasn't, he used to do things for me—he would dance with me, this sick ugly kid that I was.

"I'd come home and he'd take me in his room and put on the radio, and we'd dance. He'd tell me I was pretty. He showed me attention, I had *fun* with Tommy. I loved him. I looked up to him. But I didn't like loving him because Mama favored him so obviously. God, worshiped Tommy, her son could do no wrong. And he did a lot wrong. He was a wild, wild kid.

"His childhood, Katha? Was wild."

Katha was silent, willing Angela to continue.

"Soon as he could he hung out in the streets, in bad neighborhoods, Newark. He hated the house. He'd go from school to the streets and come home late at night. Papa would pull his chair to the window and wait for him. Tommy'd come home and they'd scream at each other. It never did any good. Tommy stayed out, Papa waited. I remember those nights I was home, I'd want to go back to school to get away from the screaming." Angela, absently, touched the lace on the lamp.

"Nick's son, Red? He got shot in a gang war. Italians and Spanish. Tommy found him—" she paused. "I don't know how involved Tommy was in the war, he was barely fifteen, but he found Red shot in the playground. He brought Red back here because Red was afraid to go to the hospital. They went to Tommy's room, but in a while they came out and told Papa, Red was bleeding so bad. When Papa came back from the hospital—" Angela looked at Katha, softly.

"I think Papa was awfully tough on Tommy. I wasn't around a lot, and I was young so I didn't know just what went on here—but that night Red got shot Papa really hurt Tommy. When they went to court the next morning Tommy had a black eye. He said it happened in the fight, but Papa took him out to the garage that night and I know Tommy didn't have a black eye before Papa took him there.

"Now when I look back, I think Mama was soft with Tommy because Papa was hard. He was a hard man, my father, thick-headed. Chain-smoked Luckies, had one lung removed and just went on smoking, working ten, twelve hours every day and so sure he gets cancer and that was it. When he went, he went fast. He wanted to go, he was *furious*. How he saw it was that's the last straw.

"My father didn't find what he expected to find in this country. He thought if he worked hard then things would be good, but they weren't so good. He never caught on to the ways. He used to pour sidewalks ten inches thick, because he thought if your work was superior, you'd be rewarded. But who wants ten-inch sidewalks?

"Tommy was ashamed of Papa for things like that, and Papa sensed it, I think. Tommy was smart, with all the imagination and the charm. But those weren't the things my father considered important. He was suspicious of that. He called Tommy a bum. They were too different, old world, new world. But I loved my father. In a way I was spared because I was a girl and he could be tender with me. He didn't expect me to be anything, just me. See that chest? My father made it. He went over it and over it, caressing the wood as if it was a woman."

Katha watched Angela's face in an effort to discern why she was telling her the story—for herself, from a sense she had of what Katha needed to know; and inside as she listened she said yes, yes, although she had never heard these things before, not in words. She'd simply known them somehow.

"My father's funeral," said Angela, "that was a scene. Nick jumped into the grave, my mother threw herself on my father when they were going to close the casket. It was mass hysteria, everybody weeping and wailing—everyone except Tommy. I remember him in his black suit, dry-eyed all through it. His mouth was set and his face was so hard as if he found what was happening ghastly, disgusting. And yeah, sure it was, but I remember thinking that day the strangest thing about Tommy. I thought he looked just like Papa—and you know they looked nothing alike, not at all. That night I asked Tommy if he was sad Papa died. He said no, I'm free.

"Here Mama is dead and I'm talking of Papa, why is that?"

Angela shifted her body a little, looked away as though trying to remember where she had left off, and, as the image of Tommy's father, superimposed on Tommy's face, pressed deeper into Katha's mind she felt Angela had been giving her a gift. Angela told her these things because somehow she knew, and even in her own grief could care, as her mother hadn't.

"I've always liked you," said Angela. "I haven't shown it very well. Neither did Mama, how could she? You took her son. She was put off by superficial things, how pretty you are." Angela smiled. "That put me off too. I imagined your looks made things easy for you. But truthfully, I always thought you were the best, the very best thing that happened to my brother. Much better than how he left here or became a success."

Tommy had kept it all a secret from his mother and his sister, thought Katha, but not well enough.

"If you can't go back with my brother," said Angela, kindly, "I wouldn't hold it against you. I know there are things in Tommy I know nothing about."

Katha wanted to cry. "I think I'll get some water. Would you like some?"

"No," said Angela, helplessly. "I'll go to sleep now, Katha. I'm very tired."

Katha stood. "Good night."

Angela lay back on the bed without taking off her dress, and as Katha left, she turned off the light.

*   *   *

Katha walked stiffly to the kitchen. She looked at her watch. Nearly nine-thirty. She turned on the water, put her face beneath the tap, and let the water run over her face. It wetted her hair. She drew her face back, her hand still holding the faucet, and thought, when you are alone people come, people come to you. She wondered why they hadn't come sooner. She wondered why she hadn't come to herself sooner. Through the window then, above the sink, she saw the garage: a separate structure, detached from the house. She saw only its outline, its dark bulky shadow. She listened to the water flow in the sink.

Then she heard the front door and her spine went absolutely rigid. She felt her hand freeze on the faucet. *Turn off the water, turn off the water,* she thought.

She turned off the water, and then she heard his steps. She felt him. She faced him. He stood in the doorway. She thought, he looks so small and so frail. He smiled and she felt her heart leap, turn over, break.

"Hi, baby," he said.

Chapter 14

Morning came. In some ways, she should have predicted it would be as it was; in other ways what happened was as new and unexpected and bewildering as any return to a person you have seen too much, known too well.

He didn't ask where she had been—he asked nothing. After he appeared in the kitchen they sat down at the table and he said, I'm glad you're here, thank you for coming. She asked—with trepidation, knowing the weighted potential of the question—how he was. He said easily, I'll be glad when this is over. Then, in the truce they had agreed upon, they talked in general of the family and of how the funeral would be. He didn't drink. Soon he went to sleep in his old room, and she slept in Angela's room, falling quickly, surprisingly, into a deep and dreamless sleep.

They weren't alone again until nearly evening the next day. As they got ready for the funeral in the morning they passed each other in the hall, and their eyes met, briefly, before they both, at the same time, looked away, almost shyly. All day, though, she watched him surreptitiously.

The funeral was short and uneventful. Demonstrations of

grief, Katha thought, had played themselves out in the days leading up to this morning. The family looked tired, restless, edgy from the extreme wringing heat of the day and the contrasting chill of the tiny dark chapel where the funeral was held; it was Sunday, and the nave of the church was holding a regular mass. Only Angela wept, and, dutifully, Tommy attended her. Katha sat with Joe and Minna, thinking that the funerals of the old were in a sense the saddest funerals of all: they often seemed a mere postscript.

They didn't go to the grave site; instead they were directed by a guide through the doors of a vast and mysterious building that stood, fresh and sterile and firm, on a crest, bare of trees, at the center of the cemetery. A straggling group, they were led down a hallway with crypts, Katha realized, at either side. These crypts, rows and rows of them with their brass nameplates, were more shocking, more startling, she thought, than headstones or crosses in the grass.

Again, they were soon in a chapel, very bare, with the coffin in front on a bier, on a carpet of green. They were given carnations. The guide read a prayer, and then, as directed, they each placed their white flower on the coffin— this being goodbye. On leaving they were given a laminated card that sealed a psalm, Theresa's picture, and the date of her death.

"I guess then they take her away," said Angela, puzzled. She looked at the card in her hand, then lay her head back in the limousine and said nothing more. Tommy stroked his sister's arm, and Katha sat opposite them, watching the tall cold place where Theresa was receding behind their heads.

They had lunch at Joe and Minna's. The younger children of the uncles, and the grandchildren exploded with energy, while the adults drank a good deal of wine. Tommy drank tonic.

Katha answered questions addressed to her evasively, feeling, by late afternoon, rather drugged—by the distance between her and Tommy that only intensified her awareness of his presence. She felt as if everyone else in the room was a shadow—ghosts, memories or props—and that the room itself existed to contain the field of energy created by herself and Tommy. She watched him talking, a cigarette always in his left hand, his right hand reaching up now and then to push his hair from his forehead.

He rarely looked at her, and if he did, he would quickly look away, though one time he came to her and asked if there was anything she needed; he asked as if she were anyone, or no one. She felt then unaccountably hurt, banished, betrayed.

Banished from what? Her right or her need to comfort him, to confront him? Tommy seemed almost—serene. He looked tired: the hollows beneath his high cheekbones were pronounced, and the outsides of his eyes very subtly drooped. But for all that his face was unusually relaxed; the tight strain around his mouth was gone. She tentatively thought that his appearance, his manner, suggested a surrender, an acceptance of—defeat. Even humility.

Then she saw him get up from where he'd been sitting with Angela and cross the room to speak to his cousin Red. When Tommy crossed the room his walk was a smooth glide. That's how she thought of his walk. She had told him so once and he'd frowned, then looked at her again, reconsidering the image, enjoying it finally. He'd come to like her perception of him as, in some ways, elegant. Often, when he was telling her something that happened at Stand at the end of the night he would say, "So I *glided* up to the bar. . . ."

Red was nearly bald, and paunchy, at thirty-nine, just a few years older than Tommy. It wasn't fair, Katha thought, that Red—a good father, a steady person from what she knew about him—looked used up already while Tommy, in spite of his thinness and his obvious tiredness, still looked almost dazzling.

She looked away, doubting her eyes. A woman at Split, years ago, had asked her how she "got him." The question was incredibly incongruous, since the woman was older, and to Katha at the time, sophisticated; Katha was nineteen, awkward, and new to the city. She remembered she giggled. The woman said, "I'm serious, what did you *do*?" Tommy was thirty, never married, and never involved with anyone else for long before Katha; Katha gathered that the woman was referring to Tommy as a "catch," and assuming an implicit strategy in the capture. How provincial, she had thought, and when she told the woman she'd done nothing to *get him* and hadn't the faintest idea what she meant, she felt superior and haughty, above that person and everyone else who suddenly stood outside of the coveted world she was part of that summer, that summer of rebellion—quitting school and becoming a model, feeling hip and gorgeous, flaunting the looks she had learned to be ashamed of, and feared, but living on instinct for once, unthinking, and running so fast, that summer when everything flipped.

"*Katha.*" Angela, erect and brittle in her faded black dress, stood in front of her. She sat down beside her on the couch and whispered, "What the hell is going on?"

Katha looked at her blankly.

"I don't mean between you two," Angela said, "that's none of my business." Last night's conversation might never have happened. "But he won't even stay to close up the house. He says we'll have to wait a few weeks or that Minna can do it, but it's something he and I should do, you know?" She lit a cigarette, blew out a fierce stream of smoke from between her clenched teeth. "Oh what am I worried about, he's a selfish sonofabitch. It's just, whatever he's got to get back to in the city so quick, if he's in trouble or something I mean maybe I could help." Her words trailed off and her eyes appealed to Katha.

But how could Katha tell her that her brother was on the

brink of prison and other calamities that were so convoluted she couldn't explain them if she tried?

"I had too much wine," said Angela. She rubbed her eyes. "He's whipped from today, so am I. He's got his marriage to worry about." She put her hand on Katha's. "Maybe we both need a break from this. I wouldn't mind going back to my apartment, maybe go to work in the morning. Take my mind off it. Hey, let's go back to the house, get our things and just go."

That was easy, thought Katha. Just don't say anything and let people come to their own conclusions. Tommy was good at that, at waiting people out until he got his own way.

So the three of them left Joe and Minna's at four and drove back to the house in Angela's car—Tommy hadn't brought the Lancia. Tommy drove, and Katha sat between him and Angela, her shoulder grazing Tommy's; she saw that his hand trembled slightly when he put on his glasses to drive, and again—putting the key in the ignition. They were both doing their best now to act natural in front of Angela—but Katha was close enough to smell him, and the mingled, harsh scent of cigarette smoke and his bleached white shirt. Their legs in the car were inches from touching.

Katha squeezed her legs tightly together, drew her shoulders and arms in close to her body, carefully, slowly, so Tommy wouldn't notice. Then in minutes the tension of holding this position made her break out in a sweat; she smelled sour to herself and felt intensely self-aware, though the windows were open and Angela, unconcernedly, smoked. Katha didn't look again at Tommy. She sat thinking, her head cloudy, about what she should do.

Angela talked about how she and Tommy were an island apart from the rest of the family. They were close, certainly, she said, but the family was from Papa's side, and she had felt the absence of anyone related to her mother today; they were in Italy, in Milan, Theresa having come here with her new husband when she was very young. Tommy and Angela had only seen their mother's blood relatives once, but Angela said that the telegrams and flowers that came from Milan had meant more to her today than anything else. Poor Mama, she said, must always have felt so alone.

When the car stopped Angela said, "You'll go back to the city with Tommy, Katha?"

Katha said, "Yes." She could have said no, could have asked Angela for a ride to the train, as she had decided she should; but, irrationally, she'd imagined Theresa's voice in Angela's question, felt herself being thrust at Tommy, so that Angela repelled her—though how could she know? No matter what Angela suspected, she couldn't know the severity of the situation. Tommy wasn't relaxed as he had appeared at Joe and Minna's. But he was controlled, he hadn't been drinking; there would be no confrontation, she assured herself—if she was careful.

At the house, Tommy held the door open for her; Angela had already gone in. "I don't mind giving you a ride," he said.

It was all right, she thought, and said, "Thank you," then put down her head because she was almost crying, and went quickly to pack in her room.

There would be no confrontation, they had agreed. Neither, she thought, would there be kind words or resolutions. She couldn't tell him she was sorry she left as she did, or ask him if he understood. She couldn't even say she was sorry his mother was dead, or say she was sorry that she couldn't help him now, though she wanted to. She couldn't tell him that, still, she wished something would drop out of the sky and change everything that went wrong.

No, nothing would be salvaged, and there wouldn't be a resolution. She'd have to live with the irresolution—he wouldn't even offer her her clothes back, she knew. She had to be punished, she *should* be punished for hoping for some sort of reason and understanding at the end of a marriage that was built from the start on unreason and misunderstanding. If only Claire had kept her bodily from coming here. She couldn't be trusted, she couldn't trust herself.

She needed a shower. She grabbed her black jeans and a blouse and rushed down the hall, without seeing him, to the bathroom; she carefully, quietly, shut and locked the door.

She turned on the shower, very hot, and let the water pound on her head, sopping her hair and matting it down around her shoulders. I come courting trouble, she thought. The steam got so thick she could barely make out the tiles on the wall or the rings at the top of the shower curtain; then they were gone. She stared into the steam and saw the slant of light at the foot of the stairs where her parents were talking in the kitchen on the night she had come back from boarding school. She stood clutching the banister and hearing the voice of her mother saying I'm sorry, but I've never understood her, and I see her becoming one of those kind of women I've never been able to trust. Her father saying Kay, you're upset. Her mother had said I'm not proud of this feeling but I'm frightened for her. Martin, if I could just love her more.

The hot water stung Katha's body. Yes, she thought, you should see what became of me, Mother. You should see the mess of my life. She smiled and said, "Kady," softly. "Dangerous."

She ducked her head in through the open car window to kiss Angela goodbye. Angela pecked at her cheek and pressed her hand.

"Don't be too hard on him for a couple of days," she said. "And keep in touch. Call me sometime and I'll meet you in the city." She turned her head away from Katha, toward the house. "See how he looks at you," she said.

Tommy, who'd gone back inside to fetch a bag that his sister had forgotten, had come out again. When he saw Katha watching him he turned away to relock the front door, then came through the yard to the curb with Angela's bag.

Katha stepped back on the sidewalk while Tommy told Angela goodbye. He'd changed into another white shirt, and a loose pair of khaki trousers that Katha had never seen before.

The engine started, then Angela's car pulled away; Katha watched the blue car getting small down the long, maple-lined street.

"Your hair is wet," said Tommy.

She turned to him, touching her hair self-consciously. "I didn't have time to dry it," she said. She noticed that the string at the top of her blouse was untied; she quickly knotted it into a bow.

"You're going to the city?" he asked.

"To the train I think. Here."

He looked at her for a moment, and then put their bags in the rear of the Lancia. They got in the car.

The hot steamy air got more rancid outside the neighborhood. "Roll up your window," he said, "I'll put on the air." She saw the heavy industrial buildings, smoke billowing above them, coming into view. They passed a bleak run-down park where a group of children struggled up a steep, rocky incline, empty swings and a slide behind them. They entered the business district and stopped at a light.

"What?" she said, feeling his eyes.

"What." His tone didn't say anything. "I'm out of cigarettes." When the light changed he pulled up in front of a candy store just down the block; two Spanish boys leaned drunkenly up against a newspaper box, drinking Cokes. She felt a hot blast of air when he opened the door. The door shut. She shook her hair and combed it with her hand, her face feeling naked with her hair wet and plastered to her head.

There was a rap at the window. She turned to it sharply, and Tommy was making a circular motion with his hand. She rolled down her window. He sighed, his hand on his hip, and tossed his hair off his forehead. She heard the two boys in back of him whistling, and she saw them walk away.

"Ah, did you want something?" he said.

"No nothing, thank you." She'd said it too fast. She watched the smooth swing of his hips, and then his hand as it reached out to push at the peeling yellow door. Oh please God, she thought. She left her window down, letting the hot prickly air pluck at her eyes.

He got in and she rolled up her window. They pulled back into thickening traffic. Sunday, she thought. She looked at the illuminated clock and saw that it was six. The smoke from his cigarette drifted by the clock, covering the numbers for a moment. The hum of her thoughts rolled incessantly by, an incantation, a chant: please, it's all right, he's trying like I am, just get away, but to where, there isn't anywhere, if I could get away from myself—what is he doing, nothing, *nothing* it's all right, a little longer—I hate you, why all the effort, why always always the effort. She saw the station up ahead. She gazed at it dully.

"Which entrance?" he said.

"It doesn't matter, the main one is fine."

"I don't see a space."

"You can drop me."

"I'll drive around."

The station was crowded tonight. People swarmed between the cars in the circular drive. He swung away and drove down the aisle of a lot and took a space at the end.

The engine died. The cool air at her ankles went dead. He

got out and she watched him walk around the front of the car, to open her door, she realized. She squeezed the door handle, but the door was locked. She unlocked it and the door yawned open. She got out a leg, stood, and then all at once she was crying, sobs heaving in her chest, ripping up through her throat. She pressed the palm of her hand against her face, and fell back in the car.

She was gasping and watching him stand there—he wasn't moving. Then the door shut and the door on the other side opened; he got back in the car. She looked over at him and saw his hands resting lightly on his thighs.

"I don't know what to do," she said, "I don't know what to do." She pushed the heels of her hands up over her cheeks and her eyes. I have to go, she thought, *I have to go.*

He turned the ignition back on and the air came back.

She leaned her head back against the headrest for a moment. "I'm sorry," she said. His hands were still light on his thighs.

"Either you're with me," he said, "or you aren't."

"Don't. You know I can't stand your proclamations."

He was silent. She said, "We'll have to talk."

"Not now." She caught a glimpse of him and the muscles were tight around his eye. He took off his glasses.

"No," she said, "we can't talk."

"And *you know,*" he said, "we can't fight."

"I'm not." She had never, never heard him say that before. "Tommy—"

"Katha, get out of the car."

She did, but he got out too. He slammed the door, then slapped his hands down on the roof of the car. His head dropped. She stood uncertainly at the other side, watching his hands and the top of his head over the low-slung roof.

"What do you want?" he said softly.

Everything was a blur but his hands and his head and the

sleek black roof of the car. She was dimly aware of people passing by.

"Nothing, I shouldn't have come."

"I'm glad you did." He looked up at her.

"You are?" He looked away. "I don't have any right to say this," she said, "because I left, but—I can't help it, I'm worried about you."

"No you're not." She went around to his side, leaned her back against the car, beside him, about a foot away.

He turned, leaned next to her. "Katha, you want—" His arms were limp at his sides. "Ah Christ. You want to come back to the city with me? Just a couple of days, until I'm—" He pushed his hair off his face. She felt the silence weigh on her, drown her.

"All right." They didn't touch, just got back in the car, and before they even got to the turnpike the strain of the day, and the preceding days, hit her with an impact that was insupportable, so she slept, and didn't even wake to the fierce city noises that used to make her jump, and when she did wake, hearing his voice, it was dark.

They had sold their loft on West Broadway last year and moved into a smaller loft-apartment on Eighteenth Street, off Park Avenue South. They had needed the cash but when they got it, it evaporated, as it always seemed to, and then, the under-the-table sum for a rent-controlled apartment was not a small amount. For a few years when Katha modeled she made good money, but that went too. Whether she worked or not, it hardly made a difference economically. Just step out on the street, people said, kiss a fifty goodbye; the city sucks money. But with Katha and Tommy it went further than that; Tommy paid out twelve hundred a month to loan sharks, the last Katha knew, and that didn't even touch the principal.

The new loft, though, was just four-fifty a month. Katha had felt optimistic when they moved there. She hoped the loft signaled a change in their fortunes; Tommy said it would give him a footing. Another delusion, she thought later.

She was convinced there was a time she would have done anything to start over with Tommy—such as leaving the city, that would have helped. But Tommy *was* the city, as he had often reminded her. He needed the city as she had once thought she needed certain things to survive—paintings, light, the ocean, gentleness. And now Claire had implanted the thought, true or not, that no matter what Katha had done it was already too late, even from the beginning, to help Tommy move away from the course he was set on.

He was never open to Katha's suggestions, except regarding the smaller decisions in their life. She had to admit she had liked that in him; she'd felt relief when he'd say, I've got it covered. For that now, she hated herself.

As they trudged up the wide stairs to the loft, she was struck with a sickening fear for what he had done to keep things going this past year, when she'd been too weak for concern about anything outside of herself—and when his own strength was ebbing, she knew, though he always denied it. Under the naked bulb by their door he looked sallow, spent. His straight nose looked too long, his clothes too loose. But something at the edge of his hair, at the hairline, where his hair met his face, looked delicate and achingly tender.

The loft had a shut-in, moldy, summertime smell. She stood in the hallway between the two rooms, staring at the goddamn pictures, of herself, that covered the wall: ten-by-twelves mostly, some matte finish, some glossy, one with her hair blowing out around her head like a fan, or like a peacock, feathers spread in regalia. The photos were stuck up on the wall with tape, and one was missing—an amateur shot that was taken in the Hamptons three years ago on a schooner, with her hair in braids and her face scrubbed clean, shining, smiling. The one picture of herself that she liked. He had ripped it from the wall she could tell because there were the pieces of tape, still holding the four ragged corners of the picture.

She called casually to Tommy, who was in the front room, "Tommy, what did you do with my clothes?"

"They're in your closet," he said.

He came into the hallway and saw what she was looking at. "You hurt me, baby," he said. "You cut me bad." He stared at the blank space sadly, then smiled. "We should open the windows." He went back to the front, where the bathroom and the dressing room, and the kitchen and their big mahogany table were.

She went to the back room, slid up the tall windows that faced a brick wall, then turned on the fan and the bedspread fluttered; the bed was unmade, and she imagined he hadn't changed the sheets since the last time she'd been here six weeks ago. She sat far away from the bed on the sagging gray couch. But for the bed, and five or six overflowing ashtrays, the room was neat—but decrepit, she thought. Sitting there watching the wall across the alley, her bones began to hurt. I hate this city, she thought, and then she thought about rainy days when they lived on West Broadway, when she had come home from a shoot, or an audition, which made her depressed, and how the polished wood floor was so smooth and comforting, and the loft warm with the rain outside, and how she felt safe there, had fresh-cut flowers on the table most of the time, even in the winter. Here it was never that way.

His steps sounded on the tile in the hallway, got soft on the rug. He handed her a tall glass of wine. "Drink it," he said.

She looked up at him.

"I'm not having any." He sat down at his desk by the window, swiveled around in the chair and watched her sip the wine. On the desk were several watercolor sets, some brushes, given to him once by a painter they used to show at Stand. Tommy had since painted occasionally, not seriously, though his paintings, she thought, were quite good. She'd hung one of them in the office at Stand, a small rectangular piece of a freeway at night—he liked to paint roads. Dirt roads, graveled, blacktops, driveways, overpasses, dead ends; roads waiting for cars. When she looked at them she felt a sort of lonely expectation, like the feeling of leaving very early in the morning on a road trip when the sky is barely light and there are few other cars on the road and where you're going seems an eternity away.

"How do you feel?" she said.

He crossed his legs, put his elbow on the arm of the chair, and rested his chin in his hand. "You want to go by Stand?"

"Not really, do you?"

His lashes fluttered downwards. "I don't know how to be with you, Katha. I've never been—walked out on before."

"Tommy—"

"No." He put out a hand, looking back at her. "I sort of admire you for doing that. I was a little off it, I had things on my mind. I wasn't paying you enough attention." He smiled, but only for a moment. He never smiled for long, just as his smile never showed before it came in his eyes. He'd smile suddenly; it would flicker on his lips then disappear and his face would be expressionless again, silently watchful, waiting. Remote. Something about this used to strike her as sexy.

"And I won't ask you any questions," he said. "But we could have talked. We could have discussed it."

"Tommy, you know we haven't been able to talk for—a long time."

"So talk," he said. "You want to talk?"

Like China

She was silent, watching the drops of condensation on her glass through her hair that fell down around her face.

"You look nice," he said. "You look better now than you used to. More natural."

She couldn't think of anything to say.

"Baby, it's just that you left when I've got all this— y'know, Mama dies and the store's not good."

Since when has the store been good? she thought. When would it ever have been a good time to leave? And his mother had been dying for years until she finally went ahead and did it. And "the store," another example of his non-affection. The club or the bar or the restaurant or what-ever it was was a "store," and he talked more like the neighborhood punks who increasingly hung out there than with the articulation he was capable of. What you are, she thought, is one complete affectation. Type: downtown. This also used to strike her as sexy.

"Aren't you tired?" she asked him.

"When I got back," he said, "and you were gone that night, Katha, it was like—you were dead. Do you, I mean, do you want a divorce?"

"You said you wouldn't ask me any questions."

"No, but just tell me, you don't—you don't want to be my wife anymore?"

"Tommy, please don't do this now. You've still got your mother on your mind, we're both tired—"

"I don't have my mother on my mind, I have you on my mind because you're the only thing in this whole rotten bloody stinking mess that means anything to me." His eyes were red. He tossed back his hair, then pushed it from his face with his hand. "I knew from the first time I saw you I'd lose you."

She leaned forward. "How can you say that?"

"How? Because I—should I say it, you want me to say it? I knew I wasn't good enough for you, I knew. Baby, what did I do? Huh?" She didn't answer; she thought, he doesn't know. He honestly thinks he doesn't know. "Okay," he said, "the times aren't good, the luck is down. We've had pressure, I know it's been hard for you—" He fumbled in his shirt for cigarettes, then leaned back and got one from the desk, lit it. "I take care of you. There's never been any other woman."

She couldn't say anything.

"Christ." He threw the cigarette on the floor; it fell halfway between them. She got up and retrieved it from the rug, then put it out in an ashtray on the chest they used as a coffee table in front of the couch. Then she kneeled, sitting on her heels by the chest. He'd put his head in his hands, his elbows on his knees.

"Tell me what to do," he said. He looked up at her. "Tell me what to do and I'll do it—within reason. My flame is running low so there are limits. If there weren't you know there's nothing I wouldn't do for you—tell me. I'm not drinking, you don't want me to drink."

"Tommy, that's not—"

"I can't afford to lose you now, this isn't the time. Christ, Kath, I was in jail a night when you were gone, what do you want?" His shoulders shook a little, but he controlled himself.

"I know," she said. "What happened?"

"It's over now."

"Is it? How could it be? Do you mean you've got it taken care of? Tommy, you take care of everything, you hold it all inside, you don't tell me anything. That's part of the problem."

"You want to leave me some dignity?" he said. "My wife leaves me, I get sloppy, someone's out for my ass, I get treated like a goddamned drug addict. Christ." He put his head in his hands.

Like China

The fan blew threads of loose hair across her damp forehead. "Do you have to go to court?" she said.

"Not now," he said. "I can't talk about it now."

"All right." There was something, she thought, between them still. "When I got to Elizabeth," she said, "Angela told me some things. About your father."

He looked at her, leaned back in his chair, took another cigarette, lit it. "What?" He observed her, cautiously.

"That he hurt you," she said. She watched his face, wanting him to, but afraid he would—make a connection. The smoke curled up around his eyes.

"Yeah, he beat the shit out of me, so?" He almost laughed.

"How did you feel about that?"

"What is this?" He did laugh, as if they were talking anecdotally about something inconsequential and rather ridiculous. Feeling hurt, she looked down at her hands. "Okay," he said, "you want to know about it? I deserved it. But the trouble was Mama, she was the root of the trouble."

She looked at him, disbelieving.

"You wanna hear the story, Kath? This is it, the sweet story. Simple. Listen." He dragged on his cigarette. "Mama. She came from those rich city people in Milan, pious assholes, and took off across the ocean with this peasant from Bari. Rash of her, yes? She thought so too. In America then she became for him the voice, the relentless and never-ending voice of her family saying to him you are shit, you're garbage, you will fail. All right. So out of frustration he slaps her around until I come along, and once I'm on the scene—because I am from the day I was born a willful and contrary child—he stops on her and refocuses on me his rage and his regret."

He tapped his ashes on the floor.

"Nothing hard to understand. No deep and hidden meaning here, Katha, except that she experiences, my mother, such immense relief when I instead of her become the brunt of his weakness, that every time I am hit she experiences a sort of—sexual thrill."

He looked at her, smiling, cruel. His smile disappeared. "Perhaps I'm overly coloring it," he said. "But here is the truth. Never from the day I was born did she do one thing to stop him when he came at me. Never. One. Thing."

Her muscles hurt they were so constricted. "I thought you loved her," she said.

"I did. I loved her almost as much as I hated her." He searched around on his desk, found an ashtray under a stack of papers, and put out his cigarette. "Katha, don't do this," he said. "It doesn't do any good to do what you're doing."

She looked at his eyes, afraid to look away.

"I've never really hurt you, Katha, you know that. The one time, the *one* time was an accident, because you don't trust. And because, my love, you don't forgive."

He smiled, it disappeared.

"You're hard," he said, "you don't forgive." And then he was crying, his head in his hands and his shoulders shaking. "I've lost you," he said. "I lose everything I touch."

She had never seen him cry, really break down and cry, but once before, just after the fire. The fan went around, and the cars outside rumbled by, and she thought, what was it he had wanted so badly? What was it they both had wanted so badly . . . God, how he cried. She tried to remember what it was in him she had once admired, really and truly, not illusions she'd created out of needs she'd outgrown. She'd thought of him once as almost noble, proud.

"Tommy, please," she said, "don't."

"I can't," he said, "I can't."

"Katha?" he said. "Just tell me you love me—or you used to love me, can you tell me that?"

She moved closer to him. She touched his arm. "Tommy."

Like China

She touched his hair. "I've always loved you. I don't know how you could have thought from when we met that you'd lose me. I've always loved you, you know I have."

He rubbed his face, still not looking at her. "Tell me the truth," he said.

"Tommy, I am."

"I never wanted to hurt you, Katha."

"I know." She stroked his hair.

"It was good sometimes, yeah?"

"Yeah." She was still on her knees, sitting on her heels, in front of him. He touched her hand that was stroking his hair. "Can I," he said, "put my arms around you? For a minute?"

"All right."

He drew her into his body, holding her, leaning down to her. Bringing her up, he stood, holding her; then he brought back his face, kissed her, softly, at the side of her mouth. She put her head on his shoulder and tightened her arms around his back. No don't, she thought, but he kissed her again and then she was kissing him and they moved toward the bed and he said just tonight—she said yes, yes, it had been so long.

He lay her down on the bed: she felt the fan, the bedspread flutter at her ankles. He turned off the light, and she felt him come down on her and his hands at her throat, then his teeth, untying the bow at the top of her blouse. He raised her hands above her head, holding her wrists, then just one of his hands was holding her wrists and she raised herself up as he unzipped and lowered her jeans. He let her go, and she listened to him in the dark, undressing—his lips on her thighs, her stomach, her breasts, on her neck, on her lips; his tongue in her mouth, the blood rushing in her head, in her legs. His hand again holding her wrists, and then he was inside her and as soon as he was she shuddered deeply, from down inside where he was, and then it went up, up in waves and she thought, the last time, *the last time*, and she felt herself slipping, withdrawing from him, from his body, his physical presence: she felt herself rise, rise up and out of herself; from the ceiling she watched him, his motions, as he labored over her passive body.

"Katha."

She sat bolt upright, pulling the sheet up to cover her breasts, and squinting at him through the harsh morning light.

He sat at the edge of the bed, fully dressed, but his face had a grayish tinge, and he was trembling; a drop of perspiration traced its way down his cheek. Katha reached out an arm and put her hand on his forehead; it was cold and moist to the touch.

"I'm sick," he said. "I feel sick."

She found his robe on the floor at the side of the bed and put it on. "Tommy," she said, standing over him now, "did you take something? Did you *not* take something? Oh God." He was really shaking. "Get back in bed," she said. "Just take off your shoes and get under the covers, okay?"

She went quickly through the hall to the kitchen and opened the refrigerator. No food, except for a couple of cartons of Chinese take-out. Three sealed bottles of Absolut. Half a bottle of wine, a six-pack of beer. She grabbed a beer, screwed off the top, and took it back to him.

"Here," she said, "drink it."

"I don't want it."

"Tommy." His teeth were chattering; his eyes were sunken and darkly ringed. "Drink this one beer and then don't drink anything else today." He took the beer. "Is there something—pills you've been taking consistently?" He took a swallow of beer. "I just mean," she said, "that if you want to stop drinking and then you—sweetheart, you shouldn't try to do everything at once."

Like China

"In the medicine chest," he said. "Bottom shelf."

She found two bottles there. One was Valium, ten milligrams, and the other was codeine. He took the codeine, two of them, when she brought it to him, and handed her back the bottle of Valium saying he didn't need it. She slipped the bottle in the pocket of the robe, then sat down beside him on the bed. He'd finished the beer.

"Lay your head back," she said. She wiped his damp hair from his forehead; he closed his eyes. "Can you rest a little bit?" He made a sound. She got up and drew the blinds down over the windows. "I think I'll go out and get something for breakfast," she said.

He sat up, alert.

"I'm just going to the store," she said. "When you feel better you should eat."

He lay back. She picked up the clothes she'd had on last night, but then tossed them on the couch and found another pair of jeans in her bag, and a fresh T-shirt. She slipped on her jacket and her shades and went outside.

Hot. This early in the day, maybe nine; a large group of people waited at the bus stop, one of them fanning herself with the *Times*.

Katha went into a grocery store two blocks away, wanting to get back to the loft as soon as she could. She bought some eggs, milk, butter, and bread, deciding against the brownish-looking bacon. After leaving the store, she went back and bought Tommy a carton of cigarettes—$16.85. Winston Lights.

"I'm back!" she called to him a few minutes later. Another beer was missing from the six-pack. Oh well, she thought, it's just beer. If he's going to quit drinking completely he'll probably have to go into a clinic. She put down the groceries on the island that separated the kitchen from the rest of the front room, and could see from where she stood that the mahogany table was dusty. The trucks outside were exceptionally loud today—or maybe she'd been out of the city too long.

"Tommy, can you eat?" He shuffled into the kitchen, then slumped in a chair at the table. "You don't have to get up yet," she said.

"Yeah, I'll eat."

She took the groceries out of the bag, got a bowl from the cupboard, started cracking the eggs.

"Kath? What would you think if I sold Stand?"

She poured some milk in the bowl, got a fork from the drawer. "I wouldn't mind." She put a pan on the stove.

"There wouldn't be much cash to play with," he said. "I thought we might get a smaller place, at least maybe a share."

Her hand tightened on the fork she was holding; she loosened her grip and whipped the eggs. She put butter in the pan.

"There's a place on the Bowery I've been looking at," he said.

She wanted to laugh, hysterically. *There's a place on the Bowery I've been looking at, for what?* To buy? With what? She knew everything Claire had told her was true. She took out two slices of bread.

"Place with music," he said, "more like Split. Art bars don't go these days, not the kind I wanted. All fuckin' gentrified nouveau bullshit. It's either music or bullshit."

I will say nothing, she thought. Nothing. She turned the flame on under the pan, watched the butter hiss and spread.

"It could have been beautiful, Kath. It almost was. Best place in Manhattan. I had it, baby, I had this one so close I could see it, *see* it. You try to do one thing well, you try and it's—it could have gone, it could have gone had I gotten one tiny *bit!* of cooperation." His hand came down hard on the table and she jumped at the stove.

Like China

The butter was burning. Instinctively she grabbed the handle of the pan, and cried out; she'd burned her hand.

"Baby," he said, "I didn't mean you. Baby, I love you." He got up and came to her. "Baby, I love you." He turned her around, smoothed her hair from her face and put his arms around her. "I'd never hurt you," he said. "I love you."

"No, I burned my hand."

"Let me see." He gently inspected the burn, then turned on the tap, held her hand beneath the cool running water. "Better?"

"Yes."

He patted her hand with a towel, kissed her palm. "It's okay," he said. "I'll make it okay. Just give me some time." He wetted the towel, wrapped her hand. "Why don't we go out to the house, Kath. Fuck everything a few days. We'll feel better . . . Don't cry."

"It's my hand. It hurts."

He held her hand against his heart, kissed her fingers. "Poor hand. Can't cook. What I'll do, I'll buy her a gorgeous lovely breakfast and take her to the sea. She loves the sea."

He turned, still holding her hand to his chest, and leaned against the sink, looking away from her, toward the window. "The fire," he said, "was a curse. It put a curse on the place. A curse, a curse. It set me back about a hundred and fourteen years."

Traffic in the midtown tunnel moved swiftly today so that soon they were out of the city and approaching Queens. On the stretch of highway through Queens it smelled even worse than Elizabeth, and at the sides of the highway for a while was the largest cemetery in the five boroughs—a necropolis; badly tended, it ran for half a mile, folding back from the road for as far as the eye could see; its monuments crowded, discolored, blending almost with the murky sky.

Katha hated it. Coming back from the Hamptons and nearing the city it lurked, and past it came the hot blast of the tunnel, then the city, rising, screaming, smashing the calm she had gathered from the ocean. When she had tried to talk Tommy out of renting a house this year, because of the expense, he had said: "You want to spend August in the city?" That ended that. She didn't know he borrowed the money to secure the rental, though she should have; he told her later. He held back such significant pieces of information, she thought, until he could use them against her.

He'd asked her to drive. Unusual. He sat slumped in his seat with his arms crossed, down from the brief, optimistic mood he'd been in back at the apartment. The cemetery came and she stepped on the gas.

"Speed," he said, and she slowed down. He'd been giving her driving instructions ever since they left the parking garage. Her stomach churned; he'd changed his mind about breakfast, saying all he wanted was to leave. He took two more codeine pills in the car and drank another beer—just his third. She had the Valium in her purse. It seemed he'd forgotten about it.

Past Queens, he fell asleep. Her hands relaxed on the wheel and the air grew clean. She began to see signs of the grayish silvery light of the Hamptons, and farmlands appeared. The traffic was so clear she thought they would make it to the Springs in under two hours. She would have to call Claire; it was Monday, she remembered, and Claire was expecting her.

Through Westhampton she smelled the salt of the bays and the ponds that rim the south shore; and the stronger smell of the wetlands, the swamps and marshes hidden by woods, beyond the low hills. With the towns of Southampton came now and again a potato field, and patches of meadow breaking soft spaces between houses standing back from the road, and the checkered mixtures of grassland and scrub.

He woke up, coughing violently. He lit a cigarette, then opened the glove compartment and took out a flask. She smelled the vodka as he drank. Not one word, she thought. It had been, after all, a mere matter of time.

They were nearing Bridgehampton, Sagaponack; they would be there soon.

"Hey goddess," he said.

She didn't answer.

"I'm talking to you. Goddess."

"What is it, Tommy."

"Don't do me any favors." He drank from the flask; it was lovely, hammered silver, a gift from a waitress at Stand. "You want to talk?" he said. "You think we should talk. Let's talk about you."

There were wisps of clouds in the silvery sky.

"Let's talk about the time I've put in on you. Where'd you go, Katha, when you deserted? Back to your loving family?"

He was waiting. "No," she said.

"So you learned one thing. Very good." He drank from the flask. "And what were you like, my goddess, my *love*, when I met you?" He answered for her: "Riding the subway downtown at two o'clock in the morning in skirts that barely covered your ass. What was your boyfriend's name, huh? What was his name, darling love?"

She felt her eyes strain at the road; felt the cords in her neck getting tight. "You know his name, Tommy."

"Katha, what was his name."

Relax, she thought.

"His name was Michael."

"And what did you do when Michael, who was happily married and the father of two and was out for, let's be frank, a quick fuck with one of his students—what did you do when he said to get lost? Katha, what did you do?" She drove slowly, because everything outside the car was receding, getting soft and blurred at the edges; she felt the beat of her heart, the wetness from her palms on the wheel.

"I stood outside his building at night, and looked up at his window. I—wrote him letters." Breathe, she thought.

"He had to threaten you finally," he said. "You'd become a disease, all that strangled, distorted love for your family, your loving family." He drank from the flask. "Then what did you do?"

"—I reported him."

"But he didn't lose his job because you were already known on the campus as a rather odd number. He did, though, lose his wife. You feel good about that?"

"You know I don't."

"You feel good about that?"

She tried to breathe. "No."

"Then what did you do?"

"I quit school." She swallowed.

"Yeah, you had the face. You had the face to fall back on. You always had the face. You made money with the face." He threw the flask out the window; it went sailing away without a sound.

"Though that of course," he said, "was beneath you and you couldn't bear it, could you, the grit of the business, the price you had to pay because, child, there's a price, for everything." His voice was low—"I have to coax her out of bed in the morning and scrape her off the floor when she huddles, weeping, it's not fair it's not fair—what's fair, what the fuck is fair in this world?"

"I know," she said.

"You know," he said. "I thought you knew, I thought you were beginning to know but I was mistaken. Again I was mistaken in you—"he laughed, shaking his head. "I've spent years, *years* attempting to make you happy. It's never enough. You say I handle everything, I—what did you say? I keep it all to myself. Because you don't want to hear, you don't want to know the reality of anything."

"I know." She felt her brain going dead.

"You know. I don't have a wife I have a child, a deceitful lying child—you loved your life with me you goddamned liar, loved the money, the scene, how I set you up with the paintings at Stand. You loved all that, didn't you, *didn't you?*"

"Yes." Her eyes darted over the road, the trees, the sun hitting the shivering grass.

"It gets a little rough you want out, you want to walk? You think you're allowed to walk out of this now?" His hands curled, uncurled in his lap. "I'm fighting," he said, "for control. I don't know if you're worth it."

Up ahead she saw the Holiday Grill; five cars parked in front, a couple coming out. "Tommy, I'm stopping at the diner."

"She's overwhelmed," he said, "oh dear-r, I'm not over-whelmed? After the fire I get nothing, no sympathy, no sup-port for what I'm going through—she's overwhelmed. Don't stop at the diner."

She hit the signal. "Don't pull into the diner, Katha." She turned the wheel but he grabbed it—"Don't pull into the diner I said!"

He got control of the car, made her steer back on the road.

"I can't drive when you're doing this!"

"Doing what." He grabbed her hair, pulled it back hard from her face. "Doing what, I'm doing what—what are *you* doing, what are you doing to me—"

"Don't!" He let her go.

"Traitor—" she stood on the brakes, yanked the emer-gency.

She threw open the door and he reached for her, but she

was out of the car, running fast across the road to a broad field in front of her. She looked back—he had pulled the car up on the shoulder—she ran, heard him shouting—a car flew by. She ran into the field and turned back; he was crossing the road. There was no place to go: there was a house, but it was too far; still, she ran, heard him running behind her in the field—it was spinning, the field, the sky— she turned and yelled, "No!"

She tripped backward a step.

He had stopped ten or twelve feet from her.

"I don't deserve this," she said, *"I don't deserve this!"*

He came closer. "Don't come near me," she said, *"Don't come near me!"*

She backed up. He stopped and said, "Katha, you left me."

"I know, I know everything I've done—*I don't deserve this!"*

He stood where he was, watching her.

She was choking, "What do I do to you, Tommy? What do I do?" The hate she had heard in his voice filled his eyes; his face was deformed with it, clenched like a fist, the skin drained of blood. "What happens when you look at me, what do you *want?*" She felt him lean forward—"I can't breathe with you, Tommy, I can't *breathe.*" He came closer—"No," she said, "don't." He came closer—he seemed to grow larger, harder with rage. She reached up her arms but he reached out and shook her: "I know about the fire!" she screamed, "Tommy, *I know about the fire!*" She was crying, choking—"Kill me," she said, "I don't care, but I know what you did—I know what you did."

She felt the force leave his hands; he released her.

She took a step back, holding her arms.

"I know," she said, low, "I know what you did."

The anger went out of his eyes, then—as if he'd been hit in the legs with a bat—he dropped to his knees, just dropped to his knees in the grass.

Like China

The breeze blew the grass; lifted his hair, let it down. She stood waiting, hearing the cars whirring by.

He said, "I want to die."

She cried, softer now. "I want to die," he said, gripping his gut with his arms. "I wanted to tell you, I couldn't. I didn't mean for them to be killed—I want to die." She watched the top of his head through the silvery light.

"Katha, I'm tired. I want to die."

"Tommy, just—just let me go. I want to go."

"I want to die."

"No." She stepped toward him. "It all got, mixed up, but you—" He'd closed his eyes and was still. So still. But then something in him came alive and he caught her by the wrist: calmer now, he was leading her back to the car.

Chapter 15

Peter eased back to the middle of the group of boys who followed Ms. Ryan through the halls from the lounge, going back to the dorm, for bed. Big Dan was walking at the rear of the group; Toby was up at the front. All night in the lounge Big Dan said get away, fuckin' leave me alone—but Peter watched. Sam had gotten permission again to play cards with Eugene. Sam wasn't here now; most nights, Eugene brought Sam back to the dorm just in time for lights-out.

Peter couldn't get close to Big Dan, and when they turned into the darker hall, with the alcove coming up, and Peter looked back again at his brother, Big Dan was gone. Peter slipped to the back of the group and at the next turn, staying quiet, he ran to the darkness of the alcove—but Big Dan was already gone and moving fast down the hall. Peter followed.

Big Dan turned a corner. Peter ran, then stopped at the corner, peered around—Big Dan stood by the room, the room Ms. Ryan had taken Peter to, and Sam was there. Sam opened the door with a key. Peter ran—

"Danny!"

Like China

Afraid, Peter stopped. Big Dan, half in the door and half out, was looking at him. Big Dan was mad. "Did I tell you to get lost?" he said.

Peter stepped toward him.

"Get back to the dorm," said Big Dan.

"No, Danny."

Big Dan took Peter's arm and pulled him into the room, where Sam was. Big Dan closed the door; it was dark. "What are you doing?" said Peter. Big Dan said, "Peter—" but there was a click and the swing of a hinge and Sam said, "Far out, I got it open with the key."

"You're a genius, Sam," said Big Dan, "a certified genius."

"Fuck you," said Sam. Big Dan had Peter's arm. "Listen," he said, "we gotta do something. I'll open the door, you go back to the dorm."

"No, Danny." They were leaving, *leaving*. Big Dan's hand got tight on Peter's arm. "I'm going with you," Peter said. It was dark, they were leaving.

"We'll be back," said Big Dan.

"No, Danny, no Danny—"

"Ah, Peter, don't cry on me now."

"I'm *not* crying."

"So let him come," said Sam, "so big deal."

"Shuttup!" said Big Dan. "Why don't you *shut up?*" His voice was a whisper, but a yell. "You're gonna get us busted, Peter. Go back to the dorm, we've gotta go *now*." But Peter didn't move, he was quiet, and he wasn't crying, and Sam said, "I'm going, man." Then Sam was out on the roof, his feet scraping the shingles.

"I'm telling you," said Big Dan, "to go back. I'm asking you—" but Peter stiffened. *"Fuck,"* said Big Dan—he let Peter go.

"I'm going *with* you, Danny."

". . . okay. Okay, Peter."

They went to the window, crawled out. Sam was lying at the edge of the roof on his belly, his legs hanging down. He eased himself down until he hung from the roof with his hands; then he dropped.

"'S all right?" Big Dan called down to Sam.

"Yeah," said Sam from the bushes below.

"Get down," Big Dan said to Peter.

Peter crouched. Sam got out of the bushes, looked up. The playground was dark. "I'm going down," said Big Dan. "Then you do like I do, hang down, I'll get hold of your legs." Big Dan did like Sam, then the swish of the bush and the thump of his landing. Then Peter went down, and Big Dan got his legs; on the ground he said go and they ran, crouching low from the bushes to where the swings were. They got to the fence. Sam went up and over. "Boost," said Big Dan; Peter climbed, the fence in his hands, and then he was over; Sam got him on the way down. Then Danny was over—they ran in the field.

"Yow!" yelled Sam. "Yah! Yah, it's beautiful!" Sam jumped and twirled in the field. Peter ran, the wind in his face.

The field stopped at a road. Across it were houses. They paused in the road, catching their breath: a three-quarter moon hung low in the sky. "Man, man," said Sam, "it's beautiful." Big Dan looked up and down the road; to the north there were lights.

"That way," said Big Dan.

They set off, walking now, up the road.

"Free free," sang Sam, "I am free as love, free as, free as, free as love." Sam started dancing, skimming the road. "Da-duh dum, da-da dum, I am free as love. Da-duh, da-duh, free as love—

"How far?" said Sam.

"Couple more blocks," said Big Dan. "Then we turn down the highway."

Like China

"Know where we're going, nerd?" said Sam. "Da-duh, da-duh, free as love—to get cash. Sweet cash."

"Knock it off," said Big Dan.

"You knock it off," said Sam. "Nurse your ulcer. There's money in the shed," he said to Peter.

Peter looked at Big Dan. "Yeah," Big Dan told him. "We get it, we split it, equally."

"Then we go back?" Peter asked him.

Big Dan didn't answer so Peter reached up and touched his arm: "We go back?" he said.

"Yeah," said Big Dan. "We—go back."

As soon as the other boys were out of the bathroom, Toby fell down on the tile in front of the urinals, moaning and holding his side. "Oh, oh!" He did it louder, "Oh, oh, o-oh! Somebody!" He rolled back and forth, "Oh-h-h, someone help!" A little boy who had just left the bathroom, wearing striped boxers and a golf cap, pushed in the swinging door and looked down at Toby. "Oh-h," moaned Toby. The small boy came in and stood beside him, watching him moan.

"Oh-h-h." The small boy adjusted his cap. He sat down.

Toby stopped moaning. "Are you mad?" he said. "Can't you see I'm in pain? Get Ryan before I expire—oh-h-h." The small boy scrambled to his feet and swung back out the door and went rushing down the hall.

Ms. Ryan came in. "Oh-h, oh-h-h."

She knelt beside Toby. "What is it?"

"Oh, it hurts over here—no! don't touch it! It's tender to the touch."

"It could be your appendix," she said. "I'll get—" her narrow green eyes swept the bathroom. "Where's Big Dan and Peter?"

"Oh-h," moaned Toby.

"I thought they were in here," she said. She got up. "Nobody's in here." She rested her hands on her hips in an ominous fashion. "Toby, get up."

"I can't—oh-h."

"Where are Big Dan and Peter?"

"I don't know, can't you see that I'm sick?"

"Don't tell me you don't know. Are they with Sam and Eugene?"

"I think it's my appendix."

"Toby, can it." Toby did.

"I'll go find Eugene," said Ms. Ryan.

"Wait!" Toby sat up, still looking vaguely ill from self-suggestion. He rubbed his sore side. "I'll tell you where they are."

"You better, buster."

"Peter's not in the dorm?"

"You know damn well he's not in the dorm. Don't mess with me, kid, I grew up in the Bronx."

"I know you did and that's why you'll understand."

"Make it fast," she said.

"There's a thirteen-year-old girl, and she's pregnant."

"Skip the story, where are they?"

"She's Big Dan's girlfriend and she needs—"

"So what are they doing, making phone calls somewhere?"

"First," said Toby, "understand the situation—"

"I don't have to understand anything," said Ms. Ryan. "I want those guys in bed."

Toby got to his feet. "Don't understand then," he said, "because we're nothing, kids with no feelings or hearts. We're wards of the court."

"Oh brother," said Ms. Ryan.

"You're a caretaker, and we're nothing."

"Don't give me this shit. My career is you kids."

"So *listen* to me. Big Dan's got some money back at his house, and he's getting it to—"

"They've left this building?"

"Yeah, but—"

"You little worm." She turned to leave, but then Eugene knocked at the door, and the door swung inward. Eugene wore the gold chain and the wristwatch Sam had won from him with three-card monte.

"Call the police," said Ms. Ryan. "The Kramers escaped."

Eugene gave a slow, lazy lift to his eyes. "All three of them?" he said. He looked down at Toby.

"Is Sam with you?" she said.

"He was," said Eugene. "So were Big Dan and Peter. They started acting up. I put them in G dorm for the night. I don't want any trouble." Ms. Ryan looked back at Toby, then at Eugene. "Aren't you supposed to be off now?" Eugene asked her.

"They're up in G dorm?" she said.

"Yeah," said Eugene. "I'll take Toby back."

Ms. Ryan glanced at Toby triumphantly. "Guess their little plot was foiled," she said, and swept out of the bathroom.

"Come on, Toby," said Eugene.

Toby went with Eugene down the hall.

"What did Sam tell you?" Toby asked him at last.

"Huh?" said Eugene. "What did you say?"

"Where are they?" said Toby.

"Asleep in G dorm. Ask me more questions, knucklehead, and I'll put you there too."

The 7-Eleven appeared just around the turn to the highway.

"So where's Artie?" said Sam.

"He'll be here," said Big Dan.

"Cool," said Sam. "I'll get some stuff to eat."

"Cigarettes," said Big Dan.

Sam went into the store. Big Dan and Peter sat on the curb at the side of the store near the dumpster. From there they had a good view of the highway.

"You mad, Danny?" said Peter.

"I don't want to talk," said Big Dan. "I'm not mad."

Peter looked at the moon and the headlights of cars and the glow of the phone booth nearby.

Sam came out with a big paper bag. "Big Dan," he said, "get some beer. Guy in there won't card you."

"I'm not in the mood," said Big Dan.

Sam threw Big Dan a pack of Camels, then sat down on the curb next to Peter. "Want a Ring Ding?" he said.

"Okay," said Peter. Sam gave him one.

"I got some sodas," said Sam. "Hey, man," he said to Big Dan, "I got you some chips."

Big Dan shook his head no, lit a Camel.

"Green onion," said Sam. "Okay, I'll eat 'em myself. Lookit this," he said to Peter, extracting a small pink cylinder from the bag. He set down the bag, uncapped the plastic container and took out a small scroll of pink paper, which he unrolled. Then he read it.

"Cool," Sam said in a minute. "Listen to this, it says: 'Get while the getting is good, don't be timid! It's time to use your talents and abilities to get the things you want! It's time to break out of the pack. Go for the best, your heart's desire. Don't doubt yourself. You've got what it takes!' Cool, or what? I mean, these are the exact things I've been thinking.

"And down here," he said to Peter, "you've got your daily forecasts, then talents, health, career, love life—oo-la-la—and, check it out. It says here under compatible signs: Libra, Capricorn and Pisces—that's you. You're a fish."

"I'm a fish?" said Peter.

"Yeah, like me I'm Aries, a battering ram."

"I don't want to be a fish," said Peter.

Like China

"It doesn't matter if you want to be, that's what you are. It has to do with the alignment of the moon and other planets when you're born. When you were born it said Pisces, so that's what you are. Pisces is a fish. The fish and the ram get along."

Big Dan got up and walked through the weeds to the edge of the highway. Peter watched the hots of his cigarette fade into the blacktop.

"Fuck him," said Sam. "Want another Ring Ding?" Sam gave one to Peter. "Hey. I'm gonna call Katha. Maybe I can get her number off information. Name's Brenner, right? Name of the people she's renting the house from?"

"Yeah, Brenner," said Peter. Sam headed for the phone booth.

"Wanna talk to her, nerd?" he called back.

"No, Sam." Peter finished his Ring Ding, licked the slick chocolate from his fingers. Even if Sam had her number, she wouldn't be there. Peter had her new number in his pocket. Sam skimmed into the booth; the light in the booth made his hair blue-black. Big Dan stood at the edge of the highway. Peter looked at the moon and considered the word alignment.

Sam came back. He sat on the curb and took a can of Orange Crush from the bag. "She can't talk," he said. "She says call another time."

"She's not there," said Peter.

"She's there," said Sam. "She lives there."

"No, she doesn't."

Sam rolled his eyes. "She answers the phone, or someone that *sounds* like her answers the phone, but yeah, she doesn't live there." Then Sam jumped up from the curb at the sight of headlights moving into the parking lot. A red Mazda.

"Yo, Artie!" called Sam. He ran to the car. Peter picked

up the bag and followed Sam; Big Dan was walking back through the weeds.

Artie's tape deck blasted U2. Sam opened the door on the passenger side. "Artie, my man," said Sam. "Wanna Ring Ding?" Peter gave one to Sam and Sam gave it to Artie.

"There's beer in the back," Artie said.

"Far out," said Sam. Peter got in the back with Sam.

Artie was the tallest and skinniest guy Peter knew; his knees pointed way up at the sides of the steering wheel. A rubber naked lady hung off the rearview.

"Say, Big Dan," said Artie.

"Say, Artie," said Big Dan. Big Dan got in next to Artie, shut the front door and turned off the music. Artie turned the music back on, but lower. They pulled out of the lot, to the highway.

"How's it goin'?" said Artie.

"Okay," said Big Dan. "Cigarette?"

Sam nudged Peter. "You wanna go by Katha's?" he said. She wasn't there, Peter knew, she wasn't in the Springs. He watched Artie's white hair, buzzed close at the back of his head so his ears stuck out.

"C'mon," said Sam, "let's go by Katha's."

"We have to get the money," said Peter, "and go back."

"So be like Big Dan," said Sam. "Me, I'm gonna have a little fun tonight." Sam guzzled his beer and started on another one. "Nice wheels," he said to Artie. "Pretty cool." Artie ignored him. "Cool tape deck," said Sam. They drove down around Westhampton and then by the Shinnecock Canal until the towns of Southampton flew by.

"How's it goin'?" said Artie again to Big Dan.

"This hasn't been my summer," said Big Dan.

"Way it goes," said Artie. "Mine's been all right. Parties. My parents went away on vacation. Cruise Asparagus Beach, get the city girls. Take 'em back to the house. It's all right."

"Any parties tonight?" said Sam.

"Shut up," said Big Dan.

"Fuck you," said Sam.

"Hot babes," said Artie. "Every night." Artie turned up the music; Big Dan turned it off. "Hey, man," said Artie.

"You've got your music," said Big Dan. "You've got your hot babes, you've got your hot wheels. You've got a great life, Artie."

"I'm hearing?" said Artie. "What'd you say?"

"Think about it, rich boy," said Big Dan.

"I don't have to take that," said Artie. "I didn't have to pick you guys up."

"Sam," said Big Dan, "give Artie ten dollars."

"That's all I've got left," said Sam.

"I'll pay you back." Big Dan reached his hand back to Sam and Sam gave him the money. "Payment for the ride," said Big Dan to Artie. Artie took the ten-dollar bill and threw it out the window; Peter watched as it fluttered away on the breeze and disappeared.

"What I think of your money," said Artie.

"Good for you," said Big Dan.

They were coming into downtown East Hampton, nearing Main Street.

"Low-life bonackers," said Artie. "That's all you guys are."

"Less than that," said Big Dan, "less than that, Artie."

They went quickly through the sparse late-night traffic on Main Street and branched south back onto the Montauk Highway. Artie drove fast. Peter felt the Springs coming closer, the ocean, the bays; the trees at the sides of the road got thicker, and dark. Sam, scowling, kept drinking beer.

Artie screeched up on the shoulder. "That's it," he said, "that's as far as I'm going."

"Thanks for the ride," said Big Dan.

"Yeah, thanks for the ride," said Sam. "And the beer."

Out of the car, Sam crunched his empty beer can under his foot and then threw it at the Mazda as it sped away. "Thanks for the ride!" he screamed. The can hit the bumper, then clattered softly to the road and spun for a moment on the white dividing line. Then the night was quiet.

The Springs was a little ways off. Peter walked at the side of the road between his brothers. Only now and again a car went by.

"One night," said Sam, "I'm walking on the highway like this, just walking, to get a little air. An' all of a sudden I see what I think must be, I don't know, a mirage or something 'cause all of a sudden at the edge of the road, on the other side, is a horse. Yeah, a horse, no rider, no saddle and no one else around. I stopped where I was and I watched him cruisin' on up the road. Big brown horse. Black mane. Really cool."

Big Dan took out his pack of Camels. "Cigarette, Sam?"

"Yeah, thanks, man," said Sam. The trees were talking. The night was clear, just a slip now and then, a whisper of fog—like ghosts, Peter thought, in the strong black night.

"He was beautiful," said Sam. "Big guy, broad flanks, head the size of a engine. Man, he was beautiful. But I didn't want to ride him or anything like that he looked so happy and content, like I was, just out for a breath of fresh air."

"He got out of his barn," said Peter.

"That's what I figured," said Sam.

"Nice here," said Big Dan. "Quogue sucks."

"Kid Artie," said Sam, "did I say he was a jerk?"

"Let's cross," said Big Dan.

They dashed to the other side and entered the Springs by Three Mile Harbor Road, Katha's road, Peter knew. He looked at Sam. Sam bounced as he walked; he smelled like beer. Over their heads the trees formed an arbor, swaying, shielding the night. Around the bend the trees parted and the night came back—

Peter saw Katha's house. The man's car was in the driveway. Her husband. Peter stopped. Sam said she was there, she could be there and her husband was there.

"Hey," called Sam from several paces up the road. "You wanna go by Katha's?"

Peter started walking again, to catch up with Sam and Big Dan, but her house pulled at his back. Peter wanted the words for fear and for longing and for dread—she was his friend.

"Her husband is there," Peter said.

"So what?" said Sam. "So we can stop by. Big Dan, we'll meet you at the house, we're gonna stop by Katha's."

"You want the money?" said Big Dan. The trees were loud. The grass at Peter's feet was wet.

"Yeah," said Sam. "We'll be there in a while."

Big Dan's eyes were very bright, his face still. "This a party, Sam?" he said. "We get the money, we go."

"What is it with you?" said Sam. "We've got all night."

"You come now, Sam," said Big Dan.

"We've got all night." Sam's face grew as still and as bright as Big Dan's. "Y'know why? Because I fixed it with Eugene, because I didn't count on some lame-ass story—some *girl* who needs an abortion, some jackass like Toby, I fixed it with Eugene—*I did it not you.*" Sam kicked the road. "You're not the only one in the world who knows something, *who can do something.* Shit." Sam was crying.

"You're drunk," said Big Dan.

"So I'm drunk, so I'm drunk!" Sam took a step, and wobbled.

Peter looked back at the dunes, the tall grass, the deck of Katha's house; there was a light on upstairs.

"C'mon, Sam," said Big Dan.

"I'm going to see this woman Katha!" said Sam. "I'll meet you at the house." But Sam didn't move.

"She could call the police," said Big Dan.

"She wouldn't do that," said Sam.

"She better not."

"That a threat?" Sam took a step toward Big Dan. "Are you threatening me, man?" Big Dan stepped back, watching Sam, and said, "Do what you want." He turned to Peter. "You coming?"

Peter looked at Big Dan, looked at Sam; he felt her house pulling at his back. "Danny, I'm going with Sam." Big Dan caught the edge of his lip with his teeth, let it go. "Don't be long then," he said. "Okay, Peter?"

"Yeah, Danny."

"I'll be at the house," said Big Dan, and he ran up the road, his T-shirt flashing white and getting small against the black of the night.

Sam sat down in the grass at the side of the road.

"We're going?" said Peter.

"Yeah, shit," said Sam. "How many beers did I have?" He held his head. "Yeah, shit." He stood swaying. "We're going to Katha's."

"Over the dunes," said Peter.

"How come?" But Sam followed Peter. "He really gets me, that guy," said Sam. "He really gets me."

From near the top of the dunes they could have seen the bay but the night was getting misty and the water was black.

"Hey, nerd," said Sam, "you go for her, huh? She gives you a feeling down here." Sam touched Peter's crotch but Peter pushed him away. Sam was drunk, Peter knew. They skidded down the last dune then went down on their bellies in the grass, and the grass was wet. They crawled through the wet grass toward the deck.

"Let's just go to the door," said Sam.

Like China

"No, Sam," said Peter. Mist floated over the boards of the deck, blurring the line of the railing. Then a light came on in the house, another light, downstairs. The curtains were shut but translucent in the light, and Peter saw shadows, two shadows in the light.

"We're going or what?" said Sam. Peter stayed where he was in the grass. Then the shadows came together, they merged, as if they were dancing, drew apart, came together again; and someone went down. "What the fuck?" said Sam. He had risen to his knees.

"He's hurting her, Sam, I saw it before. I was looking for Banjo, I was down at the bay, he put her down in the water, he was trying to kill her." She got up; the one shadow was two. Peter didn't hear sounds from the house, just the rush of the leaves in the trees. "Shit," said Sam, "*shit*—" and then there was a crash, and a shout, and the light downstairs in the house went out.

"*Motherfucker,*" said Sam. He sprang up from the grass, and when Peter turned he was running to the dunes.

"Sam," he called, "Sam!" He looked back at the house: at the darkness below and the light up above; at the trees at the sides of the house, whipping their branches like furious arms at the sky. He ran back through the grass and caught up with Sam; Sam's face was red, and wet from the grass. "Sam—"

"Peter," said Sam, "I'm getting the gun."

They were panting, breathing hard in the dark. She felt him move toward her again, then away. The overhead light in the kitchen came on. He poured himself vodka. She licked at the wetness on her lip, tasted salt—it was blood. He took the bottle of codeine from the kitchen counter, opened it, and swallowed two of the pills with the vodka.

She was down on the floor, wedged between the overturned table and the couch, near where the lamp had fallen, the glass of its bulb shattered out in a fan. Her jaw felt numb and her lip was beginning to swell. Putting her hand to her mouth, she sat up—and felt the blood between her fingers. Pain stabbed at her back; she'd struck the table when she fell, when he knocked her to the ground with his fist.

He was soaking the towel with water. He turned off the faucet and squeezed out the towel and then came to her, pushing the table aside; she drew back, painfully. Then, still on the floor, still holding her head and her body away from him, she reached out and grabbed the towel, snapped back her hand and put the towel to her mouth.

She sat up on the couch, helping herself with one of her arms. She pressed the towel to her mouth, watching him, watching him. He kept his distance. He stood at the other end of the couch, turning away in a moment, frustrated, running his hand through his hair.

"Just don't, don't—" he began, turning back to her. He held his hand lightly by his face as if about to give her the subtlest point in a difficult lesson. "Don't—"three fingers curled into his palm, one finger pointing up"—don't ever say again that you're leaving me." He went to the kitchen again and came back with two glasses. "Here," he said, holding one out to her. "I don't want it," she said.

He threw the glass to the floor, where it rolled, spilling the vodka in a trail on the floor by the shattered glass of the bulb.

"You hurt your back," he said. He'd put the bottle of codeine in his shirt pocket; he took one pill out. "It's for pain," he said. "Do you want it?"

She watched his dead eyes. She took the pill and swallowed it with spit. He turned off the light in the kitchen. He moved in the dark—but the room wasn't black in the darkness, it had a faint glow from reflections of the moon outside and from the light upstairs. His shadow moved in the room. She saw the outlines of his face, his white shirt, but she couldn't see his eyes.

"Let's stop this," he said. He was pacing. "There are things I've been wanting to tell you—for a long time, but how could I? How could I tell you?" She pressed the wet towel to her lip. He moved silently, quickly, back and forth across the room.

"I tried, I tried to get them out. I went in again and again—but the smoke, I couldn't see." He stopped; his face strained, his hands tensed, into claws, as if something was digging at him from inside. "It kept pushing me back." His voice shook. "They were *not* supposed to die, I didn't plan for them to die but they did and I knew, I knew it was over"—he almost sobbed—"what I wanted was gone, it was taken, *again, it was taken from me.*" He slumped, and stood, shaking, at the center of the room, in front of the windows.

"Listen," he said. "I'll go to jail, or if I don't go to jail they get everything, Katha—they own me." He laughed, a sound wrenched from his throat. "Do you hear me?"

"I hear you." It wasn't her voice.

"Do you know what that means? I maybe bartend the rest of my life, manage someone else's place for a pittance. Pay attention."

"I am." She swallowed blood.

"Baby, it's over."

He came to her, kneeled at the foot of the couch. "The one thing I wanted." He took her hand—she felt her hand limp, and cold. "This is my hand," he said. "Your hands are my hands. You can't leave me." He was quiet, breathing raggedly. "I never wanted to hurt you, but you—there are things you won't know, you won't learn. What you haven't learned yet is how to die." He pressed her hand to his cheek, and she saw his eyes: they were flat brown discs without light. She remembered his eyes, when she first saw him—she had thought they were the saddest eyes ever set in a face; they were gone. He kissed her hand, and she shivered.

Peter ran, the trees spinning, whirling, over his head. Near the turn onto Rappaport Lane, Big Dan was coming toward them. "I've got it!" he called. "I've got the money!" Sam ran, as if he couldn't see him or hear. "Sam," said Big Dan, "Sam!"

He caught Sam when he tried to run by. "Sam!"

Sam jerked back. "Don't put your hands on me, man." Sam's face was red and streaming with sweat. He smelled like wet earth and sweat. He was gasping for breath. "Katha—" he said, "her husband is beating her up. I'm getting the gun."

"Sam," said Big Dan, he reached out—

"Don't put your hands on me, man!" Sam stepped back. "You can go, but I'm getting the gun, from Harold's."

"Sam, we'll get to a phone, call the cops," said Big Dan.

"The cops do *shit!*" cried Sam. "They do shit, *they do shit!* And you"—Sam's eyes were wild, flashing—"he comes at her you run, *you run.*" Peter watched Sam, Big Dan, and he remembered when Daddy hit Mama, Sam throwing himself hard at Daddy, Daddy throwing him off like a bug, Big Dan running from the house, Peter hiding, and Mama, calling, later from the bed, Peter, sweet boy? Come by me in the bed Peter, honey, come sleep with Mama. Crawling out from the bed when she slept and seeing Big Dan, through the window, coming back in the cool white morning, and Daddy being gone and coming back, coming back—

"When he hit her," said Sam, "your brother, *Big* Dan, threw up in the woods. That's where he went, Peter. That's what he did."

"Sam," said Big Dan, his voice quiet, "we have to go."

"You go," said Sam. "I'm going to Harold's." Sam turned, Big Dan reached out and grabbed him by the back of the shirt; Sam lurched, tried to swing at Big Dan but Big Dan knocked him down, and then they were down in the road, rolling and fighting.

"Don't, Danny!" cried Peter. "Don't, Danny!"

Big Dan was on Sam, holding him down. "Sam, stop it," he said, *"Sam, stop it."* Sam struggled, Big Dan slapped his face.

"You can't stop me," said Sam, "you can't stop me."

A porch light came on in a house nearby. Big Dan sat up, still holding Sam. He turned his head toward the light, and then looked back at Sam. "I'll get the gun. You wait here with Peter." Big Dan got up and Sam stayed where he was on his back in the road.

"You stay here," said Big Dan to Peter, and he ran.

Sam sat up in the road. "You scared?" he said to Peter.

"I'm not scared," said Peter.

"You're not scared, *he's* the one who's scared." Sam tossed his head back toward Big Dan, who was vanishing fast around the turn onto Rappaport Lane. "When you're scared," said Sam, "put it down in your toes. *Put it down in your toes!*" he screamed at Big Dan.

Another porch light came on. Sam and Peter moved off to the side of the road where they crouched in the shadows, and waited.

What Big Dan saw first at Harold's was the flagpole, rising up above the neatly trimmed trees in the yard, the bushes, the flat red roof of the house—what he had seen from his own house, what used to be his house, what was never his house, when he went to get the money.

He'd avoided the house, going straight to the shed and digging up the ground with a spade for the stack of green bills in a plastic bag. He did it in steps, like a list in his mind he couldn't waver for a moment from: dig, get the money, go back; ignoring the voice that said run, get away, that shouted the more he ignored it.

He held the plastic bag, still clotted with dirt, in his hand. Escape money, that's what it was, had been from the time Daddy left and he'd started to save it—just in case he had to go, just in case he couldn't take it. But knowing it was there he'd been able to stay and he feared—for a moment, way back in the dark of his mind—that with it out of the ground he wouldn't go back to Peter and Sam.

With the bag in his hand he came out of the shed and looked at the house—the rusted swings in the overgrown yard, the ugly blue blocks of the house changing color in the moonlight, looking wet from the mist. The broken slab of the stoop that slanted away from the door. Then the knob of the door was in his hand and wouldn't turn; in a rage he kicked at the door, and finally went and broke a pane in the kitchen window, reached in a hand and unlocked it, drew it up, and went in. And nothing was changed, had been tampered with or moved—old garbage was there, rotting and smelling through the house, through the room near the kitchen he had shared with his brothers, in Daddy's room where he had slept alone when Daddy left. In the front room which was dark with the newspapers blocking out light from the windows but through which he moved unerringly, knowing the room.

He tore a sheet of newspaper down from the windows; the paper was old and its edges crumbled to dust in his hand. He saw Harold's house across the road, dark inside but bright in the moonlight—neat sparkling white floating out past the green of the yard and marked by the tall straight flagpole. He knew then that he could go back with Sam and Peter—even wanted it. Peter's coming tonight he saw as a sign, a sign that he wasn't to run, wasn't meant to—he felt something move, like arms that had opened. Staring at the night, at the house, he felt a new feeling inside, sort of a peace. He suddenly wanted what he didn't even want—a new home, a man and a woman who would act as his parents. Sam and Peter might maybe live near him and they would be safe. He saw he could maybe have something he had never had before, never hoped for—couldn't even imagine quite yet. But he sensed its bright outline, its shape, coming nearer, coated in mist.

As he was leaving the house he thought about leaving the money there. But Sam, he thought, Sam would be pissed. He decided to bring it for Sam. He hadn't been fair to Sam; and Sam had been right about Toby, right about the lame story and the choice of Toby. He saw now that he'd done it on purpose, almost hoping to get caught, caught running which would mean he'd go back to the youth house where he didn't want to be and hated more than anything, but still almost wanted since there, he thought, he'd be protected, locked up, protected from that thing in himself, that dark thing that wanted to run, that thing inside that seemed to keep growing and screaming and running, and growing.

The flagpole swayed in front of Dan's eyes as he ran, the money heavy in his pocket. Still though he thought that if the kitchen window was open at Harold's then he could slip in and get out with the gun and take care of the business, uneventfully, and get back—there was time.

He dashed to the side of the house, scooted up on the ledge—the window was closed. He tried it, locked. He jumped down and tried another window, another, getting too close, he knew, to where Harold was sleeping. Very quietly, he went back to the front. Harold wouldn't leave the door open, he knew. But still, he could try it. His hand was on the knob, and it turned—

The door flew back. Harold stood there, in pajamas and robe, holding the gun. "I heard you," he said. "You and him, screaming and carrying on. Come on in, boy. Come on in and talk. We'll just have a little talk before I call the police."

She knew what she was doing. She lay there on the bed, beside him, upstairs, watching the curtains at the open window move; she breathed in the air, coming in, coming in. Look, she thought, at the things I can see, I can touch—the phone by the bed. He put his hand on her thigh—no not that, she thought—but even that, anything to get him to sleep. But just think of the things I can see, I can touch—the doors downstairs and the deck and the road—

He took his hand from her leg and sat up on the bed. "It's not doing any good." He had taken the Valium, two or three. The two he had given to her she had put in her pocket when his back was turned for a moment. "I'm sorry," she said. She watched his back. Just let me get out and I'll never—no, think of the things I can see, I can touch. She watched his back. He leaned down and drank from the glass of vodka on the floor.

He got up and went to the window, turned back. "Let's go out, I've gotta get out." His face was convulsed.

"All right." She sat up, put her feet to the floor. Her back didn't hurt anymore, from the codeine perhaps. Her tongue felt thick in her mouth, her lip had stopped bleeding.

She went with him down the stairs and at the foot of the stairs he suddenly sat, seemed to collapse, and she thought he was about to pass out. But when she sat beside him he gripped her with his arms to his body and she felt the power, the strength in his arms that somehow remained. "It won't stop," he said, releasing her. He pressed his hands to the sides of his head. "I know," she said, touching his hair; it wasn't her hand. He began to get up, and she helped him. He put his arms around her again and this time he was gentle. "Don't leave me," he said. "No, no, I won't." He kissed her and mixed with the liquor on his breath was a chemical smell—it was on his skin too, in his sweat. "Maybe after a walk you can sleep," she said. "Sleep—" and he said it with horrible irony and with his quick, hard smile. He went to the glass doors, drew back the curtains, and unlocked the door; the curtains blew out. "They take it," he said, "they take it from you."

"It's all right," she said, going to him—"you'll be all right." She put her arms around him, from behind, trying to calm him. If he relaxed he'd pass out; it had happened before. She could run, and outside would be better, quieter—his ragged breath slowed.

They went out on the deck; she saw the moon through the mist. The breeze blew her hair and the branches of trees. She put her arm around him, and he put his arm around her and they went down the steps, through the wet grass and the sand to the slope that led down to the beach—like lovers, going down to the bay.

Big Dan stood swaying in the room with all the pictures on the tables, photographs, faces all around. He stood over Harold, knocked out on the floor; slivers of light from the moon outside dappled Harold's still, wrinkled face. Big Dan knelt and listened to his breathing, felt his pulse; it was steady.

It had been easy, getting the gun and then hitting Harold with the butt; easy with the strength and the power of nothing to lose. There was nothing to lose. Leave it to Harold, to Sam. Throw it all away over some damn woman—goddamn women, thought Dan. Goddamn men.

"Where is he?" said Sam. "He doesn't come soon, I'm going there myself."

"I see him," said Peter.

Out of the mist Big Dan came running, the long rifle

heavy in his hands. He held it almost vertically down, hiding it so that it almost looked like a thick extension of his leg.

"Stay down," he said hoarsely to Peter and Sam. He crouched where they hovered at the side of the road. "I walk on the inside of you two," he said. "A car comes and I hide until it's gone."

"What happened with Harold?" said Sam.

"Nothing. He didn't wake up."

"Far out," said Sam. He held out his palm; Big Dan slapped it.

"I don't want any trouble," said Big Dan. "When we get to the house you go up to the door," he said to Sam. "Peter and I'll hang back. See if she's okay. If she's not then you ask her if she wants to come with us. Any trouble, you call me."

"Got it," said Sam.

"Any trouble," said Big Dan to Peter, "you stay back and hide. You understand?"

"Yeah, Danny."

Big Dan stood with Peter and Sam. They jogged down the dark silent road. Soon, in the distance, the eyes of the beach houses shined.

He sat with her on the sand, or rather sprawled, his head thrown back and his face to the sky, and she silently said to him drop, drop back in the sand.

He took long expansive breaths, something in him still fighting, forcing the air from the night to push through his body. Drop back in the sand she said silently, please.

"Lie back," she said. She cradled his shoulders and head against her chest, pushed his damp hair off his forehead. "Kath?" he said.

"Yes." Close your eyes.

"For so long—" close your eyes, close your eyes.

His eyes fluttered shut, but then opened wide. He moved

off from her brusquely. "I'm not finished yet, it's what they think, they—" he swayed, almost swooned. "What?" He looked at her blankly, then he got abruptly to his feet and staggered away a few steps. She followed him, took his hand; he was looking at the water.

"She's dead," he said. "Wednesday." Katha didn't feel a pressure from his hand. "She's dead, do you see?" Please quiet, thought Katha, please quiet—*my legs, they're running fast down the beach running fast running hard.* "Let me look at you," he said. He took her face in his hands—and inside she said, *I'm running so fast, so hard.*

"Sweetness." He kissed and then held her. She felt his breath in her ear, softer, and hot: "Look at the water," he said. The water was black, the mist floating above it like low-hanging clouds. He pulled back—she looked at his face: his eyes had a false sheen, a brilliance that made her feel weak. He took both of her hands. Bringing her with him, he took a step closer to the water, and she felt the cold water seep through the bottoms of her shoes.

"Tommy, we're getting wet."

"Yes," he said, "we're getting wet." He looked at her mildly, intently, except for the eyes. "Walk into the water with me." She tried to pull back, but he grabbed her arm and said, "Don't." She struggled, and he pushed her down to the sand, pinned her arms and said, "Don't make me do this." She started to scream, he pulled her up and then slammed her down hard on the sand.

"You wouldn't be safe." She saw his face, above her, through the mist; around her the horrible soft lapping sound of the water on the sand. "Don't fight me now, Katha, sweetness."

He took her limp body in his arms. He laughed suddenly, shortly. "Everything I ever learned was to fight, as if it's for something, as if you'll get something . . ." His fingers went over her eyes, she cried silently.

"No, baby, don't. I don't want to go back . . ." He cradled her close. "Baby, no one will hurt you, no one will hurt you anymore."

A light, shining downstairs through the mist.
"Over the dunes," said Big Dan.
The gun rattled as they climbed.
Flat in the grass. "Sam," said Big Dan, "take it easy."
"Okay." Keeping low, Sam skimmed through the grass and pushed himself up on the deck, went under the rail. The glass doors were closed but the curtains were open.
"No one's there," Peter said—but the car was in the driveway.
Sam knocked at the door, knocked again—Sam went in.
"Jesus Christ." Big Dan leaned on the gun, almost lying on top of it; Peter smelled the gun in his hands. The trees waved at the sides of the house. Peter's blood in his body coursed strong, and slow. They watched the rectangular square of the glass, dimly lit like a stage going dark—
There was a motion. *"Come on, come on,"* said Big Dan.
Sam came out alone. He looked around, and then he jumped the rail and came back through the grass. "They're gone," he said, "but stuff is broken—there's blood on the couch." Sam's breathing was fast. Big Dan and Peter got up.
"The car's there," said Sam.
"At the bay," Peter said. "He's got her down at the bay."
"We'll go see," said Big Dan. They moved through the grass at the base of the dunes to the slope, a broad path through the grass. They hid in the scrub, near the path, and Peter saw them, sitting down on the beach near the water. The man had her head in his lap, so Peter couldn't see her face; her legs were drawn up so it seemed she was clinging to him. "I'll go down," said Sam. Sam shot down to the beach—a streak through the mist. Big Dan went down flat

in the sand. Peter lay by him, watching Sam through the gnarled brittle branches and the mist.

On the beach the mist thickened and moved. The man bolted up, clutching Katha to his chest. He moved back, dragging her feet through the sand, and then Sam was saying something, and the man was saying something, keeping Sam back. "Stay here," said Big Dan. He sprang out of the scrub and ran down the path, and then Peter ran too.

They stopped beside Sam. The man held her fast around her waist. Her hair was wet at the sides of her face; she was crying, there was blood on her mouth. "Let her go," said Big Dan.

The man looked confused.

"You wanna come with us, Katha?" said Sam. She kept crying. Her head was pressed tightly against the man's jaw. "You wanna come, Katha?" said Sam.

Big Dan gripped the gun. "Let her go." He had the gun on the man. "Just let her go, we don't want any trouble." The man squinted at them, through the mist, holding her tightly by the wrists.

"You wanna come, Katha?" said Sam.

"Yes," she said, "yes." But the man held her tight.

"Let her go," said Big Dan. The water washed softly up at the sand near their feet.

The man's face had relaxed. "Are you kidding me?" he said. "Who are you?" he said to Big Dan. "Tell them to go," he told Katha—"Go," she said, "go." Big Dan cocked the gun. *"Get the fuck off,"* said the man. Big Dan shot into the sand; the sand flew and the shot echoed loud in the silence of the night. Sam took a step—

"Sam, get back," said Big Dan. Sam moved back with Peter, in back of Big Dan. Peter watched the man. He was angry; his lips were pulled back from his teeth. He held Katha so hard that her face was getting white, very white in the darkness; but she had stopped crying.

"This is my wife," said the man, "you understand?" Big Dan took a step—Katha's head turned, and the man jerked it back, jerked it up by her hair. "Come on closer," he said, "go ahead." He was pulling her hair.

"I'm telling you," said Big Dan, *"let her go."*

The man let her go, but he came at the gun—he had thrown Katha forward so Big Dan couldn't shoot—he grabbed for the gun and it fell to the sand; Big Dan smashed himself into the man, knocked him down to the sand. He was holding the man, calling, "Sam, get the gun, get the gun—" but before Sam could move, maybe even as soon as the gun hit the sand, when Big Dan hit the man, Katha got it. She took a step back, the gun in her arms, raised it up; the gun shook, then it steadied. "Tommy, get up." Big Dan let the man go. The man got to his knees. Big Dan moved back. "Get up," she said. The man got one foot up, still down on one knee; he looked at her.

"Get up," she said. She pointed down with the gun.

The man stood and faced her; his eyes glittered in the mist. "Good, baby," he said. "These friends of yours? You can tell them to go." He looked at Big Dan. "She's my wife."

"Tommy, give me the keys to the car."

"I don't have them," he said.

"Take the keys from your pocket and give them to me—throw them down in the sand."

The man smiled. "Katha, give me the gun." She brought the gun to her face, put her eye at the sights. "Oh," he said, smiling, "you learn that at camp?" She cocked it, he started for her, and she shot him straight through the chest—blood burst out at the sand. The blast of the shot threw him back, then he rolled, down to the water. She sat in the sand, knocked down by the force of the blast, and then over the sound of the shot that still rang in the night came a piercing, wailing sound from far away. Peter looked at Big Dan, saw the sound of the sirens, alive, in his eyes; he saw him run. He looked back at Katha, she was dragging the man by the arms from the water. Sam called, *Peter, come on,* and the sirens were coming.

She had the man back from the water. Blood was all over. She let go of his arms and sat down beside him. She started to cry, a deep choking sound—and again Sam called *Peter, come on,* the sirens were coming. But Peter couldn't go. He kept looking at the man. Sam's voice went away. Peter sat down in the sand, near Katha, near the dead man. Then the sound of the sirens went away, and all Peter could hear was her crying, now soft and high. He sat with her there until the lights came, coming down from the dunes to the beach.

Three months later

A gray day, leaves on the ground, a promise of snow. It was only November. Winter comes late to the island. Peter knelt by the swimming pool, stretching the rake to catch leaves that had gathered at the center of the tarp. He'd pull all the leaves to the sides, then rake the dry grass until it was clean. Every day new leaves fell to the ground and Peter cleared them after school. This was his job. There were oaks and maples in the backyard; and near the house by his window, like looking through lace before the leaves fell, was an elm.

He learned this in school, the names of trees. He learned math and reading and stuff about volcanoes. Mrs. Talbert said he had never had a problem with learning, he had just had a block.

The rake scraped the ground, pulling back leaves. Peter made ten neat piles and then stopped for a break. He sat down and took the new letter from Katha out of his pocket. First the letters had come from a place called Katonah upstate. Now they came from the city. She said she had a job in an art gallery, and hoped soon to go back to college. She'd crossed out a sentence in the letter. Last night Peter held it up to a light and saw what it said: I'm still sad all the time. Peter was sad. When he was in school or working in the yard he didn't feel it so much. He missed the ocean. In October the Talberts took him to Main Beach in East Hampton, but everyone was gone, gone back to the city.

One day a friend of Katha's came to see him. She brought a little girl who wore a purple raincoat that Peter sort of liked. Katha's friend asked if there was anything she could do. Peter said he hoped someday to go to the city with Katha, as she'd said they would. Claire said to give Katha time, that maybe Katha couldn't see Peter yet because he would remind her of things she needed to forget. Peter thought he'd ask the Talberts to take him to the city.

Peter liked the Talberts, though Mr. Talbert was sort of a geek. He called Peter Pete and always asked Peter to go down to the plant. Peter didn't care about the plant, though Sam said he should. "You see the size of that thing?" Sam said. "The guy's rich." When Sam got out of the youth house he moved in with a family who worked for Mr. Talbert in the Riverhead plant.

The leaves were stirring. Peter raked two of the piles into one, catching the leaves that flew off from the rest and pulling them back with the others. Sam talked too much. He always said things about that night—how Big Dan had lost him on purpose that night, and how if it weren't for Peter he'd be gone with Big Dan. They never would have caught him. Peter tried not to think of that night, or later when he talked to the judge, or saw Katha again. How her eyes had looked. What it seemed like since then was days full of waiting and still he was waiting. It should have been simple, easy for the cops to find Big Dan. He'd gone to the city—Peter knew it. He was there now. Who cared what Sam said, how Big Dan was maybe down in Texas or west on the coast. "I can see him," said Sam, "making big bucks and scoring with all kinds of women." But Sam didn't know. Sam didn't know anything about Danny.

Peter worked hard, bringing together the ten piles of leaves. Every now and then he looked up at the sky; bursts of white light were pushing at the thick gray clouds. When the leaves stopped falling, he thought, it would snow. From inside the house he heard the dog's barking. Last week Mr. Talbert bought him this dog, something called a wire hair terrier—something like that. It was too small and too skinny and it made Peter nervous. Mr. Talbert took the dog out for walks, when he got home from the plant.

The leaves were one pile. Peter went around the side of the house to the garage for the blanket; he'd wrap the leaves in the old wool blanket and take them to the street. A blue Schwinn leaned up against one wall of the garage near the trash cans, by Mrs. Talbert's car. He thought he'd take the bike and go over to Sam's when he finished working. Even though Sam made him mad. Peter thought Sam wouldn't be so bad if he just wouldn't talk all the time, would just learn to sort of leave things alone. Sam was mad at Big Dan, mad at Peter. Sam was even mad at Katha, who he used to say he loved.

Coming out of the garage with the blanket, Peter paused for a moment and looked at the street, at the trees in bunchy lines on both sides; a couple of squirrels skittered over the grass in the yard across the way. All of the yards were big like the Talberts' yard, not too big, not big like some of the lots in the Hamptons, but they had enough space; and most of the houses were brick, solid looking, not new but not old. They looked like they'd been there awhile and were there to stay. They looked like the Talberts; the Talberts weren't young but they weren't that old either. Peter wondered what Danny would think of this place. The air was fresh and crisp. The neighborhood was quiet, though some of the kids in Peter's school lived not far away. A couple of guys he rode with on the bus lived three houses down. They were okay.

Peter saw Mr. Talbert's tan Mercury coming slowly up the street. He took the blanket and went back around the house. He spread out the blanket on the grass. He raked the leaves on the blanket, then pushed them to the center with his hands. He took the corners of the blanket and pulled them up over the leaves, hearing the sound of the leaves, smelling the wool of the blanket and the dryness of the leaves. The blanket was a big soft bed for the leaves.

"Pete!" Mr. Talbert was at the back door. Behind him the dog was barking and jumping up and down.

"How's it goin' there, Pete?" The dog tumbled down the steps, wagging his stump of a tail. "Just about done?" said Mr. Talbert. He walked over to Peter. "Easy boy, easy," he said to the dog. The dog was jumping and spinning around Mr. Talbert's long legs. Mr. Talbert squatted down and patted the dog, letting the dog lick his face and rub his square muzzle up against Mr. Talbert's plaid shirt. "He gets restless cooped up in the house," Mr. Talbert said.

Peter didn't say anything.

"Nice job," said Mr. Talbert. He patted the dog. The dog had a dullish coat, short curly hair black and brown. "The weekend's here," said Mr. Talbert. "Anything special you'd like to do?"

Peter thought about it. "I've been wanting to go to the city."

"Hey, good idea. I'll check with your mother."

Mr. Talbert didn't look like a rich guy, Peter thought. He looked like any other kind of guy who worked at the plant. His hands were dirty, and under his nails, like he worked pretty hard.

"Any place in particular, Pete? Radio City, the Empire State?"

"I don't know," said Peter. "The planetarium."

"Now that's a place I haven't been in a while." He rubbed the dog's head; the dog made little whining sounds. "I used to have a great interest in space. Comets, that's what I liked. How they orbit the sun. Their tails shooting out in a stream." Mr. Talbert drew his hand through the air in an arc. Leaves rustled, flew off the trees and blew over the grass.

"You know what they say?" said Mr. Talbert. "That comets come from a place far outside of our solar system and sometimes, after they've circled the sun, they come back." The dog whined and rolled in the grass. "Interstellar travelers," said Mr. Talbert.

Peter thought of Big Dan. The dog jumped, all four of his legs coming up from the ground. He did it again. "Better take this guy for a walk," said Mr. Talbert. "Let's go, boy." The dog jumped and circled Mr. Talbert as he started off around the house. "You need a name," he said, "don't you, old boy?" The dog barked.

"Mr. Talbert?" called Peter. "You can leave him out here if you want to." Mr. Talbert turned back.

"Thanks," he said. "I'm beat if you want to know the truth. You'll give him a run?"

"Sure," said Peter.

The terrier whined for a moment at the door when Mr. Talbert went in. "Come on, boy," said Peter.

The dog ran to Peter, wagging his tail expectantly.

"You need a run?" Peter said.

The dog jumped, straight up from the ground.

"Sit, boy, *sit*."

The dog sat, then jumped, then sat again, his head cocked. "Good boy." Peter looked at his face. His eyes were perfectly round, dark and moist; they looked just like his nose.

Peter looked around in the yard for the tennis ball he'd seen a few days ago. He found it and threw it for the dog. The dog ran, flying through the grass. He nuzzled the ball, but then he took it in his mouth and came running to Peter.

Peter took the ball back, threw it high in the sky. It caught light in the sky. Peter watched it, coming down, the dog barking. The light had a power. Big Dan said a mind was like that, like a searchlight, and that you had to run it all over until something took, the thing that you wanted, the thing that you chose. But Big Dan was gone. Sam said it was Katha's fault, that if it hadn't been for her the whole thing never would have happened. Peter said that it wasn't, it wasn't her fault. Sam said, whose fault was it then, Peter? Think about it. Whose fault was it?